FAMILY SECRETS

FAMILY SECRETS

JOLYNN ANGELINI

iUniverse®

FAMILY SECRETS

iUniverse books may be ordered through booksellers or by contacting:

iUniverse
1663 Liberty Drive
Bloomington, IN 47403
www.iuniverse.com
844-349-9409

ISBN: 978-1-6632-2411-8 (sc)
ISBN: 978-1-6632-2489-7 (hc)
ISBN: 978-1-6632-2410-1 (e)

Library of Congress Control Number: 2021916002

Print information available on the last page.

iUniverse rev. date: 08/13/2021

Family is everything.

Prologue

Josie stood in the floor-to-ceiling window of her very modern and very large Manhattan apartment. So many thoughts from her past were racing through her head. Thoughts of how hard her past would be to face. She watched all the cars on the street below. All the people walking by with their computer bags. Some walking their dogs. Some with shopping bags. Some just out for their daily run. She wasn't an animal lover and she definitely didn't run. She was a writer, with her office right there in her apartment. She envied them, though. She would rather be any one of them right now, doing any of those things that she didn't normally do.

She flashed back to her past again. This time they were good thoughts. Exhilarating thoughts of her first love. Maybe her true love. *Good times*, she thought.

Coming back to reality, she noticed that her palms were starting to sweat. Her stomach started rolling. She tried to calm herself, but it was so difficult. The next few days were going to be a nightmare. She didn't quite know how she was going to get through it alone.

She knew she was not actually going to be alone, but she might be, in the end. This complicated trip was going to be heart-wrenching. Beyond heart-wrenching. There was too much from the past that would infiltrate this trip. This trip *was* the past.

She saw a couple pushing a stroller and tears pricked the corners of her eyes. *This is too much*, she thought. *How am I going to get through this? Why am I even considering going?*

She felt her palms start to sweat again, and this time she thought her breakfast was going to come right back up. She took a couple deep breaths and looked over at her suitcase waiting by the front door.

Whether she was ready or not, it was time. Time to face her past and meet the challenges it would bring, head on. She grabbed her bags, picked up her phone, and realized that she had a text message. She had been so lost in the thought of the sorrowful events that would be taking place over the next few days that she must have missed the ding.

She tapped the message bubble. With a quick glance at the number, with no name attached, relief struck her heart but dread filled her gut.

Chapter 1

Mrs. Paretti sat in the funeral home, wondering what she'd done to deserve losing a child. Where did she go wrong? How could she have let this happen? She feared the investigation would go on forever. Her family had been through enough over the years. She thought they were in the clear, and now this. This was the worst to date. This was the unimaginable. Mrs. Paretti brought herself back to the task at hand—rehearsing in her head all the things she would need to say to everyone. *This is a very sad day*, she continued to say to herself.

The spouse is always the first suspect, said the whispers around town. She laughed at that one. Even now, at such a horrifying moment in her life, she laughed out loud. Her daughter-in-law couldn't grocery shop without a catastrophe occurring. The thought that she could have actually done such a horrific thing to her son was more laughable than anything.

She sat in front of the closed casket. She had told herself she wouldn't do this, but nostalgia got the better of her, and she started to reminisce about when Carmine was a little boy. The doctor had told her she would never have children, but she didn't want to believe it. She didn't want to face the fact that something she had always wanted was never going to happen. She had prevailed. She showed that doc who was boss: she went on to bear three wonderful, healthy children . . . well, maybe not wonderful, but healthy. They loved their mother. Their father, on the other hand, was a different story.

Did they not love him because he didn't love *her* enough? Did they finally understand as adults why she had been so bitter and cynical for so long? They did. At least they said they did. She certainly didn't have the life she always wanted. Kids, yes, but the marriage was far from what she always wanted. It was great for a while, but then it all went to crap. Mrs. Paretti had blamed herself for so long for the marriage falling apart, but her therapist explained it all. She understood, finally, after years of therapy and getting a boyfriend.

Yes, the boyfriend. How liberating. She figured, if her husband could have a girlfriend, why couldn't she have a boyfriend? This was the answer to her happiness. This would be her magic elixir. This would make life OK until it wasn't OK.

How disrespectful could I be? she thought. *I am literally thinking about my own selfish ways instead of grieving for my child.* She figured this was some coping mechanism that her brain was using to get through the grief. Who could do this to her sweet boy? *Her sweet boy*, that was a laugh.

Her ex-husband, and the father of her children, worked from home. He was a pharmaceutical sales rep for a very large global pharma company. He traveled about half the time, mostly out of town and overnight. It wasn't a surprise that he strayed. Although his sales job was his main source of income, there was another job that they had done together. Working together was exhilarating. It started as just a small thing and grew as the years went by. They really worked well as a team; she hated him for screwing it all up. They had continued to work together here and there after they split, but the chemistry had faded significantly.

So now it was just Mrs. Paretti and her grown children. Although she loved them, she didn't always like them.

From the outside looking in, her children—what was left of them—all seemed to have their lives together. Little did everyone know what was actually going on. Mrs. Paretti usually took the blame for spoiling the kids rotten with all the money that their father had earned. She certainly had a hand in making them who they were today. Just like every other parent on earth. She was slightly saddened by that.

Mrs. Paretti was pulled from her thoughts by the ruckus coming from a room behind her. Her stomach dropped. She loved her children because they were hers, but sometimes, being around them made her want to vomit.

The funeral home allowed Mrs. Paretti and her family to visit the day before Carmine's actual service to make sure everything was in order; it was just Mrs. Paretti's luck that everyone insisted on being there.

Jackie came through the door first. She was daughter-in-law number one, scared of her own shadow, and, on account of being newly widowed, would now have to raise her kids on her own. She dressed like she was homeless most of the time. She used to work. She was an artist, and she was pretty good at it, too. She quit once she had the kids; not that she wanted to, but Carmine ran the house like it was 1950. No wife of his was going to work when she had kids to care for and a household to run. Not to mention taking care of Carmine. He was like having another child. Mrs. P was not quite sure how this was going to shake out. She would have to hire a nanny for Jackie, or maybe even help her herself. Either way, the woman was going to need some sort of guidance.

"Hi, Jackie."

"Hi, Mom." Mrs. P found it so odd that Jackie called her Mom, but since Mrs. P did not have any daughters of her own, she did not mind terribly. Jackie gave her a good caring hug and Mrs. P invited it. She knew it made Jackie happy.

Her second son, Marco, followed Jackie into the room, trailed by his wife. He was the middle child, but didn't fall into the stereotypical disaster category. He was quite successful but didn't always have his priorities straight; although, priorities set by Mrs. P's standards were so high it was hard for anyone to meet them. He was living quite the extravagant life, but with no children, of course he could be spontaneous and spend more money than most people. His wife on the other hand . . . she was sort of awful. Marco certainly had his issues, but Mrs. P was actually quite partial to one of his vices. Or should she say *someone* of his vices. Mrs. P did not condone this behavior, but Marco had a way of keeping his past a constant part of the present.

Marco's wife, Lexi, was daughter-in-law number two. Though a fairly intelligent woman, she was so full of drama and couldn't keep her mouth shut, even if you stuck a sock in it. The woman could not shut up. Talk, talk, talk was all she ever did. She wasn't necessarily gossipy or malicious, she just babbled on for no good reason. Mrs. P smiled to herself; she had a pretty good idea that this week was not going to be very kind to Lexi, and that was OK with her. Lexi deserved every bit of what was coming to her. Mrs. P didn't bother leaning in for a hug. That was not Lexi's style anyway. She was so stuck up, with her shoes and her handbags that were more expensive than an average mortgage payment. Sickening.

Jimmy came in the door to the funeral home last, the baby of the family. Usually, the firstborn was the favorite, but in this family, it was Jimmy. He was the most normal out of all the boys; normal was a relative term, but Mrs. Paretti never had any problems with Jimmy. He was well-behaved, always did his homework, and had excellent grades. He was the only child who used his brain to succeed instead of trying to pull one over on his teachers, or better yet, his mother and father. She laughed to herself at the word . . . *father*. She was obviously still bitter.

Her ex-husband hadn't bothered to show. Mrs. P wasn't surprised—he'd never been much of a father or a husband. She pretty much raised the kids on her own. He was a hard worker, and she always loved him for that, because that was how he made her feel important. The harder he worked, the more he was able to give them. It took her a long time to realize that was his way of showing love.

Her feelings were split because, while he supported the family and mostly did what was right, he slipped up. Just because he wasn't home didn't mean he was always working. Whatever he was doing, he made more money than she could have ever wanted, and she made sure she got enough of it when they parted ways. The children, the grandchildren, and maybe even the great-grandchildren would be set for life if they were smart about their share. He never spent quality time with her or the kids. This was her main reason for leaving him.

Then there was Josie. Always in Mrs. P's heart. She was not family . . . not yet, anyway. She would not be there today, but she would be there when it mattered most. Tomorrow.

The Parettis all waltzed farther into the funeral home like they owned the place, carrying on as if they did not just suffer a huge family loss. As if their mother never taught the boys how to act in a situation like this. She gave up long ago trying to parent them. They never listened anyway. They took after their father's side of the family in that regard. She just rolled her eyes and was thankful Jimmy would be there for her. Jimmy, without Marco, was a sweet boy.

As they reached the casket, Mrs. Paretti looked at her family with a somber expression. She was pretty sure they all knew how she felt, but at her age, she didn't care who liked her or who didn't. Whether they were her children or in-laws or not, they had all better be nice to her if they wanted to keep their names in her will. They might need her money more now than after she was dead.

Chapter 2

As Josie arrived in front of her parents' house, Mrs. Altieri swung open the front door with a big smile on her face. Josie's dad stood behind her mother with his hand on her shoulder. They looked so happy to have her home. It was no wonder; the only time they ever got to see her was when they visited her in the city. She hadn't been home in over seven years. It had been too long.

"Honey, I'm so glad you're home!"

"Hi, Mom." She threw her arms around her mom and dad. "You're acting like you didn't just see me last week," Josie said.

"I know honey, but you haven't been home since . . ." Mrs. Altieri trailed off as her husband lightly elbowed his wife as if to say, "Don't start on her."

"Are you hungry, Josie?" her mother asked.

"It depends, what did you make?" Josie asked with a sideways smile.

Josie's dad added, "She's been cooking since we heard the news."

"Mom, I just told you yesterday morning that I was coming home."

The Altieris glanced at each other and her father nicely said, "We were pretty certain you were going to come home. Even if only to see . . ." As if on cue, in the distance they heard the low growl of a diesel engine. As the sound grew louder, the windows steadily shook from the pounding speakers.

"That didn't take very long. You've been home what, ten minutes? Some things never change," commented Mr. Altieri. Now it was Josie's mom's turn to elbow her dad.

"What did you used to call him, Dad? That spoiled—" Before she could finish, her dad cut her off.

"Alright, alright, I guess I was wrong about him. He turned out pretty well."

"Yes, he did."

Josie welcomed the conversation's calming effect; her stomach was in her throat in anticipation of whether the truck was going to stop for a visit or just honk the horn and drive by.

Mrs. Altieri looked at Josie holding her breath. She knew how hard all this was for Josie, and it was only the beginning. She was hoping she would stay home for a while. But then again, maybe that wouldn't be the best idea. There was so much history. Mostly wonderful history, but some bits were too painful to relive.

The growling engine began to settle down as the truck crawled to a stop in front of the house.

Josie's palms were damp with sweat and her heart was pounding. Her mother was baffled at how her daughter, a brilliant, independent, confident woman, could let this boy—well, now a man—get to her like this.

There was a very loud knock at the door from his bear-sized fist.

Josie swallowed hard and braced herself for the tornado that was about to blow through the door.

"Would you like to get the door?" her mom asked.

Josie didn't even answer. She put her hand on the doorknob and turned it, pulling the door toward her.

She steadied herself to make sure her voice wasn't too shaky. She didn't bother to wipe off her sweaty hands; she would end up in his arms before he even got into the house.

The door opened wide, and Josie exclaimed, "Hi, Marco!" as he scooped her into his arms.

Chapter 3

Marco engulfed Josie in an obnoxious bear hug while the Altieris slowly slipped out. Against his better judgment, Mr. Altieri was coaxed by his wife to leave the room. Though he wasn't comfortable leaving them alone, Mrs. Altieri knew better than to worry; anyhow, they needed at least some privacy.

Marco lowered Josie so her feet could land back on the hardwood floor. She smiled up at him and he kissed her on the forehead, like always. Her body came alive with the feeling of Marco against her. He was just shy of six feet and he was full of solid muscle—not in an over-the-top body builder way, but an athletic way.

"Hi, yourself. How long has it been since we've seen each other?" asked Marco. Josie raised an eyebrow and tilted her head. He knew darn well when they had seen each other last.

From where the Altieris sat in the kitchen, they couldn't help overhearing the conversation. Mrs. Altieri said, "He doesn't seem too upset for just losing a brother."

"Kate, look who he's with. The world could be ending, and he would have a smile on his face with Josie by his side," Mr. Altieri replied.

"This is all so unsettling. She could be in danger." Her wheels were spinning.

Mr. Altieri gave his wife a reassuring pat on the hand and said, "She might be, but you know there is no sense in telling her what to do. She won't listen. Besides, as long as Marco is around, she'll be just fine."

"I suppose you're right, Joe, but you know I'm still going to worry," she said.

"I know, that's all you usually do." He sat back in the chair. "Although, soon enough you really won't have anything to worry about, if all goes to plan."

She nodded her head firmly and confidently said, "Looking forward to it." And then, playfully throwing a hand towel at her husband, Mrs. Altieri said, "Let's make some lunch."

In the living room, Josie and Marco were looking at one another like school kids. Josie did her best to snap out of it so they could talk for a while; after all, Marco came to tell her what the next few days were going to look like. She knew she should pay attention.

"So, my brother's viewing is tomorrow." His face fell. "I can't believe this is happening. I can't believe it's real."

"You always had a knack for ignoring the truth."

"Really? You're going to bust my stones at a time like this, Josie?"

"No, no, I'm sorry. I was just pointing out that you have a great defense mechanism for ignoring catastrophe. Now, more than ever, you'll need that."

"You really get me."

"Duh, isn't that why we . . ." Josie stopped herself. Saying it out loud felt incriminating.

Josie felt sick to her stomach at the prospect of seeing Marco's whole family again. It had been years since she saw everyone. All in the same room, anyway. The funeral proceedings weren't something she even wanted to be part of, but she knew Marco would want her there, even though it wasn't her place and she really didn't belong. She was going to have to find a way to blend in and not be seen. A difficult task, but one she would at least attempt.

Marco's phone buzzed in his pocket, but he ignored it.

"How are we going to do this?" Josie asked Marco.

"I don't know. We'll just have to figure it out, I guess."

"I don't think that's going to work. Lexi is going to be furious the minute I step foot in there."

"You know I don't care. She doesn't have any place to talk after I discovered her little secret." Josie could hear Marco's anger at Lexi in his voice. Except he wasn't angry for himself, but for the family.

"Yes, but she doesn't know that you know, so as far as she's concerned, I'm just there causing trouble," Josie pointed out.

"That's true. Do you not want to come, Josie?"

"I don't want to come at all, but I know you want me there."

"That's the only reason you're coming?" asked Marco.

"No, I should be there for Carmine. I know he would be over the moon to know I was there. And for your mother, of course." Josie smiled. She knew how much Mrs. P liked her.

"Just come for a while and then leave. I don't expect you to be there all day. I want you there all day, but that's not very realistic and I know that."

Josie breathed a sigh of relief; he had given her a partial pass.

At the lull in the conversation, Marco's thoughts went to an extremely inappropriate place, especially given the circumstances. He knew it was so wrong, but he couldn't help it.

Josie saw the look on Marco's face, and she was all too familiar with it.

"Are you serious right now?"

"What? I can't help it. You are the best part on my life right now," Marco protested.

"I am not part of your life," said Josie.

As if on cue, Marco's phone buzzed again, and again he ignored it.

Marco, obviously upset, said, "Do you really have to start about that now?"

"I wasn't starting anything, I was simply reminding you of the reality of our situation. Of your situation." She corrected her statement; she wanted him to know that he was not going to control her.

"You know the deal."

"Yeah, yeah. *You just need time.* That's what you've been saying for too long to mention," Josie said.

Marco's expression fell. He was sad, and not for his brother. He'd put Josie in a really crappy situation, and though it seemed like she was willing stay in it, he would have to make a change if he was planning on keeping her around.

Marco put his hand on Josie's face. "You have to believe me when I tell you—"

Josie's mother came barreling into the room, and Josie and Marco quickly turned their heads. Marco dropped his hand.

"Marco, honey, I think something is wrong."

He pulled his phone out of his pocket; he had a number of missed calls from his family.

"OK, thanks Mrs. Altieri." He looked at Josie, rolling his eyes at the added family drama, and said, "I'd better go. I'll call you later."

He walked out the door and Mrs. Altieri looked at Josie with overwhelming concern. "I hope you know what you're doing."

Chapter 4

Marco walked out the door and tapped his brother's name on his phone's missed call list. As the phone rang, he got in his truck and started driving.

Jimmy answered. "You're not going to believe this."

"What now?" asked Marco.

"I just ran into John at the gas station across from the pier."

"John who? And why should I care today?" Marco blurted out.

Jimmy was silent on the other end. He knew Marco was preoccupied with Carmine's death and Josie's arrival, but even the mention of John should have gotten his full attention.

Sure enough, Jimmy's silence snapped Marco out of his inattentive haze.

"Are you kidding me?" Marco's voice thundered through the phone. "What in the hell is he doing back here?"

"Something about his dad's boat. They're moving it this weekend down to his father's new place in the Carolinas somewhere."

"I can't believe this is happening. Did you say anything about Carmine?" Marco asked.

"No, and he definitely didn't seem to know. He didn't say a word about it and I'm fairly certain he would have. Although he did put a hand on my shoulder and ask me how I was doing, so maybe he does know."

"Yeah, especially because the two of you used to be buddy-buddy." Marco knew it was total bull that John didn't know about Carmine. He was certain that he did. *Even if you move away from this place, you always know what is going on. All the time*, Marco thought. He was certain that Jimmy wasn't lying though, either.

"Marco, are you serious? With everything we are going through right now, you're going to rag me about that?"

Marco felt like an ass. Especially because he'd just barked at Josie for doing the same thing to him. Different issue, but the same ragging. Marco thought he was beginning to see a pattern, one he'd have to correct sooner or later.

"I'm sorry, Jimmy, but my head feels like it's going to explode. First the funeral home this morning, and seeing Mom there sitting in front of the casket like Carmine was going to just open it up and walk out of it. Then Dad not being there, and now that ass John blowing into town. I don't think I can take anything else right now."

"The next few days will most likely get much worse. Do you have a missed call from Mom?"

Marco checked his phone quickly and said, "Yes, why?"

"You better call her back, Marco. You are definitely going to freak out when you hear what she has to say."

Marco ended the call with Jimmy just as he pulled into his driveway. Lexi was sitting on the front porch, waiting for him. Marco sighed. The last thing he wanted was to deal with her nonsense right now.

He got out of the truck and stabbed at his phone to find his mother's number.

"Marco?" Lexi called. Lexi was thrumming her perfectly manicured nails on the handle of the rocking chair. Her long, brown hair flowed over her shoulders in big, high-maintenance waves.

"Not now, I need to call my mother."

Of course you do, Lexi thought. "Your mother is always more important than me. Lately everyone is more important to you than me.

Anyway, I just got a call that I need to travel for work this week, but I was able to push it off until after all the services," Lexi explained.

Marco heard what she was saying as he walked away from her. "Thank you, Lexi," he called over his shoulder as he opened the front door. Lexi, frustrated at his disinterest in talking with her, followed him in, but Marco walked into his home office and slammed the door in her face.

The phone rang and Mrs. P answered. "Hi, honey."

"Hi, Mom, I got your message and Jimmy said I should call you. What's happening?"

Marco's mother muttered her news on the other end of the line. Marco just shook his head and said, "I'll be right over," and hung up on her.

Marco walked out of his office door, hoping that Lexi found something else to do other than bother him. He walked through the house and out the front door, thinking a quick walk around his property to clear his head would be just the thing before heading over to his mother's house.

He walked out to the flower garden and threw himself on the hammock. He could see his very beautiful, very large house from the garden where he was lying. So many windows, the spiral staircase, all the things that he'd ever wanted. He exhaled sharply with a smirk on his face as he thought, *Everything that Josie always wanted too*. He closed his eyes and thought he had everything, everything he and Josie always wanted. Except for Josie.

Chapter 5

Josie found her way to the back of the funeral home. She was confident in her decision to go and pay her respects. She would get some hugs and kisses, certainly, but she was also expecting some dirty looks and maybe an evil eye or two. She was prepared for the worst. She could handle it. Seeing the Paretti family would be the most difficult part on so many levels. She practiced what she would say to each one of them.

Lexi would be the biggest obstacle to today's pleasantries. Lexi was not a fan of Josie, and Josie enjoyed every minute of discomfort she could inflict on Lexi. Lexi was the devil, and Josie had known it for quite some time. Her mind drifted to the possibility that Lexi was responsible for Carmine laying in that coffin. Bitch.

Josie was going to hug Marco whether Lexi liked it or not. She knew Lexi wouldn't make a scene, especially not in front of Mrs. P. *God forbid Lexi get taken out of the will, that money grubbing . . .* "Ugh," she sighed. Josie had always been convinced that Lexi married Marco for his money.

She slowly made her way through the line towards the casket. She saw a few friends that she went to high school with and exchanged some pleasantries. She noticed that Mrs. P wasn't sitting up front with the kids. There was an empty seat for her, but Josie didn't see her close by. She wasn't surprised, given the heavyhearted and chaotic history of this family.

Through the people waiting in line, she got a glimpse of the casket, and tears quickly filled her eyes. She and Carmine were such good friends in high school. They had attended the same college, lived in the same dorm, and spent a lot of time together. They had done some really stupid things. *Those were the days*, she thought. She couldn't believe he was gone.

She wasn't sure why the casket was closed. She would have to ask Marco.

She was up. She knelt in front of the casket like the good little Catholic girl she wanted everyone to think she was. She made the sign of the cross and bowed her head. The tears were coming a little faster now as she continued thinking about all the good times they had together. She could not believe something like this could have happened to him. As she knelt there, she was struck by the thought that she was going to get dragged right along for the ride to find out what happened. The shitstorm that was coming was something she needed to put out of her mind. For today anyway. She was thankful for the closed casket. She didn't believe she could bear to see him like that.

Josie stood up from the kneeler and walked a few steps over to greet the family. Jackie, Carmine's wife, was the first in line next to Mrs. P's still-empty chair.

"Hi, Jackie. How are you holding up?"

Jackie looked at Josie with unfocused eyes and slowly said, "Josie, it's nice to see you."

Josie took Jackie's hand, noticing that Jackie was struggling to communicate. "If you need anything, Jackie, don't ever hesitate to ask."

"Josie," Jackie's speech was slightly slurred, "I'm glad you're here."

Jimmy was next in line, and he could see Josie struggling to make heads or tails of Jackie's odd conversation.

"Hey, Josie," Jimmy said while gently guiding her away from Jackie.

Jimmy hugged Josie so softly, like he was afraid he was going to break her. Knowing full well that Marco practically broke Josie's ribs whenever he hugged her, Jimmy wanted to be a little gentler.

"Sorry about that," Jimmy bobbed his head towards Jackie. "She is taking something the doctor prescribed to calm her down."

"Oh, that makes a lot of sense. She's practically catatonic compared to usual."

Jimmy couldn't help but laugh. "Josie, this is the exact reason you needed to be here today." Josie smiled. She knew she was still loved by this insane family.

"Jimmy, how are you holding up?" Josie felt like a broken record. "How many times did you hear that today?"

Jimmy smiled at Josie. She was trying to be comforting and it was working.

"I'm OK. Carmine wasn't exactly brother of the year." Josie just nodded and shrugged her shoulders. "I just wish this would all be over. The police investigation gets further from any idea of what happened with each day that goes by. I'm not sure they will ever really figure it out. They aren't telling us anything."

Marco, waiting next in line, was trying to keep his cool with Josie so close, but he could barely keep his composure.

Josie ignored him until she was done talking to Jimmy. Marco knew she had to. It only made sense. She didn't want to call any added attention to them.

Josie moved on to Marco with a consoling smile, leaving the racing emotions connected to her heart out of the conversation. Marco wrapped his arms around her.

From a distance, Mrs. P smiled, a true smile for the first time in a few days, as she eyed Josie and Marco hugging. She was even happier to see Lexi standing right next to them.

Lexi, fuming, kept quiet. She didn't bother saying a word. She didn't want to upset Marco, in plain sight anyway. Lexi's eyes drifted to the casket. Suddenly overwhelmed, she sat down and just cried. Carmine's death was going to cause some serious issues for her. This family was going to go off the rails. How was she going to get through this?

Chapter 6

Josie and Marco, noticing Lexi's reaction, rolled their eyes at each other. Lexi, unable to sit there any longer, excused herself and disappeared into the crowd.

"Part of me wishes she would have made a scene instead of being so pathetic. How can she even live with herself?" Josie asked.

"I know," said Marco. "Think about how she set us up for the future though. This is all going to work out in the end. Barring no extreme circumstances."

"Speaking of extreme circumstances, where is your mother?"

Marco laughed. "She's in the back somewhere with Tessa. She said she wants to talk to you without people watching her every move. I think she wants to ask you something." Josie, craning her neck around Marco's large shoulders, saw Tessa, Mrs. P's oldest friend and partner in crime, standing near the back with Mrs. Paretti.

"Oh boy, about what?"

"I'm not really sure. She wasn't really clear about it and I didn't ask."

"How could you send me into the lion's den like that?" Josie joked.

Marco laughed again at Josie, then said, "I'm sure it's nothing really crazy. You know she loves you."

"I know, but you never know with that woman. What should I say if she asks me how much I know?"

"You can tell her the truth. I'm pretty sure she knows I told you everything I know, so it won't get me in trouble if you tell her."

"That's a relief. I feel much better now."

The conversation came to a halt as Marco and Josie realized they had been standing in a slow dance embrace the whole time they were talking.

"We better separate ourselves before people start staring," Marco said.

"Too late," said Josie with a smirk and a raised eyebrow. She dropped her hands, resisting the urge to kiss him. "OK, I'll see you later."

At the back of the room, Tessa had gone to the ladies' room and then to make a phone call. Mrs. Paretti was sitting by herself, memories of the past forty years flowing through her head. She remembered bringing Carmine home from the hospital just like it was yesterday. He was rotten, even as a baby. But he was hers and she did everything she could not to kill him back then. She soon came to the realization that almost every mother, at one point or another, had that thought about their small children.

She felt a tap on her shoulder. She turned and, seeing Josie's smile, she relaxed. Josie was here. Her dear Josie.

"Hi, honey! How are you?" Mrs. Paretti managed the best whisper possible while maintaining her excitement. She was so happy to see Josie, but she didn't want to fall all over her. She knew it would be completely inappropriate; they were at a viewing, after all.

"I'm very well," said Josie.

Knowing how Mrs. P was feeling, Josie didn't bother asking. She was pretty sure Mrs. P did not expect her to, either. Josie just looked at her, and closing her eyes shortly and giving a quick nod, Josie put her hand on Mrs. P's.

"Honey, I have to ask you something. I would like for you to be totally honest with me."

Josie sat next to her. The woman she wished was her mother-in-law. Long ago she was sure that's where life would take her.

Mrs. P embraced Josie with a tight hug and a kiss on the cheek. "Took you long enough to get back here."

Josie laughed. "I didn't know you were back here. I had to ask Marco. I thought you would have been up front."

Rolling her eyes, Mrs. Paretti said, "I couldn't take the hypocrisy."

This was worse than Josie thought. She always thought she was fully aware of all this family's issues, but now she was beginning to wonder if there was much more to it all. Even more than Marco knew.

"So, back to my question that you so rudely ignored," Mrs. P teased, nudging Josie's elbow.

"Sorry," Josie said, smiling shyly. "I was hoping to avoid it."

"You don't even know what I was going to ask you," Mrs. P said with a smile.

"I know, but I have a pretty good idea of what it is, and I was just stalling."

Mrs. P laughed. "You are lucky I like you so much."

"If you didn't, I wouldn't have ignored you." Josie smiled again.

"So, what's happening with you and Marco?"

Even though Josie knew the question was coming, the abruptness of it left her unprepared to provide an answer.

"So, we're just jumping right into that question, at your son's viewing no less?" Josie took a breath to gain some composure and crafted an acceptable answer in her head. She just needed to make it come out sincerely.

"What do you mean, what's happening with me and Marco?" Josie said, still stalling.

Mrs. P looked at Josie and very seriously said, "You are joking, right?"

Defeated, and with a look of resignation, Josie replied, "I honestly don't know. I'm not in the business of sleeping with married men, so the real answer is nothing, at least until he figures out his situation."

"By *situation*, I assume you mean Chatty Cathy?"

Over Mrs. Paretti's shoulder, Josie saw Tessa approaching them. Catching the tail end of their conversation, Tessa evidently decided to leave again. She turned on her heel and walked off.

Following Josie's gaze, Mrs. P turned and looked at Tessa. Josie and Mrs. Paretti looked back at each other, both smirking.

Josie said, "Yes, you assume right. I'm not going to nag him. I do have my own life in the city and I need to just stay grounded and focused during all this."

"Oh Josie," Mrs. P said, with a very dark look on her face. "You won't have to worry about Lexi much longer."

What the hell does that mean? Josie thought.

No sooner had her heart rate begun slowing down than Mrs. P, looking towards the back of the funeral home, said, "Oh no, look what the Ghost of Christmas Past dragged in."

Josie turned her head and spotted John.

"Oh shit," said Josie.

Mrs. P braced herself. This was about to get interesting.

"How are you going to handle this one, kid?"

"Any ideas?" Josie asked.

"I'll keep Marco's attention while you talk to John. Then I'll try to get Marco away from the front of the room so John can see Jackie and Jimmy."

"Now I know how this family has kept their shit together for all these years."

"Smoke and mirrors, kid. Smoke and mirrors." Mrs. P mused with a wink.

Josie smiled.

"Oh, and by the way," said Mrs. P, "Carmine's not even in the casket."

Josie's mouth dropped open, and Mrs. P let out a snarky laugh.

Chapter 7

Josie made sure she caught John's eye before she approached him so he was ready for her.

"Hi, John, what are you doing here?" asked Josie in an unpleasant tone.

"Nice to see you, too," said John.

"I'm sorry, I just didn't think you would have shown your face here after—"

John cut her off. "It's been years since all that went down. We were practically still kids. Plus, I'm here for Jimmy. He and I are friends."

"Were friends," corrected Josie. "When was the last time you saw or even spoke to him?"

Very proudly, John puffed his chest slightly and said, "This morning, at the pier."

Josie rolled her eyes in disgust. "That is not what I meant."

"I know," said John, "But it's the truth."

"You ass. I know you want to pay your respects and support Jimmy, but you really shouldn't be here. Marco is going to flip his shit when he sees you."

Josie crossed her arms and turned her head away from John. She couldn't help but think back to what actually went down right before she went to college. She hadn't been prepared to see John again, and not like this. And even though John and Jimmy were friends, John was definitely still the odd man out in this place.

"Josie, why are you so worried about it? And better yet, what are you doing here? Since you asked me, I'll come right back at you with the same question."

"Carmine and I were friends. You know that."

"Yes, don't remind me. Shouldn't you be blaming Carmine for making you lose Marco a million years ago?"

"No, I blame you, and of course myself. I take responsibility for what I did."

"I would hope you blame yourself. It wasn't my fault I asked to see you and you caved."

"I caved because Marco and I were always fighting, and he didn't want to talk about me moving to the city and going to college. Our relationship was over before that less than perfect night with you," Josie shot back.

"Well, now that we got the pleasantries out of the way, maybe I should ask you again. Why are you here?"

"Lay off, John. Why do you always have to do this?"

John smirked. "What, try to get you away from Marco?"

"Yes. I mean, no!"

"You don't really know, do you? Don't forget that you were mine long before Marco came on the scene. And by the way you're looking at me right now, I think it's safe to stay that you might still be mine."

"Are you out of your mind, John? Do you have any idea what you're talking about?"

Josie stood there in front of John, fuming, but wondering if he was still the same amazing kisser that he was all those years ago. She couldn't help but notice his still-sparkling hazel eyes. His broad shoulders used to be so comforting. His face was just as easy on the eyes as it was when they were in high school. *Are you serious right now, Josie? Get yourself together*, she thought.

"Josie, your mouth still gets the size of a dime when you give me your angry face. If you didn't still care, you wouldn't be angry at all."

Good God, Josie, think of something fast so this arrogant jackass doesn't get his way. As it turned out, she didn't have to. The large bear-sized hand on her shoulder was enough to say, "Here I am to save the day."

"Hello, John." Marco reached out to shake his hand.

"Hey, Marco, how are you holding up?"

"As well as can be expected. I assume you're here for Jimmy?"

"Yes, Josie and I were just discussing that." John gave a cocky smile. "How is that beautiful wife of yours?"

Josie, still fuming, fidgeted a little. Marco could see the anger in her eyes. She didn't say a word, but he knew she was pissed.

"She's up front. You can ask her yourself when you get up there," Marco said to John in a condescending tone.

John lightly touched Josie's shoulder and, excusing himself, made his way to the casket.

Marco appeared calm and collected, but Josie could see in his eyes that he wanted to rip John's head off.

Josie squinted and through partially gritted teeth said, "Marco, you better go sit with your wife before John tries to steal her, too." And she walked away.

Marco hung his head.

As Josie moved to the back of the room, Marco watched, hoping that she would stay a while longer. He noticed Josie's old high school friend, Louisa, walk in the back door of the funeral home. His emotions, already high, began to simmer again. Ten minutes ago, he was sad about Carmine and Josie, but now he just felt defeated. There were too many people from his past. As Louisa hovered near the back, Marco recalled that he wasn't very fond of Louisa, for reasons the whole town knew and surely remembered. Louisa never thought Marco was good enough for Josie, and didn't have any trouble telling anyone who would listen. And he couldn't blame Louisa for not trusting him. He was a complete hellion when they were in high school, and paired with his wandering eyes, Marco certainly had a knack for trouble.

He wasn't going to let Louisa ruin a chance with Josie for him again. He would stop her, no matter what he had to do. First John tried to ruin things, and now Louisa. *This might be over before it even begins*, Marco thought. He needed to figure out his next move with Lexi before he lost Josie, once and for all.

Chapter 8

Josie gave Louisa a big hug before sitting in the chairs at the back of the funeral hall to catch up.

"Has it been a circus today?" asked Louisa.

Josie laughed. "Strangely enough, it's nowhere near as bad as I thought it would be."

"Are you still on the outside looking in?" Louisa asked the question with a playful smile, but it didn't quite reach her eyes. She wanted Josie to be happy, but everyone knew she didn't approve of Marco.

"Why do you have to rain on my parade?"

"Someone needs to keep you in check." Looking up, she caught a glimpse of John. "Whoa, is that John up there?"

Josie said, "Yep."

"Jeez, how did that go over? His face is still intact, so it must have been somewhat amicable."

"Yes, you could say that. It was uncomfortable as all hell. John still has feelings for me, and he is not going away quietly this time."

"What the hell? Talk about history repeating itself," said Louisa.

"You're telling me. I was talking with Mrs. P when he walked in. She saw him before I did, and then very calmly orchestrated a plan to make sure Marco didn't strangle him."

"That was nice and deranged of her," Louisa joked. "Sounds like the Parettis are as crazy as ever."

"Oh, I think they're worse. Can you blame them after all that has happened over the years?"

"It always amazes me how you can just bring that up so nonchalantly," Louisa said. "Like it wasn't one of the most humiliating and hurtful experiences you ever had."

Josie just waved her hand and blew it off. She didn't want to rehash that awful day with that awful man. Not many years had passed since the incident, but sometimes it felt like it was a lifetime ago. And despite Louisa making it sound like the Parettis had caused it, it wasn't them at all. Marco had nothing to do with it, and it was actually Mr. Paretti who retaliated after the fact. Josie didn't know if Mr. P would have even gotten involved in the bigger problems if it weren't for that awful day. Truthfully, Josie had him to thank for that awful man getting what he deserved.

Louisa didn't press Josie to talk about it, and instead said, "Lucky for you, you don't really have to be involved. Now you can walk away any time you want. Are you staying with your parents?"

"Yes, I am. They are thrilled, of course."

"How long are you staying?"

"Probably just a few more days. Since opening night of the movie is in two weeks, I'll have to get back to the city in time for all the events."

"Josie, I'm so proud of you. You wrote a best-selling novel, and it was picked up by a production company to be made into a movie. How amazingly cool is that? The hubby and I are so excited to attend the premiere. We can't thank you enough for the invitation." Louisa couldn't help but gush over Josie. She was one of Louisa's closest friends.

Josie smiled, happy to know that she would be surrounded by family and friends, not only for the movie premiere, but for her next book launch also. Her work got to be tiring at times, so she needed lots of support and laughs.

"Of course. I want you by my side during such a momentous occasion," Josie said. "I'll warn you now, though, that Marco might be there."

"What? Why?" asked Louisa.

"Well, he's been handling my finances during the movie deal and process."

"Josie, are you serious? Why would you do that?" Louisa was having a hard time hiding her irritation now. "I know you are all caught up with him, but how long are you going to keep this up?"

"Keep what up?"

"Josie, come on. Are you going to tell me that nothing has been going on since you hired him to be your accountant?"

Josie's face flushed; she didn't have to say a word.

"I can't believe you. How could you get involved like that again with him? Never mind that he's MARRIED!" Louisa raised her voice.

"Shh," Josie hissed. "Keep your voice down." Josie didn't really have to worry; it didn't matter how loud Louisa got, it was like Grand Central Station in here. The people sitting next to them didn't even notice that she was being so loud.

"Josie, we've been friends for a very long time, and I would never tell you what to do with your life, but as a friend, I will always try to protect you. I won't say I told you so when this whole thing blows up in your face. I will just be there to pick up the pieces."

Josie sheepishly smiled and said, "Thanks. I don't know where all this is going to take us. There are some things that I need to tell you. You do know who we are dealing with here."

"Yes, and that's all the more reason for you to just watch your back. This is not a good idea and you know it," Louisa cautioned.

"I know. When you come to the city, we can talk it all out and then you'll know what's happening. But I do need you to know right now that Marco and I are not sleeping together."

"Josie, you don't need to explain yourself to me. I love you, even if you should have a scarlet letter on your chest," Louise mused. "It's not that I don't like Marco; I just know you can do better. I don't want you to miss out on someone better for you because you don't want to let go of him."

"Ha, ha, very funny. I know, but we really aren't sleeping together, and I just wanted to make sure you knew that. I know you are only looking out for me, and I really appreciate it."

"OK," Louisa said, smiling, "I better get up there and pay my respects so I can get the hell out of here."

"Come to my parents for dinner tomorrow night. I know they would love to see you," Josie said.

"I would love that. I'll bring my hubby. I know your dad is obsessed with him."

Josie laughed, "Definitely."

They hugged goodbye, and as Louisa walked away Josie thought, *Time for me to get the hell out of here as well.*

Chapter 9

Josie walked out of the funeral home. She couldn't give one more fake smile, answer one more person's question of, "How is the family holding up?" It wasn't her answer to give; after all, she wasn't family. She knew Louisa was right in everything she said but she also knew, in her heart, the only way she would walk away from Marco was if she learned the hard way. She had so much going on in her own life that however it worked out, she would make it out OK. There would be no one there to hold her back. She needed to focus on her work right now.

Driving through the streets, and after the stress of the morning, Josie craved a giant latte with enough calories to make her work out a half hour longer tomorrow. She was ecstatic to find a new coffee shop had been added to the growing place she called her hometown.

She walked into the new cafe and let her eyes run over the comfy couches and small tables with decorative chairs. It was charming. This would be the perfect environment to continue writing her new book. She'd brought her laptop with her, just in case.

When the barista finished making Josie's drink, she took it from the counter and settled into a table in the corner and got to work, starting with her email. It was mostly housekeeping items. Like usual, she worked from the bottom up. Two emails from the top, Josie stopped, a shiver running up her spine.

In all caps in the body of the email, it read STAY AWAY FROM HIM!!

Josie froze. Her heart felt like it was going to pound out of her chest. As she was staring at the screen, she realized that she was chewing on her fingernail. She never chewed her nails.

She certainly wasn't expecting anything like this today. Especially today. She looked at the time stamp; it was sent about an hour ago. There wasn't any information about the sender, and the subject line only had the word *Daffodils. What does that even mean?* she thought. She assumed it was helpless stunt by Lexi. She hadn't thought she needed to worry about Lexi, but now she wasn't so sure. Maybe she really would have to watch her back, like Louisa had said. Come to think of it, she really didn't know what Lexi was capable of doing.

About an hour or so later, Josie's latte was long gone and she was ready for a break. She took a few moments to look around, taking in the fun little place. If she still lived in town, she would be here every day.

Her phone buzzed, pulling her out of dreamland. Josie glanced down at the screen; it was a text from Marco. She ignored it, not ready to talk to him. She knew he would ask when he could see her, and she wasn't ready to answer that, either.

Her phone buzzed again, too quickly for it to be the same message. She looked at the screen again to see a message from her mom.

Mom: Honey, are you coming home for dinner tonight? I just want to make sure I have enough food.

Josie: Yes, Mom, I am. I'll be home around 6.

This would give her enough time to herself and to deal with whatever might pop up in the meantime.

She was glad she'd planned her day the way she did.

Josie turned back to writing, only to have her phone distract her a few minutes later. Her phone buzzed, showing a call from an unknown number. She waited to see if the caller would leave a voicemail.

She went back to her writing again, but couldn't concentrate knowing there was an unanswered text from Marco just sitting there among the rest of her messages. She picked up the phone to answer him. All she typed was, "Hi."

Marco replied and they messaged back and forth for a while. Marco wanted to see her tonight, but all Josie could promise was that she'd text when she was done with dinner and see where he was. He agreed. There wasn't much else he could say.

Suddenly remembering the call from the unknown number, Josie saw the notification for a voicemail. She stabbed at the phone screen to retrieve the voicemail and heard John's calm and persuasive voice coming through the other end of the phone.

"Hey, it's John. Call me when you get this."

First, she thought, *how in the hell did he get my number? And second, why in the world is he calling?* Josie was getting angry. There was no reason he should be calling her.

She opted not to call him back. Nothing good could come from her calling him, and she really didn't feel like hearing his crap.

Out of the corner of her eye, she could see someone getting closer to her. She looked up to see John about a foot away from her table.

"Oh brother, now what do you want?"

Chapter 10

Jackie got in her sensible crossover vehicle in the parking lot of the funeral parlor. Her parents had offered to take the kids for the evening so she could just be alone for the night and get some rest.

She got home and kicked her shoes off by the back door, feeling relief that she was here instead of at the funeral parlor. She'd left the viewing early, at Mrs. P's suggestion, and didn't care what anyone thought. Tomorrow was going to be a very long day, and she needed to get some rest before facing all those people again.

She and Mrs. P hadn't been the closest over the years, but she had been very kind and helpful to Jackie during this time. They'd even developed a friendship over the last few months. They seemed to have a specific goal in common. Life must go on after you lose, or part from, a controlling, selfish husband. Carmine had been the poster child for the phrase, The apple doesn't fall far from the tree.

Strangely, Jackie didn't really feel sad about Carmine's death. She was at ease knowing that the very large insurance policy would be coming her way shortly, and she was very grateful to have that. But she couldn't quite put her finger on what exactly she was feeling.

While she continued to ponder her feelings, Jackie decided to make a cup of coffee and take it outside. She walked out on the very large deck with a panoramic view of the mountains. She wasn't sure where life would take her now that Carmine was gone. Maybe she would get a part-time job. Maybe she would stop making excuses that she didn't have enough time to work out, or enough time for herself. This was just the beginning of what she hoped would be a stress-free life. She would need to control whatever she could and everything else she would just have to deal with somehow.

And she would be able to start creating her art again. That was hard to believe, but very exciting. Maybe she would be able to go back to the art gallery.

A stress-free life wasn't exactly possible with two kids, but she would let whatever she could roll off her back. Either way, she needed to focus on herself from now on. The kids would still come first, but she would make time for herself.

Another big smile crossed her face as she thought about all the money that was coming her way. She would pay off the house and then figure it out from there.

Mrs. P was the one who suggested that she get the insurance policy set up in the first place. After Mrs. P cut Carmine out of the will years ago, Mrs. P figured if anything ever happened to Carmine, Jackie would be taken care of with the policy. Jackie did just as her mother-in-law said. She left it up to Mrs. P to take care of the details. Jackie didn't even have a copy of the policy. It made sense, but now that she thought back on that conversation, she couldn't help but shiver. *How sick is that? she thought. That was years ago. Long before . . .*

With a sharp inhale, Jackie put a hand to her mouth. *She knew*, Jackie thought. *Mrs. P knew then what was going on.* Jackie's eyes filled with tears at the thought of the disgusting way Carmine lived his life. As she put the pieces together, it was far worse than she thought. Mrs. P knew. She knew the whole time. Jackie couldn't bear the thought of how long her husband had been keeping his twisted life from her.

Chapter 11

John didn't answer. Josie, sounding tired and a bit singsongy, asked, "What are you doing here, John? Didn't you take the hint when I didn't answer your call?"

"It was an unknown number, so I assumed you weren't going to answer."

"Then why did you bother calling me?"

"I just took a chance. I hoped you would answer." Josie rolled her eyes.

"Well, now that you're here, John, what is it that you want? And how'd you get my number?"

John, trying to keep the peace despite Josie's obvious annoyance, said, "You have the same number from high school."

"Yes, but how did you know that?"

"I didn't, Josie, I still had the old number and just took a shot."

"Wow. A lot of trial and error today for you," Josie said, her mouth in a thin, straight line.

"Yes, I suppose so. Listen, we should talk."

"Good God, John, why? Why, after all this time, should we talk? After everything that has happened and all the time that has gone by? And now you want to talk?"

"Well, you left so soon—"

She cut him off. "I needed to get out of there. After you showed up, I didn't want any more surprises."

"I wasn't talking about the viewing, Josie. I was talking about . . ."

"Stop right there, John. We are not doing this. Not today, and maybe not ever."

"Josie, that's not fair. We never talked about it. I'm here now, and I need some sort of closure."

Really feeling angry now, Josie spat out, "What closure do you need? What else is there to say? It was like, a million years ago."

"I don't know, Josie, maybe a thank you?" John seemed to match her anger with his frustration.

"Thank you?!" Her voice was elevated with the question. "Are you serious? What are you talking about? What on earth would I be thanking you for?"

John's frustration suddenly dissipated. He looked at Josie with pure surprise. He'd thought it was a possibility that she didn't know what he had done for her back then, but he hadn't known for sure. In the tone of her question, it was now confirmed for him that she had no idea what happened. Should he just let it go, or should he tell her?

Thoughts raced through his mind as he stared at Josie in silence. Should he tell her that he discovered what Anthony had done to her, and when he confronted Anthony, he hit him so hard he thought Anthony was dead? Anthony. That vile, vile man who tormented Josie and her family.

What a time that had been. It was when John worked for Josie's dad; Anthony was always hanging around. At the time, John hadn't understood any of it, but now . . . now he knew exactly what was going on. What John didn't know was just how deep into the criminal world Anthony really was.

And then John had lost Josie, again, almost lost his summer job before college, and looking back on it, John could have lost his life. Back then, Anthony was dangerous and John was just a cocky kid with nothing to lose . . . nothing except Josie.

Josie's voice brought him back to the present. "John, honestly, what are you talking about?"

John reeled himself back in, preparing to give her a bogus answer. "When I was leaving the funeral parlor, James—you know, Mr. Paretti—showed up, just as I was walking out to my car."

John noticed fear in Josie's eyes.

"Are you OK, Josie?" asked John.

She cocked her head to the side while rolling her eyes.

"Really, John? Just the thought of that man makes me want to crawl in a hole and hide."

And really, Josie didn't even know the half of it. She had no idea what that man was capable of. Rumor was, he had more corrupt connections than the Mafia.

Josie asked, "Did you talk to him?"

"Very briefly. I didn't say too much. I shook his hand and gave him a one-armed hug. I told him how sorry I was, but he cut me off before I could finish. He said that he doesn't accept betrayal, whatever that means. I just looked at him. Naturally, I didn't know what to say. He said the only reason he was even there was for Antonia."

Josie piped up then. "For Mrs. P? She hates him. Why would he be here for her?"

"He didn't really say why, but it seemed like he didn't want to disappoint her."

Josie laughed. "That's funny, considering that man wasted her life away with all of his lies and womanizing."

"At least she's free from his grip now, after all these years."

"I guess. But it was twenty-five years of a life spent mostly miserable." Josie trailed off. Her head was filled with thoughts of James and Antonia toward the end of their marriage. It was so awful. Throwing things and yelling. Jimmy was the one that dealt with most of it because he was still living at home. Carmine and Marco were already out of the house. Far away at college and protected from the misery of their parents. Jimmy only had another year before he was out of there, too, but at the time, it couldn't come fast enough.

"Earth to Josie," said John.

"Sorry, I just got lost in my thoughts. Thinking about how bad things were back then with that family."

John said nothing.

"John, was there something you came here to say?"

He opened his mouth to speak, but stopped when Josie, facing the door, dropped her face to her hand. John turned to see Marco stroll in, hands in his pockets, very calmly approaching the table. John shut his mouth.

Chapter 12

John was angry. Not ready-to-throw-a-punch angry, but angry enough that he might tell Marco to leave Josie alone.

"Marco, what are you doing here?" asked Josie.

"Listen, I didn't come here to fight. And I'm not here to tell you what to do, Josie. I know John doesn't mean any harm. Well, maybe not to me," Marco said, shooting them both a playful smirk. "I thought I might find Josie here, but to tell you the truth, I'm glad I found you both."

Skeptically, John and Josie glanced at one another, sharing the thought that this probably wouldn't be anything either one of them would want to partake in.

"Marco, you have to be joking," John said.

"No, really. Just hear me out. I think I'm going to need your help."

John, very sarcastically, said, "Why on earth would I want to help you? What could you possibly need my help with?"

"Listen, I realize how strange this seems, but if you can keep your pompous mouth shut, I'll explain."

"OK, OK, let's get to it then," Josie said, tired of their constant jabs at each other.

Marco continued, "Something just doesn't seem right. I know the medical examiner is still working on the extended autopsy, but something just is not adding up for me."

Josie quickly jumped in. "What do you mean, Marco? Like, you think Carmine was murdered?"

"Yeah, I think. I think that's exactly what happened."

John, confused, cut in. "But what makes you think that? Wait, how can there be an extended autopsy when the viewing is today, and the funeral is tomorrow?"

Marco glanced at Josie. He knew she wasn't going to say anything, but he was always afraid that trust might be broken at any time.

"Yeah, John, about that. Carmine isn't in the casket," Marco confessed.

"What?" yelled John. He looked around and saw people staring. Taking a deep breath, he lowered his voice and asked, "Are you shitting me? Look, I just came in here to talk to Josie. I don't want to be caught in your mess, Marco."

"It's not my fault you came in here. It worked to my advantage, but I didn't ask for it," Marco said with a smug smirk. "Listen, I know it sounds really crazy. We know there was no gunshot wound and he was not stabbed. There was no dramatic scene or car accident. We know there was no sign of foul play, but think outside the box. These are some of your traditional murder weapons, but what if something else happened?" explained Marco.

Josie and John were on the edge of their seats, taking in every word of Marco's story. "I can't help but feel like someone is hiding something. I've been mulling this over in my head for the last few days, but I can't quite tell you why. I also can't come up with any reasonable explanation. I know it sounds crazy, but I can't get it out of my mind. I feel like this is something that I need to pursue."

"Marco, how can we help? And where would we even start? We certainly aren't detectives. None of us even has any background in criminal justice. How are we going to figure this out on our own?" Josie's words tumbled out. She couldn't get over the shock of what Marco had said.

Of course she wanted to help, but it wouldn't be easy for her to focus on this and her real life, especially with her launch coming up soon. Truth be told, she didn't want to be bothered with this right now. She felt oddly comforted by John's company today. At least they were in the same boat—equally as surprised by Marco's request.

"I'm not sure why you want my help, given the circumstances," John pointed out.

Josie shyly looked away, avoiding eye contact with both of them.

"Well, John, you're good at meddling where you don't belong. I thought you'd be the perfect person for the job."

John rolled his eyes and shot Josie a look that said Marco was being very tiresome.

Trying to bring them back to the conversation at hand, Josie asked, "So, Marco, where do you suggest we start?"

"Well, don't they always say you should start with the spouse?"

Josie drew in a breath and nearly choked on her gum. "You can't be serious, Marco. I don't think Jackie would kill a fly, never mind her husband. Plus, he was her cash cow. What's she going to do without him?"

John shifted uneasily in his seat. His financial planning experience had shown him more than enough times how families could be torn apart after the death of a loved one. He wasn't about to get too involved and lose his job because of this nutcase family.

"That's why we need to start digging."

Chapter 13

Mrs. Paretti let out a disgusted snort as her ex-husband, James, strolled into the funeral parlor. He made his way towards her and sat down. Neither one of them said a word for several minutes. Tessa eyed them from not too far away, and deciding to keep her distance, took a seat near the front where she still had a view of the couple. *This will either be World War III or, by some miracle, they will get along civilly*, she thought.

Tessa had been friends with Antonia since they were teenagers. She'd been with Antonia all along, and she still couldn't believe that these two were at each other's throats as much as they were. They'd been the perfect couple. James and Antonia won every dance contest they ever participated in. They built a perfect home together. They had stars in their eyes for one another since the day they met. *What a shame*, Tessa thought.

Antonia didn't even look at James, never mind speak to him. They were no longer together, and for good reasons—more reasons than she would like to recall at the present moment. She sat there with her arms crossed, hoping James would take the hint to not speak to her unless he had something important to say. Antonia glanced at him for a split second, and out of nowhere, she felt a pang in her heart. Not liking that one bit, she pushed it away, replacing the pang with anger.

She felt the need to tell James to go up to the casket. To make sure he did the right thing. He used to look to her to know what the right thing was.

"Don't you think you should go up there? Just for the sake of the situation?" Antonia urged.

"After all this time, you are still telling me what to do. How can you possibly . . ." He stopped, seeing her look of sheer disgust. James knew she was right. He shut his mouth and made his way over to the casket. As she watched James walking to the front, Antonia thought about her ex-husband. She still despised him, even though nine times out of ten he did what she asked. James needed her to keep him on track. But the very things that he needed her for, he ended up resenting her for; it had never been fair to Antonia.

James approached the front of the casket with not much emotion at all. He thought back to when Carmine was first born. He was a bastard from the day he came out. Getting him to go to sleep was impossible. He was always fussy. He hardly ever ate for them. He never listened. As he knelt there in front of the casket, he wondered if he hadn't given up on Carmine as a child if he would have turned out better. It was too late to fix. As he glanced up, he caught Antonia's eye and recalled her complaining about him being around more for the kids. This was obviously what she was talking about. He was a putz and in this moment, he became much more aware of that.

He stood up, unsure if he should go talk to the kids. They hated him for the most part and he knew it. As he looked in their direction, he noticed only Jimmy was left. Jackie must have already gone home, and Marco and Lexi were gone too. He learned not to question years ago when he realized how ridiculous his children could actually be sometimes. His daughters-in-law weren't much better. He bobbed his head at Jimmy and walked back to Antonia.

He sat down next to her. "Where did we go wrong?"

"Are you serious? You were hardly ever home. You never bothered to try and discipline them, the small percentage of time you were actually home and not hiding in your office."

"Are we really going to do this here?"

"You asked a question you already know the answer to. Why did you even bother asking?"

He looked at her with raised eyebrows and shook his head. "I don't really know. I guess maybe I was looking for an excuse to be emotionless at my own child's viewing."

Antonia had an overwhelming feeling of relief wash over her. She was happy it wasn't just her who felt that way. She softened towards James. "It makes me feel better to hear you say that."

He looked at her with surprise. "Did you really just say that? Are you feeling OK? That might be the first time in years you agreed with me without your usual condescending tone." He smiled at her. She smiled back and said, "You said something that made me feel good for once in a very long time."

His face fell. As much as she couldn't stand him most of the time, Antonia felt bad for his defeated expression. She thought fast to lift his mood slightly and said, "You know, it's not all our fault. We never raised Carmine to purposely do the horrible things he did in his forty-odd years of existence. We may not have shown each other enough love, but we showed them love."

"I know that. But think of the horrible things he has done to us. I have never forgiven him for that and now I don't ever think I will," James said.

"I won't either. At least we agree on something."

"Man, you are relentless, aren't you, Antonia?" He nudged her elbow with his and shot her his boyish grin. She was never able to resist that look. Even after all these years and all the bad memories, she still found him attractive, even if his smile had less of an effect on her now.

The smile on James's face became a frown as he thought about Carmine and his antics. "You know, stealing money from your parents is one thing, but to steal from your in-laws is another. I really thought the drug dealing took the cake. That was earth shattering enough, but then to find out—" Antonia put her hand up, stopping him.

"Don't say it out loud. It's just awful. I don't want to hear you say it."

"I'm sorry. I just can't get over the whole thing. I can't help but feel like justice is served. I never thought I would say that. I never thought I would be happy to lose a child, but if it had to be any of them, he would be the one I would have chosen."

She looked at him with her mouth in a straight line and just bobbed her head up and down.

The small piece of doubt Antonia had been harboring inside her quickly vanished. This was all she needed to know that it was OK that Carmine was gone out of their lives. More importantly, to know that James was OK with Carmine being gone out of their lives. Even so, it was still going to be a long road ahead.

He nudged her arm and nodded his head toward the line to kneel by the casket. She turned to see who he was gesturing towards. Antonia noticed a tall, handsome man in a decent suit with jet-black hair. He glanced in their direction without making a fuss. His piercing blue eyes were hard to miss. Antonia knew he wouldn't go unnoticed by this nosy, meddling crowd.

Antonia and James continued to make small talk and watched as the man made his way up to the casket. When he was done praying, he stood up, made a small nod in the direction of whoever was left in the receiving line, and walked out of the funeral home.

Chapter 14

The funeral was over, and Josie could not pack up her car fast enough to get out of town. She was longing to get back to the city and away from the chaos. Small town nowhere should not be more chaotic than the big city, and yet the past few days had been too much for her to deal with. She knew it would be rough, but she hadn't anticipated John showing up.

"Alright, well, I've just got one stop to make on my way out of town, and then I'll be out of here," Josie said. She hugged and kissed her mom and dad.

"Goodbye, honey. Don't wait so long to come home again," said Josie's mom, knowing full well there was a chance she would be coming home sooner than she thought. Josie's dad patted her mom on the arm as if to say, "It will all be alright." Josie's mother looked at her husband and let out a huge sigh.

Josie smiled and got in the car, closing the door with a triumphant slam. She waved goodbye to her parents and blew them a kiss. At the end of their quiet little street, she slowed to a stop at the sign. She could make a left to head back to the city, or she could take a right and head to Marco's. He was expecting her, but she didn't know if she had the energy to deal with him. At least she wouldn't run in to Lexi. Marco had texted that Lexi left right after the funeral for a work function out of town, so he'd be home alone.

After a few seconds of overthinking the situation, she tapped her blinker in the direction of Marco.

She pulled up in front of Marco's towering house. Her place in the city was twice as much as this and a small fraction of the size. It was ridiculous how high the prices were in the city. But there, you didn't need a vehicle and there were more things to do in one city block than there were in this whole town; she was so happy to be going back.

Marco was sitting on the front porch, no doubt waiting for her. She knew how much he still cared about her. How could she not know, with all the things he'd done for her in the past few years? Helping her get the business set up. Helping her move into her new place.

She wasn't proud to be taking up the time of a married man, but she still cared deeply for Marco. She wasn't going to apologize for it, especially after Lexi's ridiculous behavior and her horrible little secret. Josie had always suspected that Lexi only wanted to be with Marco for the family's money. How could Josie not think it was so, given Lexi's past relationships?

As Josie approached the porch, she noticed another car in the driveway and she knew exactly who it belonged to. No sooner did her foot touch the first step to the porch than Mrs. Paretti came out of the front door. "Oh, hi!" Josie exclaimed. "I didn't know you were going to be here. I'm so glad. I felt awful leaving town without saying goodbye."

Mrs. P walked closer to Josie and hugged her. "Try not to let so much time go by before coming home again."

Josie smiled. "My mother said the same thing. I'll try. You could always stop by when you're in the city. My big launch is coming up. I would love for you to be there."

"I would love that."

"It's settled. I'll send you the tickets."

"Looking forward to it," said Mrs. P. She hugged Marco and got in the car. Marco held his breath, waiting for her to drive out of sight.

He pounced on Josie like a cat, hugging her and trying to kiss her, but Josie wasn't having it.

"What's the matter?" asked Marco. Without giving her the chance to answer, he kept talking. "Josie, I'm confused here. We talk and text often and now you are home and I just want to be close to you. One minute you're all about us and now you're pushing me away. What gives?"

"Listen, Marco. I've been thinking about all this and you need to figure out what's happening with you and Lexi before we spend any more time together. I'm not going to be your second choice any longer, and if you choose her over me, so be it, but I don't want to go on like this any more."

Marco was panicked. He wasn't prepared for this. Frantically, he grasped for something, anything, that he could say to change her mind.

"I understand, Josie. The situation sucks and I know it sucks for you even more. I'm working on it."

Josie snapped at Marco. "No, you don't know. You don't know what it's like to be on the other side."

"Oh, no? I don't?"

"Marco, don't you even go there. That was years ago, what happened with John. None of us were married and I chose you in the end anyway." Josie flashed back to when she and John were dating off and on, and Marco was in between. There was an awful misunderstanding involving another girl that broke up her and John in the end. Josie thought John was cheating on her and he wasn't. He never did anything of the sort and she ended up breaking up with him over the other girl. For no reason at all, it turned out in the end.

Marco knew she was right. There was no fighting her on this one. He cared about her so much that he didn't want to argue any longer. He needed to shift the conversation again. *Josie's too smart to fall for it, but I can at least try*, Marco thought.

"Josie, do you remember that time we—"

"Don't even, Marco." Josie cut him off. "Don't try to sweet talk me like we're having two different conversations."

Damn, I knew she wouldn't fall for it, he thought. Now he was going to pull out the big guns. He knew this would make her angry, but that's what they did. They fought and then they made up. They needed this right now. He needed to keep her with him right now.

"Fine. I've kept my mouth shut until this point about John."

"Him again? Really? Are we going to do this again?" barked Josie.

Josie was furious. She was so mad she stormed off the porch and headed for her car. She wasn't wasting her time on this conversation any longer. She needed to get back to the city. Back to her life.

Marco raced after her. *I'm going to lose her*, he thought. *I'm going to lose her and I don't even deserve her in the first place.* How did this get so out of control? Marco asked himself every day why he didn't go after Josie when she left, all those years ago. Why he just let the years go by. He met Lexi not long after he and Josie broke up and just stayed with her. He shouldn't have married her, but he did anyway . . . knowing he never stopped loving Josie.

"Wait, don't go. I'm sorry. I'm an ass," Marco called to Josie.

"Why does almost every argument we have end in you saying those words? It's getting very tiresome. Not to mention it's starting to bore me." Josie managed a small smile and raised an eyebrow.

Relief filled his head and partly his heart to know he hadn't lost her for good. But Josie was just tired of arguing about it. She certainly wasn't interested in arguing about John right now. This was about her and Marco.

She didn't want to leave him. She never wanted to leave him, and certainly not on bad terms. But she needed to stand her ground and hold her boundaries. She also needed to work out the nagging feeling she had about John. Josie quickly pushed John from her thoughts. *I can't think about him now*.

Marco gave Josie a huge bear hug, lifting her off her feet as usual. Once he lowered her back down to the ground, he kissed her on the forehead. He knew better than to try to get Josie to give him a real kiss. She was getting the hell out of there now, before anything else happened to hold her back.

"Please, stay in touch and let me know when I can come and see you, Josie."

"Well, if you leave your godforsaken wife from now until my launch, maybe you can come." Josie's comment spilled right out. She was never usually this blunt with him, but she really did love him, and she was sick and tired of waiting around. She was tired of being second best.

Clued in by her bluntness, Marco knew Josie was at her wit's end. He was hoping that she wouldn't leave so angry, but he was resigned to the fact that there was nothing he could do to lift her mood. He let her go and she got in the car.

Josie sped off Marco's large property as fast as she could without wrapping her car around a tree and killing herself. She needed to get out of there.

She cranked her radio and got lost in her road trip playlist. She was outside the town in no time, only paying attention to the road in front of her. Lucky for Lexi, Josie never noticed her in the rearview mirror.

Chapter 15

In a fit of rage, Lexi barreled down the highway, following Josie's car closely. She wasn't going to let Josie steal her husband. There was no way she would let that happen. It was bad enough that Marco never stopped loving Josie; Lexi had always known that was the truth. Lexi had long believed that Marco may have loved her at one time, in the very beginning, but his love for her could never push the love he had for Josie aside.

Lexi had always wanted kids, but anytime she brought it up, Marco said he wanted it to be just the two of them. She knew better than to think that was the truth; kids would only tie them together forever, and he would never let that happen.

But if he really didn't love her anymore, why stay? It would have been easier if he just left. It would have given her closure and that would be better for the both of them.

It was hard to judge Marco for his faults; after all, Lexi was no angel. She had plenty of her own secrets. If they were still secrets, that is. She wasn't sure who knew, and at this point, driving at high speeds as she mirrored Josie's movements, she really didn't care. Her life was pretty much over anyway, so why try to hide it anymore?

For years, Lexi had been taking anxiety medication as well as something else to control her mood swings. It was a way to control something in her relationship with Marco. Of course, she was convinced that there wasn't anything actually wrong with her. She blamed Marco and his never-ending relationship with Josie for all of her issues. She hardly ever took personal responsibility for anything. Today was different though. She was thinking much more clearly now that she stopped taking her medication. It had only been about a week, but she had never felt so free, so alive!

Lexi was gaining momentum in the giant SUV. She was just getting closer to Josie when suddenly, her cell phone rang.

Without looking to see who it was, she barked, "Hello?"

"Lexi, it sounds like you are driving. Did you rent a car? I thought someone from the office would be driving you."

"Marco, um, hi. What are you doing? Are you OK? What's the matter?"

"Nothing. Why are you so on edge?"

"No reason." Lexi tried to keep her cool, but Marco hardly ever called her, especially when she was traveling. The last time he called her was to tell her what happened with Carmine. She didn't know how much more she could take. "Did you need something?"

"I forgot when you said you were coming home, and you didn't put it on the calendar like you usually do," Marco said.

Think fast, she thought. She couldn't believe she'd forgotten to put it on the calendar—then again, she wasn't actually traveling.

"I must have forgotten with everything going on with Carmine . . ." She barely choked it out. She was trying to hold back tears now. She hadn't been sure how she would react to things like this without taking her meds. Obviously not that well. She was trying to hide the tightness in her throat.

"Lexi, I don't have all day. When are you coming home?" Marco's voice came loud and angry through the phone.

Get a grip! Don't give yourself away. Marco's a very intelligent man. Don't give him a reason to look into why you are acting so crazy, Lexi thought.

"I'll be home tomorrow," she finally squeaked out. "Around noon. Why?"

"Nothing is wrong. We just need to talk."

It certainly sounded like something was wrong. But Lexi wanted to get off the phone; she couldn't take this anymore.

With a note of defeat in her voice, Lexi said, "OK, Marco. Whatever you want."

She knew damn well what he wanted to talk about. This was it. He was going to leave her. All the more reason to get rid of Josie once and for all. If she couldn't have him, neither could Josie.

Chapter 16

Josie's phone was ringing, but she just ignored it. Whoever it was would call back if it was important. She was in the zone, her tunes cranked up and thinking of ideas for her new novel. She felt free. Freer than ever before. She had laid it all out on the line for Marco and he knew where she stood now. She'd had the chance to catch up with her parents and she would be seeing them when they came into the city in two weeks. All was well in the world of Josie.

One small thing tugged at the back of her head: John. She wasn't going to deal with that now. The feelings she apparently still had for him were now large enough to harp on. *It will all work itself out*, she thought. *He's in the city, too, so it will make it easier to see each other if the time comes. And I won't have to worry who is watching. No nosy, small-town gossip in this city.*

Her calming thoughts were interrupted by the damn phone ringing again. She glanced down at the screen and rolled her eyes. It was Marco. What could he possibly want now? She had left him no more than forty-five minutes ago.

"Hello," she said, as chipper as she could be; she didn't want another fight. She didn't want to burn their bridge just yet. There may still be hope for them.

"Listen, I just got off the phone with Lexi and she sounded very frazzled and off-balance. She's supposed to be traveling for business, but something just seems off. She's driving herself around and she never does that."

"Marco, why are you telling me this?"

"She might not be taking her meds and I want to make sure you watch your back. Just in case. I know I might be way off, but when I spoke to her, she was very on edge and I'm not sure what she is capable of."

"Seriously? Are you for real right now? Is this some sort of last-ditch effort to talk to me?"

"I wish it were, Josie, but I'm just worried about you, that's all. I know you like to listen to your music and detach from reality when you have a long car ride and I just want to tell you that this time, you should keep your guard up."

He knows me well. That's exactly what I'm doing. King Kong could come and plow over my car and I would never see him coming, Josie thought.

"OK, Marco. Thank you for the warning." Just then she remembered the email. "Hey, I wasn't going to say anything, but I received an email from someone I didn't recognize, with the word *Daffodil* in the subject, and the body of the email said STAY AWAY FROM HIM! I'm guessing it was from Lexi, because who else would care what was going on with me and you?"

Through the silence on the other end of the phone, Josie could picture Marco trying to work it out in his head. Defeated and exhausted, Marco shook his head and said, "Do you see what I mean? I don't know what she is capable of." Marco could feel the anger rising alongside his desire to keep Josie safe. He didn't want her to go.

"I'll see you soon, I hope. If you remember, can you text me when you get back to the city, so I know you got home safely?" Marco asked.

"Yes, if I remember."

"Miss you," Marco said, and hung up. He wouldn't give Josie the chance to not say that she missed him, too.

Josie wasn't going to let that phone call get her out of her zone. She was making progress on the book idea in her head, and she wanted to keep it that way.

As the miles added up, though, Lexi and her jealous rage kept popping back into Josie's head. No matter how hard she tried to focus on the new book, she just kept thinking about Lexi.

Out of the corner of her eye, she saw a giant SUV crossing all three lanes of traffic, headed towards her on the fourth lane of the highway. "Oh my God," screamed Josie. She swerved to get out of the way of this maniac. She didn't know what was happening. *Was that Lexi?* She couldn't believe that Marco might be right in saying that Lexi would actually come after her. But like this? On a busy highway, in the middle of the day? Lexi could get them both killed. She shivered at the thought. *Maybe that's what she wants. Maybe she wants us both dead.*

She had to get as far away from this nutjob as she could. Where was the SUV? She searched and searched in her mirrors and out the windows. The SUV was nowhere to be found. She sped up a little to try to lose the car if it was trailing far enough behind. Maybe the driver was just trying to scare Josie. Job well done, if that was the case.

A few minutes later, Josie saw the SUV coming up behind her, gaining speed far more quickly than Josie thought that tank could handle. In her rearview mirror, she could see the driver. "Lexi! It's Lexi," Josie yelled. She pushed her foot harder on the gas and pulled away from the SUV.

Lexi switched lanes to get next to her, but Josie was still ahead. Too far for Lexi to reach her. Even if she swerved to hit Josie, Lexi would miss. There was no way she could get her from where she was.

Lexi pulled back into Josie's lane. Josie's terror was now turning to anger. Her blood was boiling. Lexi was so close to Josie that the front end of her SUV disappeared in Josie's review mirror. Josie could only maintain her speed, as traffic was now unforgiving. There was no escape from Lexi.

Lexi got as close as she could and tapped Josie's bumper with hers, just enough to get Josie to swerve, but Josie kept control of her vehicle. The car in front of Josie merged into the lane to the left, and Josie sped up. She pulled away from Lexi, far enough to get away from her. Traffic was now moving between them and Josie wasn't sure if Lexi was letting it happen or if she was losing control. Either way, it didn't matter. Josie changed lanes, still craning her neck for any sign of Lexi.

As luck would have it for Lexi, traffic was breaking up a bit near the freeway off-ramp and Josie was approaching a car up ahead that was going much slower than both of them. There was nothing else for Josie to do but to slow down. Thinking quickly and checking her mirrors to make sure she wouldn't get hit, Josie slammed on her brakes, leaving Lexi speeding forward. Josie took the exit and got off safe and sound.

"What the hell!" shouted Josie. Lexi was clearly loony tunes, but Josie was realistic enough to know that Lexi only had herself to blame. It was pretty safe to say that the email came from Lexi.

She pulled into the parking lot of a fast-food restaurant to calm herself down. *How did Marco know Lexi would come after me like that?* He said it was just a bad feeling. Maybe it was true, but what would make him even think Lexi would do that to Josie? What in the hell was Lexi doing? Did she want to die, or did she just want to torment Josie?

She didn't know what else to do, and she wasn't going to call Marco, so she dialed the next best person: Antonia Paretti.

Chapter 17

Jackie had invited Mrs. P over for lunch, and it worked out well because Mrs. P wanted to see the grandkids. She was doing all she could think of to give Jackie a break. She offered to stay with the kids in the morning so Jackie could go shopping, get her nails done, and go for coffee. Whatever Jackie wanted to do. Mrs. P thought it would be good for her to get out of the house. Not only to deal with Carmine's death, but because she wanted to make sure Jackie was in the right frame of mind to handle everything that might come her way now that Carmine was gone. For everything to work out the way she wanted, Mrs. P needed Jackie to have a clear head through all this.

Jackie was so pleased by the offer that she took Mrs. P up on it and said she would make her some lunch. Jackie would get some groceries while she was out. They could have a nice relaxing meal on the oversized deck and chat.

It wasn't that Mrs. P didn't like Jackie. Actually, she was quite fond of Jackie. During the recent unfortunate events with Carmine, Mrs. P saw an unexpected strength in Jackie that she had never seen prior. She liked Jackie, but she'd always struggled to respect Jackie. Jackie was very dependent upon Carmine. It wasn't because she didn't work. It wasn't because they relied solely on Carmine's income—not that he had a respectable income. That's not even what really bothered her.

What bothered Mrs. P is that Jackie ran the household and took care of the kids and still asked for permission from Carmine to do things. She did not stand for that. She and James had always had an understanding that he worked, and she ran the household. They stayed out of each other's way. Not that they had a perfect marriage by any means, but that was one thing in their marriage that worked. Mrs. P did not ask for permission to do the things she wanted to do.

Maybe Carmine just had some hold over Jackie. Mrs. P thought this might be true, but Carmine had no room to talk. He did whatever he wanted, whenever he wanted. It really wasn't fair to Jackie at all. Jackie never seemed to be the type to need all this money and all the material things. Mrs. P just couldn't quite understand why she lived the way she did. Maybe she would find out one day.

Jackie arrived home, pulling into the four-car garage with new nails and a handful of grocery bags. She really did feel refreshed and ready to take on the world.

She walked into the house to a greeting from Mrs. P. "Hello, dear. How was your morning?"

"Oh, Mom, I can't thank you enough for suggesting this! It was wonderful. It was nice to not have to worry about anything for just a few short hours. Thank you so much."

"You are very welcome, honey. You looked like you needed it and I wanted to spend time with your maniacs." It sounded like a backhanded compliment, but Jackie decided to blow it off. Seconds later, her crazy children came screaming through the living room, playing cops and robbers and almost knocking over the end table. Mrs. P just smirked at Jackie as if to say, "See for yourself that they are, in fact, maniacs."

Mrs. P gave Jackie a nurturing smile. "It will all be alright from here on out, Jackie. Now you can live a life you actually want. I know I said

I would not talk about this again, but everything is in motion and you won't have to worry about a thing."

Jackie was a little caught off guard by hearing Mrs. P talk so bluntly of tying up loose ends. To be nurturing was very out of character for Mrs. P. Was there a catch? When was the ball going to drop? Did she expect something in return for her kindness? Jackie's head was spinning now. *Jeez*, she thought to herself, *just calm down and roll with this. You don't want to do any of this alone. Take all the help from this woman that she is willing to give you. After all, you both owe each other now.*

Even though they were not supposed to talk about it, Jackie opened her mouth to ask Mrs. P a question, but Mrs. P's phone began to ring.

Chapter 18

Mrs. P picked up her phone and said, "Hello, honey. How are you?"

Josie was trying to stay as calm as she could. She didn't want Mrs. P to freak out. She thought it would be better to call Mrs. P instead of Marco, but Josie regretted dialing the number as soon as Mrs. P answered.

"Hi. I, uh, wanted to reach out and let you know what just happened." Josie's voice was very shaky, but she didn't sound frazzled.

"I can tell something is wrong. What is happening?" When Josie didn't answer right away, Mrs. P continued, "You practically just left. What could have happened in such a short period of time?"

"So, I was driving along the highway, minding my own business, and a car tried to run me off the road. I'm fine and my car is fine."

"Oh my God!" exclaimed Mrs. P. "Thank God you are OK. Did you call the cops? Are they on their way? Where are you?"

"I didn't call the cops. I thought I should call you first."

"Why me? Why didn't you call your mom and dad? Do you need me to come and get you?"

"No, no. I called you because the driver trying to run me off the road was Lexi."

Mrs. P's concern switched to steaming anger. She was so angry she could strangle Lexi with her bare hands. She told herself to calm down. She had to keep her cool in front of Jackie. How dare Lexi do this to

Josie. She had had it with Lexi. She wasn't going to let her get away with this.

"Mrs. P, are you there?"

"Yes, honey, I'm here. Where is Lexi now?"

"I'm pretty sure I saw her run off the road, but I don't know what happened after that. I didn't stick around long enough to see if she smashed into the guard rail or not. Frankly I didn't give a shit. For all I care, she could have killed herself."

"What do you want me to do, dear?"

"It doesn't really matter to me, but I thought you would have a good idea of how to proceed. I didn't call Marco, for reasons I'm sure you can understand. I'm sure you don't want one son six feet under and another behind bars in the same week."

Mrs. P smiled. She liked Josie's sense of dark humor at a time like this. "OK honey, I'll take care of it."

"Thanks Mrs. P. I'm not going to call the cops and press charges or anything. I just want to get home and put this behind me. Put these past few days behind me."

"Please keep in touch, and I hope to see you soon. And Josie, you won't need to worry about Lexi for much longer."

"I will. See you soon." *What in the hell is that supposed to mean?* Josie was starting to get the idea that Mrs. P had a master plan in place. She didn't know what Mrs. P was planning, but she was sure of one thing: shit was going to hit the fan.

Josie hung up, and Jackie was staring at Mrs. P with stress-filled eyes, wondering what the hell could be happening now.

"What is it, Mom? What's going on?"

"That was Josie. She just told me that Lexi tried to run her off the road."

"Wait, where? Isn't Lexi out of town traveling for business?" asked Jackie.

"Apparently not. She obviously lied about traveling today. She must have assumed that Josie would visit Marco before leaving town and decided to follow her."

"Wow, I thought I had problems," said Jackie. "What does she want you to do about it?"

"She didn't really want me to do anything. She just wanted to tell me what happened."

Jackie eyed Mrs. P, wondering if she'd been sharing information with Josie. Mrs. P could see on Jackie's face that there were questions flying through her head now. Mrs. P narrowed her eyes and looked straight into Jackie's. "Do you know me at all, Jackie? Don't be stupid."

Chapter 19

Marco left his house and headed for the restaurant where he would be meeting Jimmy for lunch. He was looking forward to catching up with his little brother somewhere other than a funeral parlor.

He pulled into the parking lot and saw a car that looked like it belonged to Lexi's boss. He was sure it was him. It was the most ridiculous shade of green that he had seen around here, ever. He rolled his eyes and shook his head in disgust. He hated that man. He really thought his shit didn't stink, and he was a weasel to boot.

Marco was suddenly overwhelmed by the feeling that something wasn't right. As he continued to look at that horrible green car, Marco realized that Lexi was supposed to be traveling with her boss. Why was he here? This pretty much confirmed his suspicion that Lexi was lying for sure this time. Oddly enough, he didn't really care.

Marco walked into the restaurant and saw Jimmy waiting for him at the bar.

"Hey, you made it," said Jimmy.

"Yes, of course, did you think I wouldn't show up?"

"I wasn't sure. I know you're so busy all the time. I was hoping you didn't get called into a meeting or something."

"Oh, I'm sorry. I must not have mentioned that I took today off as well. I worked from home for a few hours this morning and then . . ." Marco trailed off. Jimmy got judgmental when he talked about

Josie. Jimmy loved her—everyone did—but he was annoyed that Marco couldn't let her go.

"Then what?"

"Then what, what?"

"You said you worked from home and then, and then you stopped," said Jimmy.

Marco didn't want to lie, so he just spilled it.

"Lexi is traveling today and she is supposed to be home tomorrow." Sheepishly, Marco said, "So Josie stopped by before she left town."

"Marco, you are an ass. You should not be tying that poor woman down when you're married. Let her move on. She doesn't need you and our insane family issues cluttering up her life."

Marco knew he was right, but he just couldn't let Josie go. She just meant so much to him, and if she was willing to keep seeing him then he would take advantage of that. Although the conversation today was not so good, he was confident that they still had a chance to be together.

"I know, Jimmy, but it's complicated."

"Marco, it's not complicated at all. You still love her and we all know it."

Marco was shocked. "What?"

"Marco, you're not serious, are you? You didn't really think we don't all know that you're still in love with Josie, did you?"

"Well actually, I thought I was hiding it pretty well, up until now."

"Marco, we would all be pretty stupid not to see it. Just the way you look at her and the way you talk to her."

There was no denying it, especially to his little brother.

"I didn't know it was that obvious."

"Uh, yeah, it's that obvious!" Jimmy wasn't going to bring up Lexi. She didn't deserve to be brought up in this conversation. She certainly didn't deserve Jimmy sticking up for her.

Jimmy disliked Lexi for causing the mess that Marco was in. Of course, he disliked her for many other reasons too. But Marco had been a bad kid and he completely turned his life around. Jimmy looked up to him for that, and Jimmy couldn't help but feel bad that Marco was in a crappy marriage and unhappy.

"Jimmy, why are you looking at me all stupid?"

Jimmy laughed out loud at Marco. "I'm so proud of you."

Marco was shocked at his little brother's comment. He wasn't sure how to react or what to say.

"Thanks," Marco said; it was all he could really come up with. Jimmy's comment felt like it was out of nowhere. He knew he should have said more, but all he said was, "You basically just told me I am an idiot for holding on to Josie, and now you tell me you are proud of me. How am I supposed to react to that? Are you taking your meds today?" asked Marco.

They both laughed. Marco knew full well that Jimmy didn't take any meds. Jimmy had his shit together, more than any of them.

"Let's get our table," Marco said to Jimmy as he put him in a headlock right there at the bar.

The hostess took them to their table. As they sat down, Jimmy asked, "Isn't that Lexi's boss over there?"

Marco didn't bother to look. "Yeah, that's him."

"You didn't even look."

"I saw his car in the lot when I pulled in, so I knew he was here somewhere."

"Oh, that makes sense. You seemed a little off when you walked in. You still hate him that bad?"

"I don't really hate him. I just think he's a pompous ass."

Jimmy laughed. "Oh, like our brother?" It just came right out. He wasn't even sure why he said it. There was obviously some hatred left for Carmine within Jimmy. Jimmy was unsure of what Marco would say, so he was ready to apologize based on Marco's reaction.

Marco just looked at Jimmy, blinking in wonder.

Jimmy started but Marco cut him off. "Is there something you want to talk about?"

Jimmy said, "No, not really. I just don't understand what happened to him. He was the best brother ever when we were little. Well, when I was a kid, anyway. He always took care of me if I needed something. He was always there to talk to, and he gave the best advice. I don't know how his life could have taken such a hard turn. I know it's not from Jackie. She wouldn't hurt a fly. She certainly didn't want him for the money. With all the money they had, she didn't dress flashy. She didn't even buy expensive things. She could have done without the money."

Marco said, "Well, Dad was always very critical of him. Dad thought that if he constantly ragged on him to do better in school, always dress properly, act like a young man and all that, it would set him up for success. Carmine didn't really work that way."

"What do you mean?" asked Jimmy.

"What I mean is Carmine was extremely intelligent, but he never wanted to do anything the conventional way. He never wanted to follow the rules. He always wanted to do things his way. If it took three steps to do something, he would do it in ten just to say he did it his way."

"Why do you think he was like that?"

"Just to be defiant. I think he wanted to have control over something and because he couldn't control our family, I think he figured if he could control his own actions, it would make him less crazy. After a while it all just got out of hand and he just started crapping on everyone."

Jimmy looked at Marco, trying to see if he knew what Jimmy knew. If he had any idea. Marco didn't let on that he knew anything. Either Marco was great at bluffing or he really just didn't know.

"I don't know how he could have done the things that he has done over the years. How heartless could one man be?" Jimmy asked.

Marco looked at Jimmy and said, "That's what a boatload of money does to some people. Once they have so much of it, they want more and will stop at nothing until they get it. More is never enough."

"But hurting your friends and family?"

"Sometimes you get in too deep and there is no way out," Marco said sadly.

Jimmy caught Lexi's boss getting up from his table to leave and Marco looked in that direction as well. Jimmy could see Marco's wheels turning.

"What's eatin' you about him?"

"It's not really him that's on my mind. It's Lexi."

"Oh, wow, now you're going to start thinking about your wife with concern on your face?"

Marco threw his napkin at Jimmy.

"No, it's not concern, it's just . . ." Marco trailed off.

"What then?" Jimmy was thinking about Lexi and the horrible things he knew about her. Why would Marco be disgusted if he didn't know? Jimmy didn't want to come right out and ask him.

"I mentioned earlier that I took some time to see Josie before she left town."

"Yes, you did but—"

Marco cut him off. "Lexi was supposed to be traveling with her boss. So why is he here, and better yet, where the hell is she?" Marco exclaimed.

Jimmy looked at Marco, the panic causing his eyebrows to rise. Jimmy knew Lexi was capable of some horrible things, but this raised serious concerns.

Chapter 20

John was back in the city and settling into his office for the day. He was thinking about Josie and wondering how he was going to convince her to have dinner with him. He was racking his brain, trying to figure out why she was still hung up on that nutcase, Marco. He was nothing special. He certainly didn't have more than John. Not to mention the fact that Marco was married. The thought of them together, romantically . . . again . . . made him almost angry.

John could understand if Josie didn't want anything permanent, but she wasn't the type to sneak around with someone else's husband. So why was she doing it, and how was he going to get her away from Marco?

John was looking out the window of his office, and his mind drifted to the last conversation that he and Josie had before they both left for college.

"Josie, wait! Can't we at least talk about this?"

"No, John, there's nothing left to say."

"How can you say that? We could talk for two days and there would still be more to talk about."

"John, there is nothing we can do about what happened. All I can say is thank God it's over."

"Thank God it's over? How can you say that? You just told me today. I literally just found out minutes ago."

"Well, I've been dealing with it for a week, so for me, I'm just glad it's over."

"Josie, I can't imagine what you are going through, nor would I ever try to understand, but at least talk to me about it."

"I'm sorry, John, but I don't have anything to say. Do you want the gory details? Do you want to know how I figured it out? What exactly is it that you are looking for?"

John knew that Josie didn't blame him for when she cheated on Marco with him. She took full responsibility for what she did.

That wasn't the worst of things to happen though. John's feeling of sadness was unavoidable whenever he thought about the last thing she had told him before she left. Josie had a miscarriage, and John's heart broke for her every time he thought about it.

His continuous sadness only reinforced his feelings for her each time he thought about what she said. He knew the baby wasn't even his—the timing was way off—but he still felt sad. Not anger or hate. Just sad.

And even though Josie didn't blame him, his deep sadness for the situation was because it was his fault that Josie and Marco broke up. He blamed himself. He always thought that life would have been easier for Josie if he would have just left her alone. She was happier without him than with him. Even though Marco came between them, John was the reason Josie and Marco broke up for good in the end. Maybe Marco's family wouldn't hate John so much if he would have just left her alone too. They cursed him for pursuing Josie while she was with Marco. Typical for that family to not take responsibility. They loved Josie, and blamed her too, but they didn't want to face the fact that Marco was clearly pushing her away.

With that horrible question from Josie echoing in his head, he snapped out of his thoughts and wondered how he could have been such a putz. Why didn't he just leave her alone? Would it have made any difference? It's not like she would have talked about it or stayed with him if he didn't push the issue. She was leaving no matter what, and so was he. Both going at least two hours away from home. He didn't dare bring up that old conversation.

And there was Anthony. The most vile man they had ever known. He needed to talk to Josie about that too, but he would need her to bring it up. The past would need to be dealt with if they had any hope of moving on together, but it would have to be on her terms.

Then there was Marco's request of him and Josie. John was fixated on it. How were they ever going to figure that out? They were two people who hadn't been in town for years and certainly hadn't spoken to Carmine in those years. Where would they even begin? Being a two-hour drive away from their hometown gave John no lead. He couldn't speak for Josie, but he was pretty sure she didn't have any clue where to start either. He thought it was safe to assume she probably wasn't even thinking about where to start.

He was staring at his computer, seeing the piled-up emails and the files on his desk and he could barely focus. John needed to get out of there. He was just not in the mood to do anything at all, not to mention to do actual work. He thought he would run down to the coffee shop on the corner and grab a coffee and maybe a breakfast sandwich before he dug into the pile of crap on his desk. He should have done it before he even got into the office, but he was trying to cut down on the coffee these days.

Hearing a noise down the hall, John peeked out his office door to see the light was on in his boss's office. It was way too early for him to be in the office already, but there he was. John was trying to figure out how he could sneak by his boss without being noticed. Not that he would have any issue with John leaving, but he would want to tag along, and that was the last thing John wanted.

John was just about to get up to leave the office for his unplanned breakfast when a new message popped up saying he had a file to review.

He had every intention of waiting to open it until after he returned to the office, but something about it caught his eye.

He clicked to open the message and began reading. Most of it was the usual jargon of a normal insurance policy, but as he continued reading, he began to panic. He kept reading a particular paragraph over and over; the more he read it, the more he panicked.

He stood up and started pacing around his office. Forgetting that his boss was in early that morning, John nearly jumped through the ceiling when he saw him standing in his doorway. “John, is everything alright?”

Chapter 21

Josie was with Marco in his jeep, Marco driving too fast as usual. They pulled into the parking lot at the lake. Well, where the lake used to be. It was drained, for reasons she didn't know. She saw a piece of land that used to jut into the water, but without the water, it was just another mound of sand. She wasn't sure why they were there, but she had a feeling, and she was becoming angry with Marco. "Let's go," said Marco.

Josie looked at him, puzzled. She got out of the jeep and walked towards Marco. He took her hand and pulled her over to the waterless land. He picked her up in his big bear hug and swung her around. He put her down and held her for a while.

She was so lost in the moment. He kissed her on the forehead, but something just didn't feel right. She was there, but not all there.

Josie's eyes started to flutter open, and she rolled over to the sunlight beginning to creep in through her bedroom window. It took her a few moments to realize she was dreaming. She hardly ever dreamed about something that actually happened.

Today, she had a number of things to do to plan for the premiere, but she was able to do everything from her apartment. She was getting very excited; she wanted to take it all in and enjoy each moment. She made sure her calendar was clear of any calls and appointments for the day.

As she lay there staring at the ceiling, she recalled the fact that she didn't bother to text Marco when she got home last night. She was not going to give him the satisfaction. She thought she might regret it when she woke up in the morning. Nope! She was still pretty happy with herself that she stood her ground.

She was going to have to figure out what she really wanted. She really liked having Marco in her life, but this was getting out of hand. She knew he loved her, but if he didn't make steps to leave Lexi, she was moving on.

Of course, her thoughts drifted to John. He was the perfect guy, if there was such a thing. He was single, still obviously crazy about her, and he had a great job. Sure, time can change people, but he was still a gentleman. She knew by the way he acted at the viewing. Josie hoped maybe he would call. She knew she couldn't reach out to him. She didn't want to go chasing after him without knowing what her intentions would be for them. She didn't want to lead him on. She felt it would only work if he initiated any communication.

She was beginning to see a pattern that was concerning her. Each time she thought of Marco and Lexi, her mind would drift to John. As great as John was, was she only entertaining getting to know John again because she couldn't have Marco to herself? She rubbed her temples with her fingers.

They were both very polite. Who was better looking? Would that matter when they were old and gray? No, it wouldn't. Who made her laugh more? Definitely Marco, but John was deeper. It always seemed he had more interesting things to talk about. Marco was distracted at times.

That was enough about that for now. Josie was unhappy that she wasted this precious premiere planning time on them today. She rolled out of bed and walked into the bathroom to get ready for the day. After she showered, she threw on a pair of jeans and a sweater, and didn't bother to do her face. She didn't need make up anyway.

She made herself a cup of coffee and opened her laptop.

Chapter 22

John looked at his boss in complete embarrassment. He didn't quite know what to say. With his boss staring at him like he was a lunatic, he stammered out, "Hey, I mean, hello, good morning."

His boss asked again, "Are you OK, John?"

John, clearing his throat, replied very cautiously, "Yes, I'm fine. I was on a roll this morning and my hands began shaking and I realized I hadn't eaten breakfast yet. I stood up to head out to get something to eat and got an alert on the computer saying I had another email and I was just contemplating whether I should address that first or just run downstairs to get something to eat quickly."

"Why don't you just head out to grab something to eat? Maybe the walk will help you calm down a bit."

"Good idea, boss. Thank you, and I'll be right back." John blew out the door directly past his boss and didn't care that it might be rude that he didn't ask him to go along. He would patch it up when he got back. He needed to be alone right now. He needed to think.

He got off the elevator and ran out into the fresh air. He felt slightly better, but he knew the feeling would be short lived. He was hoping the corner coffee shop wasn't too packed. He just wanted to eat his breakfast in peace and figure out how he was going to talk to Josie about what he may have just discovered. He knew it would make Josie angry if he got in the way of whatever she was doing with

Marco, and he wasn't trying to do that, but he needed to make sure she was safe.

As he thought back, it seemed like everyone was always trying to protect her. She was worth protecting, but why was she always caught in the metaphorical crossfire?

He was going to have to choose his words very wisely. He needed to have a full understanding of what he was reading before he went to her with this horrifying document that just fell into his lap.

"John!" John turned, brought out of his deep thought. The woman behind the counter must have been trying to take his order.

"Sorry, uh, yeah, oh, sorry about that. I'll take, uh, yeah, my—"

She cut him off. "Do you want your usual, John?"

"Yes, please, Jamie. That would be great."

"Are you OK?"

"Yes, I'm fine." John looked at Jamie behind the counter. He certainly wasn't going to get into it with her. He didn't want to be rude either. "I'm sorry, Jamie. I'm really busy at work for some reason and I just needed to get something in my stomach so I could focus for the rest of the day."

She handed him his breakfast sandwich and a large black coffee, and he was gone before she could say goodbye.

When John got back to the office, his boss was waiting for him, right where he'd left him. There was no avoiding it; John just walked past him and sat down at his desk.

"Thanks, boss, I just needed to eat something," John said, finishing the last few bites of his sandwich.

"So, you're better now?"

"Yes, I believe so." John calmed down a bit and made his best effort to show his boss that he was fine and ready to get back to work for the day.

"OK, good," he said and walked back to his office.

John let out a sigh of relief. Now that his sandwich was eaten and his coffee was cooling, it was time to dive right into this new file and see exactly what the hell was going on. His first lead.

Chapter 23

Lexi woke up in the hotel she stayed in after her poor attempt to scare Josie to death. She was definitely not in her right mind. It was time for her to get a grip and put things into perspective. *How did things get this out of hand? How did I let it get this bad?*

She knew it was ridiculous to blame Josie for anything. She drove Marco away with her nonsense. It was Lexi's fault that all of this pain was going around. Maybe not totally her fault, but she had enough of a hand in all the grieving. Most importantly, she was grieving and there was no one to blame but herself.

She was afraid to go home. She knew if Marco already knew what happened that he would go crazy. She didn't fear him physically, but she feared what he was capable of doing, the people he knew and the connections he had. She shuddered at the thought. She feared the others more, but he would be behind whatever were to happen to her.

She'd have to go home and face him, sooner or later. Now was as good a time as any, and why not just get it over with? Still in bed, she took her meds for the first time in a week. *More of a chance of getting somewhere with the conversation if I'm focused*, she thought.

She showered quickly and got herself together. She packed up her little bag and got in the car to head home.

As soon as she revved up the engine, her phone buzzed, alerting her that she had a text message. She wanted to ignore it, but it was time to face the music.

It was from Mrs. P. Her heart sank with worry. As she read the message, she began to calm down. Mrs. P was asking to get together for lunch some day next week. She thought it would be a good idea to get Jackie out of the house one afternoon. She asked Lexi to check her schedule and see what day would work best for her.

Maybe Josie kept her mouth shut after all and just went back to the city where she belonged.

Lexi pulled out of the parking lot and started driving. She hadn't spoken to Marco since his call yesterday. *He's probably working; what else does he do?* she thought.

She was still trying to blame Marco for her antics. He worked too much or never paid enough attention to her. *Stop blaming everyone else, Lexi. You need to be responsible for your own actions.* As all of this was running through her head, she briefly forgot about Carmine. As his memory floated back into her head, she choked up. She thought she was all cried out, but the tears kept coming.

Lexi pulled into the driveway, and Marco's car was missing. She was relieved, but also bothered. The countless days that she had come home and he wasn't there pulled at her nerves. She wanted to talk to him and get this off her chest. She would just have to wait until he got home. Whenever that would be.

She sat down at the kitchen table and fired up her computer, checking her calendar for lunch with her lady-in-laws. She would rather stick a fire poker in her eye than have lunch with them, but she figured she better play nice for a while until the dust settled.

She picked up her phone to reply. She typed out, "Those dates work for me. Pick one and let me know where and when."

Her stomach started churning. She knew Marco had to know by now what happened. If he did, he was going to be so angry with her. So angry that this might be the breaking point for them. It was just as well. If this was the end of them, so be it. They would both be better off apart anyway. She was beginning to feel numb to their whole relationship.

She heard Marco's car pull up outside. This was it. Possibly the end of her marriage.

Marco walked in the house and saw Lexi sitting at the table.

"I thought you weren't coming home until tomorrow," he said.

Lexi was confused. She didn't know why he was so calm. She had told him yesterday that she was coming home tomorrow, which would be today. She chose her tone carefully. She didn't want to sound as though she was blaming him for not listening.

"Oh, I'm sorry. When we talked yesterday, I thought I told you I was coming home tomorrow, meaning today."

Marco just nodded.

"You can't just let her go, can you?" The words poured out of Lexi's mouth like wine into a glass. This was not the angle she was supposed to take for this conversation. She was not planning on blaming Josie, but the words just came out.

"Who? What are you talking about?"

Lexi did not utter another word. At that moment, she realized that Marco had no idea what happened. He didn't know she tried to run Josie off the road. She needed to choose her words very wisely if she wanted to keep this marriage alive.

"Marco—" Lexi began, but Marco cut her off.

"Where were you?"

"When?"

"Yesterday," said Marco with disgust. "Where were you yesterday?"

Lexi was confused. He obviously didn't know about Josie, but he knew she wasn't actually traveling for work.

She already knew he hated her. No matter what she said right now, it would be wrong. She took a deep breath to gain some composure.

"Marco, I wanted some time to myself and I just needed to be alone. I know how that sounds and I'm sorry. Everything hit me at once and I realized how stupid and selfish I have been to you and your family."

Marco stood there, stunned. He had never expected her to say anything like this. She'd never admitted how selfish she had become over the last few years. She always just blamed him. Was she taking the blame now? Would it matter? In his mind, there was still no way to save this marriage.

"Marco, we have been through a lot, and mostly because of me. Our marriage, if you can still call it that, is in total shambles. Not like I have to tell you that, but I don't pretend to think that there is anything left." She stopped talking, half expecting Marco to walk away and slam doors or race out of the house and peel off in his car somewhere unknown; but he just stood there staring at her. This was what she wanted.

Marco eyed Lexi cautiously. He knew she was hiding something, but he had no idea where to even begin to figure it out. He wanted to see where this was going so, he let her keep talking.

"Maybe it's time we just call it quits. We don't need each other any longer, and thank God you never wanted to have children."

That stung Marco. Right in the heart. He always wanted kids, but not with Lexi. His mind drifted to another time and, of course, another girl. He reeled himself back to the conversation. If this was the end of them, he should pay attention.

Lexi wasn't looking at Marco while she was talking. She was too afraid she would start to cry. "I was always so lonely, and I know I did some really stupid things, but I want you to know that I loved you once. You were truly in my heart for quite a while. I never felt inferior to Josie, but I know you could never love me the way you loved her."

Marco felt a very small bit of sadness for Lexi. He was a shithead, after all, and clearly never saw how it affected Lexi. Talk about selfish.

The horrible thing she had done to him was possibly because of him, and he began to realize it for the first time.

"Lexi, please don't say that."

"Marco, it's true, and I've come to terms with it. That's why I'm telling you that we should just walk away before we kill each other." She came into the conversation planning on saying the exact opposite of what ended up coming out of her mouth, but Lexi was groveling. She had her own secrets, secrets far worse than Marco's, and she was not willing to bring them up now.

Marco said, "If that's what you want, then that's what we'll do. I can't argue with any of what you just said. Let's try to agree to not let this thing get nasty. After everything we have been through over the years, we can have enough respect for one another to keep it civilized."

Lexi agreed, knowing full well that was not how she was planning on playing this game. This wasn't over, and she was going to make sure of that. She was going to make him suffer if it was the last thing she did. That's what she thought, anyway.

Chapter 24

John sat at his desk, mouth gaping open in complete disbelief of what he was reading. He had so many questions. He contemplated reaching out to Marco, but if Marco was involved somehow, he did not want Marco to know he had this information.

This was too much to handle by himself; even if it wasn't, he thought Josie should know. This was going to crush her. Just bringing up this creep's name was going to upset her. Anthony Scarano, one of the shadiest men John had ever met. He was one of those guys who had a lot of money, and no one ever really knew why or how he got it.

Of course, you'd think Mafia, but it didn't add up. This man infiltrated Josie's childhood and somehow was connected to her father. Again, a situation of who knew how or why. All John knew is that Josie hated him, and she had every right to.

John toyed with the idea of calling her. He wanted to tell Josie what he had found, but he was afraid of how she might react. And he knew that she'd hang up on him if the name Anthony came out of his mouth. He had to do it, though. No question. He knew that if he didn't tell her and she found out he knew, she'd be mad anyway. Either way it was a lose-lose for him. He would rather get it out of the way now so they could move on. He wanted to be honest with her.

John picked up his phone and dialed Josie's number. His palms began to sweat. Suddenly he realized that he was sitting on the edge of his office chair, almost hoping she didn't pick up.

"What do you want, John?" A soft yet annoyed voice came through the phone.

"Hi, I didn't think you would pick up when you saw it was me calling."

Josie paused before she answered. "Well, if I ignored you, you would just keep on calling."

John couldn't argue. She knew him well. He bashfully laughed and got on with it.

"Josie, I discovered something today at work and I need to talk to you about it. I know you probably don't—"

Josie cut him off, "And you want to meet up for dinner to show me, or tell me, or whatever you are up to?"

John was baffled that she just said it like that. He was hopeful that she was willing to meet up, but he thought he had a better chance of seeing God before she threw it out there.

"OK, John, where do you want to meet and when?"

Still baffled by Josie's response, John was silent. He knew he better speak up before she got angry and she changed her mind.

"Can we meet tonight at the Thai place on 37th Street? Say seven?"

"I'll see you then, John."

"Don't you even want to know what it's about?"

"Carmine?" she asked.

"Yes," replied John.

"Goodbye, John."

Before he could say goodbye, Josie was gone.

That was much easier than I thought it would be. What is she up to? Maybe nothing. Hopefully, nothing. Josie knew what John did for a living, so he figured she already thought he found something important.

He looked at his watch. He had plenty of time to gather a lot more information and get home and take a quick shower before heading out to see Josie.

John was grappling with the fact that there was a good chance that he was not going to end up with Josie, but he wanted to play nice in this whole situation. Also, he was beginning to think that he wanted to help Marco out of the kindness of his heart. With all the issues they had over the years, he was starting to feel Marco's concerns. He'd been doing this job a long time and he knew what this stuff could do to families. He wasn't doing it just for brownie points with Josie anymore. He was putting a lot on the line for them. He was going to have to be very clear that if he shared this info with her and someone found out about it, he would definitely lose his job, or even worse.

Chapter 25

Josie sat back in her chair, wondering, *How bad could it really be? Carmine's death has nothing to do with me; it really doesn't affect my life at all.* Her life, for the most part, was back to normal. She'd hear some details from Marco and now whatever John had to say, but no matter what, she knew, ultimately, it would not have any bearing on how she lived the rest of her life.

She had so much to do in the coming months. She would be so busy with the movie premiere and the launch of her next book. The last thing she wanted to worry about was all this.

Her thoughts continued to drift back to John. She didn't want to be thinking about him, but for some reason she kept going back to him. How things ended with them and how she just left for college and never turned back. This was the first time she had the smallest bit of regret about how she left things.

There was no way she could let the past get in the way of her future. She needed to focus on her professional career and continue to leave the past in the past.

She would meet with John, just to hear what he had to say. She would eat some good food and she knew she would have a pleasant evening with John, if nothing else. She would hear him out and try not to get sucked back into the chaos. It was awfully ironic to her that John was at the center of things now. And Josie couldn't help but wonder why Marco would want to get John involved, anyway. Why John, after everything that happened in the past?

Just then, it dawned on her what John did for a living. Her heart rate increased, and she realized she was pacing. *Did Marco know something? Did he know that if he asked John to keep an ear open for any inkling of foul play, and John agreed, he would get information from him that he wouldn't otherwise be able to acquire?*

That could be the only logical explanation for Marco to want John involved in this, even if he wanted to see if something was going on with John and Josie. There were a few angles that Marco could have here, and her anger was building. If she wanted something to be going on with John, she could have it, and there was nothing Marco could do about it. She sighed, feeling like maybe she was jumping to conclusions now. Making excuses again and pushing Marco away.

Her mind wandered right back to John and what shocking news she was going to have to prepare herself to hear. She would also be prepared for John to possibly ask her out again. *Was this a date?* she thought. *Probably not. John sounded way too serious on the phone for it to be a date.* Although, the way he looked at her at the viewing was enough for her to know that he still had feelings for her.

She looked at her watch. Her stomach did a small somersault for a reason she was unsure of, but for now, she was going to put the anxiety away and just wait to see what he had to say instead of trying to figure it out on her own.

Chapter 26

Mrs. Paretti sat outside the office of the forensic pathologist, waiting for the circus to arrive. They'd be a smaller group today. Jimmy and Marco were driving together, and Jackie had excused herself from coming; she just could not bring herself to attend. Mrs. P had offered to pick her up, but Jackie refused. And Lexi had made herself scarce since the funeral. Just as well for Mrs. P. She would be meeting Jackie and Lexi for an early dinner instead of lunch later today.

James would be strolling in any minute. Antonia felt a twinge of excitement at the thought of the conversation they would eventually need to have. As much as she despised him, they always did work better as a professional team than a couple.

Marco and Jimmy strolled in, quietly for once. They had become closer as Jimmy had gotten older and Mrs. P was glad for that. With Carmine gone, she wanted them to be close. She wanted them to always have each other.

They hugged their mother at the same time, and each gave her a kiss on the cheek. Marco, in his usual fashion, looked as though he had better things to do than be there.

She let it go. She was not going to say a word. He had every right to feel the way he did about Carmine. Just like the rest of the family.

In sync, they all whipped their head towards the door when it opened. Mr. P strolled in, looking like a million bucks as usual. His somber facial expression did not match his clothing. He shook hands with his sons and put an arm around each of them. He knew it was too little too late, but he wasn't going to stop trying. Mrs. P could see he was making an effort, and that lifted her mood.

He kissed Antonia on the cheek, just like the boys had, and whispered, "Let's get this over with." As much as she had despised this man for a long time, they were still connected. Just like in the old days when they used to plot and scheme together, unbeknownst to the boys.

Marco and Jimmy shared a sideways glance as their father kissed their mother on the cheek. Marco rolled his eyes and shook his head. This was the last thing he had time for right now.

Once they were all settled, the receptionist said, "The pathologist is ready for you now."

As they were walking in, Marco said, "Mom, I don't understand why you would want this autopsy. You're incurring all this extra cost on your own for them to tell us what we already know."

Mr. P turned his head away from Marco so he was unable see his smirk. What he knew was not for the kids to know, or anyone for that matter, except Antonia.

"Marco, please just appease your mother," his father barked.

Jimmy said, "Wait, aren't we going to wait for Jackie?"

Mrs. P replied, "Oh, she won't be coming. She texted me earlier saying she just couldn't deal with this today. I'll see her later anyway, and she didn't exactly agree with me about having the autopsy done. She said the initial ruling was a heart attack and she didn't want Carmine to be cut up just for them to say the same thing."

Marco agreed with Jackie and thought his mother was crazy for having this done on her own dime. The death was ruled a heart attack from the beginning and it seemed a perfectly legitimate reason. Maybe she assumed foul play, but the cops weren't sold on that theory. They had no evidence that led them to think it was anything other than natural causes.

The door opened and in walked the forensic pathologist. He shook hands with everyone and offered them all a seat.

He was an average height man with a shaved head. He had compassionate eyes and looked well-prepared to deliver the news.

He said, "Thank you for coming in today. I know that things like this are not easy and you all seem to be holding up pretty well."

At the pathologist's remarks, the boys shifted in their seats and Mrs. P cleared her throat. Everyone was holding up fine; they just wanted to get this over with.

He began again, "My findings are in line with the original cause of death, so I am ruling this a heart attack. I don't see anything else that should cause alarm. There is nothing that would lead me to believe that something other than his poor health would have factored into Carmine's death. It is my professional opinion that no other parties were involved in Carmine's death."

Mrs. P smiled slightly, pleased that she decided to have this done. Now she could rest easy knowing that the results had been verified, shared with the family, and written in the report.

"I do have one question, and I noticed that the deceased's wife is not in attendance today. I'd planned to ask her, and I'm not sure you would know the answer."

Mrs. P said, "I can get her on the phone, if you would like."

"That's fine with me, but I will need to ask her some questions to verify that it is actually her. I am sorry to do that, but—"

Mrs. P cut him off, "Don't be sorry, we understand."

She dialed Jackie and waited for her to pick up. When Jackie answered, Mrs. P put the phone on speaker and told her what was going on. She then handed the phone to the pathologist.

"Jackie, hello." He introduced himself and fired away with his questions to verify it was, in fact, Jackie. "Carmine's medical records show that he was taking heart medication."

"Yes, that's correct," answered Jackie.

"Did you notice if he took his medication every day as prescribed?"

The hair on the back of Jackie's neck stood up. *Pull yourself together, Jackie*, she thought.

"I'm sorry, but I don't really know the answer. I didn't physically see him take it, but I would pick up his prescriptions every month, so I'm sure he was."

"His blood work was abnormal. The levels of medication in his system were not consistent to the dosage of prescription. He also had a high level of calcium in his system. This is another reason for his heart malfunctioning. So, my pronouncement stands: he had a heart attack."

Mrs. P made eye contact the pathologist. She gave him a very subtle but curt nod, careful not to let the others see. Everything was falling into place.

Jackie was stunned. *That's it?* she thought. *He didn't take his medication? Case closed?*

Chapter 27

When Mrs. P got home, she dialed Jackie to check on her and make sure they were still on for an early dinner with Lexi. The phone rang but went to voicemail. She left a message. She didn't panic. She did a few things around the house and then Jackie called.

"Hello, Jackie."

"Hi."

"You doing OK?"

"Yes, I'm OK. I'm just glad that it's all over. I could hardly stand the wait. Even though I didn't want to be there today, it's been eating at me something awful."

"I know, Jackie. I hated putting you through that, but, well, you know I had my reasons."

"I understand, Mom. I'm just glad it's over."

"Are you still coming for dinner?" Mrs. P asked.

"Yep, I'm all set and my mom is coming over to stay with the kids. I'll be over in about an hour." Jackie was revving up to ask about the call, but she ran out of time.

"Great, see you then." Mrs. P hung up.

Lexi sat at the kitchen table, wondering how she could possibly get out of going for dinner with the good witch and the bad witch. She would rather stay home and be judged by Marco than spend the evening with those two.

She was on a deadline for work and wanted to put her nose to the grindstone and get it done. She was on a roll until the thought of Carmine slipped into her head. *This is it. Now he will no longer be on the earth. He'll be in it. What a morbid thought.* She couldn't shake it. She was sad but becoming angrier as the time went on. She had bitten her nails down to stubs waiting for Marco to tell her what the autopsy results showed. She had her own suspicions of what happened, but that was totally off the table for now. At least until she found out the truth.

The second hand ticked by on the clock, and with every tock, the knot in Lexi's stomach got bigger and bigger. She wanted to talk to Marco before she left for dinner. She wanted to be prepared for how dinner would play out. She knew she'd have to be very careful about how she asked Marco. Maybe she'd be lucky and he would just tell her. She exhaled strongly with a scoff at that thought, knowing he never just offered the information. God forbid he communicate.

She heard the back door open and knew he was home.

"Hey," said Marco as he came around the corner.

"Hey, how'd it go?" she asked.

"It went. The ruling is still a heart attack, as they originally thought." He refused to mention the rest of it. She would have to get more details at dinner.

"Oh," said Lexi with relief, but also sadness. She was looking for someone to blame.

She glanced at the clock on the computer and saw that it was time to leave.

"I'm heading out for dinner with your mom and Jackie."

Marco's eyebrows lifted. "Wow, that sounds exciting."

"Yeah. I'll see you later." She waved goodbye to Marco. The days of them kissing hello and goodbye were long gone. She grabbed her bag and out the door she went.

When the doorbell rang, Mrs. P opened the door and invited Lexi in. Lexi felt so uncomfortable. She didn't belong here and she didn't want to spend the majority of her evening making nice with two women that certainly weren't her favorites.

"Hi, Lexi." Jackie greeted her with arms out for a hug. Lexi hugged her reluctantly. She was even more uncomfortable now. They had to be up to something. But what?

They sat down to eat, and Mrs. P made her family favorite, chicken piccata. It paired nicely with the two bottles of white wine Lexi had brought; she was prepared to drink heavily to get through the evening. Mrs. P would have more if the conversations got particularly unpleasant.

The night moved on quickly. She was careless with her alcohol. Her eyes were almost shut. She was very drunk. She realized how badly she was sickened with grief.

"Lexi, I think I better take you home. You certainly are in no shape to drive. Jackie can follow us to your house to bring your car back."

Lexi was embarrassed, but she knew Mrs. P wasn't going to take no for an answer.

"OK, thank you." Lexi muttered.

Mrs. P smiled slyly at Jackie, expressing that this was the right thing to do, even though they both despised Lexi for her actions leading up to this night. She had become such a dreadful person. Mrs. P lamented about how nice she used to be when she first came into the family. She kept coming back to the same question: What happened to her? Lexi seemed to be so innocent and shy when she and Marco first started seeing one another. As the years passed, she became so obsessed with money and material things. Was it a way to cope since Marco was still in love with Josie?

The cars pulled up to Lexi and Marco's home, and Mrs. P and Jackie carried Lexi inside. Marco, sitting in the living room, heard the commotion. "What's happening?" he called out as he entered the room. Marco took in the scene before him, his mother and sister-in-law holding Lexi up between them. Just when he thought he couldn't be more disgusted with this woman and her actions, he was repulsed by her limp, drunken body.

Mrs. P said, "We ate dinner and had a few bottles of wine. She must not have had enough to eat today."

Jackie chimed in, saying, "We brought her car back."

"Thank you," Marco managed. He picked her up and put her on the couch. "I'll let her just sleep it off."

"I don't think you have much of a choice, honey," said Mrs. P.

Marco saw them out. Coming back into the living room, he considered smothering Lexi with a pillow but decided she wasn't worth going to jail for. Instead, he picked up his phone and called Josie.

Chapter 28

Josie wanted to get to the restaurant before John, but she knew there was a fat chance of that happening. Sure enough, she walked in and there was John, waiting for her at the end of the bar.

"Hey there," said John, pulling Josie in for a hug and a kiss on the cheek. He wasn't letting her out of that. He needed her to know he was there for her, no matter where this twisted story turned.

"Hi, John." She gratefully welcomed his enthusiastic embrace. Being with John was very easy. No drama, and hardly ever any distractions. She was beginning to dismantle the wall she put up around herself to keep John away. All he wanted was to help, and she was fully aware of that. She didn't know how tonight was going to go, but she braced herself for whatever he had to say.

They sat at their table making small talk. They looked over their menus and put them down at the same time. They smiled at one other. They had both forgotten how easy things could be between them. At the same time, they both started to speak, blurting out each other's names then breaking out into laugher at what they had just done.

"You go first, Josie."

"I'm not sleeping with him," Josie said a little awkwardly. "I mean, if you were wondering what is actually going on with Marco, it's not that."

John raised his eyebrows, hoping she would elaborate. "Um . . . thank you?" he questioned, just as awkwardly.

She giggled, knowing how ridiculous she just sounded and tried to make light of it. "I saw the look on your face when you realized something might be going on with Marco and me at the viewing and I just wanted to tell you what's not going on. You know me well enough to know I wouldn't go sleeping around with someone's husband."

"That's exactly what I thought to myself when I thought something might be going on. I knew you weren't. It did cross my mind, but my exact thought was that there was no way you would do that. It's none of my business, but since you are back in my life . . ." John stopped. At that, Josie could have thrown her drink in his face and stormed out of the restaurant, but she didn't.

She stayed and said, "John, before we go jumping to conclusions here, let's just take it one step at a time." His heart jumped a little. Knowing there could be a chance for them made him very happy.

"Josie, I know I don't have to say this to you, but if you have to explain yourself to someone, then you are probably better off without the person who needs explaining in your life."

"Thank you, Mr. Life Coach." She smirked at John. "I plan on enjoying this evening for as long as we have, and I don't want to rush it. Let's get the awfulness out of the way and hopefully it won't ruin the rest of the evening."

"OK, Josie, whatever you want, I'll do."

She liked knowing that he was willing to conform to her needs. At least for tonight.

John continued, "OK, so this is what happened. I'll start from the beginning of my day." He went on to tell her how he lost all concentration at his desk and how he was heading out to get breakfast. He had just stood up to leave his office when he received the notification that he had a new file to view.

"Josie, I stopped dead in my tracks. I was literally just about to get out of the office, even though I had only been there less than a half hour, when this file arrived. I don't think I have to explain again that I could lose my job for sharing this with you, but given the circumstances, I could never keep this from you. Things like this happen more than you think, and I just hope I'm not the one to get caught doing it."

"How bad is it, John?"

"It's sort of awful, but it's far more bizarre than awful, I think. You are going to really hate one piece of it, but other than that it's just odd."

"OK, so hit me with it!"

"Here it goes. So obviously every insurance policy has a beneficiary, right?"

"Yeah, of course," Josie agreed.

"Well, there was an insurance policy taken out on Carmine. The weird thing is who it was taken out by." He paused. He hated having to be the one to say his name to Josie. "It was taken out by Anthony." He didn't bother to say the last name. She knew damn well who he was talking about.

Josie just sat there, stunned. "Why?" she managed to question.

"Josie, that's not even the weird part. That was the awful, now comes the bizarre." John's voice became higher, even though he tried to calm down. "The beneficiary is Lexi."

Josie didn't bother to speak, and John wasn't expecting her to.

"Sadly, I'm not done. The second listed beneficiary, if Lexi is no longer alive, is Jackie."

Chapter 29

Marco sat in his living room, flipping through the TV channels. He was so annoyed that Lexi was drunk and passed out. He puffed out an angry breath while shaking his head.

He wondered how it all got to this point. What was to come? *How will I get out of this ridiculous marriage without Lexi making a complete mess out of any attempt at civility?*

He glanced at his phone, fighting the urge to call or text Josie. Again. She ignored him when he called her earlier. He wanted to so badly, but he knew she wasn't exactly happy with him right now. He was trying to give her space. Ultimately, he knew that leaving Lexi was the only option he had for getting Josie back for good. That was going to be a process, but he was actually working on it this time.

He picked up the phone and started texting, then erased it. He tried again. He started typing. Then erased it again.

Forget it, he thought. He picked up the phone and just called her. Again.

Her voicemail picked up, and his heart ached. He knew it was a possibility that she would ignore his second call, and she did.

His phone rang immediately after he put it down and his hopes rose. He looked at the screen but didn't recognize the number, so he just ignored it. *Guess I'll head to the home gym for a workout*, he thought.

Josie was enjoying her dinner with John until he dropped the bomb about Lexi. During a break in the conversation, Josie's phone started buzzing on the table. She checked the screen, as did John, and he stared at her, wondering if she was going to answer it or let it go to voicemail.

Josie wanted to answer it so badly, but she didn't want John to think their time together wasn't important to her. How important was it to her, really?

She needed to just put Marco out of her head for the time being so she could focus on John and all the information he was giving her. She promised herself she wouldn't keep this from Marco. She had every intention of telling him when they spoke again. But for now, the information John just blurted out about Lexi was something she was still trying to process.

Marco was working out, and all the while becoming angrier about the mess surrounding him. He was preoccupied and didn't hear the voicemail alert on his phone. It was from the unidentified number.

He decided to shower quickly and then listen to it. When he got out of the shower, he briefly thought to check on Lexi, but then thought, *Why bother?*

He picked up his phone, typed his passcode in, and began listening to the message.

"Marco, son, it's your father." Marco's pulse ticked up a few notches. "I have a new number so I'm sure you didn't recognize it. Call me as soon as you have the chance. Now that Carmine is gone, you and I are going to have to start getting along." Marco thought, *Really? Now you want to get along? This is just stupid. What an insult. My brother needed to die for my father to pay attention to me?*

Marco's father continued his message. "We have some things to talk about, and things are going to get ugly. Your mother knows I'm calling you, so call me when you get a minute."

What is the hell is he talking about? Like things aren't ugly enough? He wished Josie would have picked up her phone. He could really use a few minutes of just hearing her voice sweetly chirping on the other end of the line. He didn't even care if she was screaming at him. He just needed her.

The last thing he felt like doing right now was speaking with his father. *God only knows what this is about.* Against his better judgment, he decided to call him and get it out of the way.

He was just about to push the redial button on the phone when a text came through from his mother.

Mom: Marco, please call your father back.
Marco: I'm on it, Mom. Calling him now.

"What in God's name is going on?" Marco puffed through gritted teeth. He tapped the number for a call back, and his father picked up on the first ring.

"Hi, son."

"Hey." Marco was not going to give him the satisfaction of pretending that they were one big, happy family.

"I'm glad you called me back."

"No problem, and Mom just texted me, too. I don't understand how the two of you hate each other but work together like Bonnie and Clyde."

Marco's father laughed, even though this was no time for laughing, and he knew Marco would rather be doing anything other than talking to him.

"Marco, this is not the time to discuss your mother and me. I have something very important to speak to you about." Marco was silent, hoping that would cue his father to keep talking so this would be even quicker.

"We all know your brother was no saint." Marco rolled his eyes. He was sick of this conversation already and it had only just begun.

"Yes, the money, you guys, the in-laws," listed Marco.

"Marco, it's far worse than that. It's worse than any of us could have imagined." His father's voice faltered a bit. He was holding back a sob and Marco could hear it.

"Dad, are you OK?"

Mr. P was now unable to hide the crackle in his voice. He was not one to be in touch with his feelings, and for most of Marco's life, he wasn't sure his father actually had feelings. Marco sighed, urging his father to get his composure.

"Marco, our relationship has been under great stress for some time now. I know I said it was no time to talk about your mother and me, but I can make time to talk about you and me."

"Aren't they the same things, really?"

"No, but if you want to be angry with me about the issues between your mother and me, that's up to you. You know how difficult relationships can be." Mr. P wished he could take that comment back, but it was too late.

"Whatever," said Marco. "It's not just about Mom. It's about you never being around. You spoiled us with everything money could buy but you were never home. You were never there when we needed you. I understand that you worked, and Mom took care of the house. You never realized that Mom had to be a mom and a dad. Do you know what it's like having to talk to your mom about guy things? I don't hold a grudge and I'm not even angry at you anymore. I've learned to let go of the past, but that doesn't mean that we can automatically have a relationship. That is something that needs to be built over the years, and once I went to college, it was too late. You still weren't there for us."

"I understand, Marco. I wanted you kids to have more than what I had growing up, and I got so caught up in working harder to make more that I didn't realize that what you needed was me. I'm sure you didn't complain when I spent more on you kids for Christmas than most people made in a year," Mr. P tried to explain.

"Really? At least you were there for Christmas. Don't you remember us trying to play with our new toys with you? Spending time with you is what we wanted."

"I know that now, but back then, I didn't realize. I was too stupid to realize that was what your mother needed too. I threw myself into my work and worked as hard as I could to be a good provider."

"Listen, Dad, I'm not sure what's happening with you and mom, but I was not prepared for this phone call."

Marco uttering the word *Dad* lightened the mood, and Mr. P was feeling more at ease to speak freely. "That's why I'm calling."

"Oh great, this ought to be good," Marco huffed sarcastically.

"You know your mother and I have known each other for a very long time. Our history and past is something that will always be a positive part of us. Since Carmine has . . . well, since Carmine, she and I have been in touch more often. We believe there is a lot more to Carmine's death than appears on the surface."

"What does that mean? Where are you going with this?"

"We believe Anthony is involved somehow," Mr. P said.

"You have to be joking. I need to get in touch with Josie. She's not returning my calls. She won't even text me back. What if something happened to her?"

"Marco, she's out to dinner with John."

"Are you having her followed?"

"Yes."

By Marco's silence, Mr. P knew the much-dreaded question was coming. He never wanted to have this conversation with his children, but he knew eventually it would chase him down.

Chapter 30

Josie sat at the table, blinking at John. She wasn't quite sure what to say. Should she tell him what she knew? She didn't want him asking a million questions, and lately she didn't want him thinking there wasn't a future for them. *How could you be so selfish at a time like this?* she thought. Finally, she managed to say, "What the hell?"

"Josie, are you OK?"

"John, there's something you should know. It's not exactly my place to tell you, but I feel like you need to know. It will make some of this a little easier to understand."

"What is it, Josie?"

"Lexi and Carmine were having an affair." It just tumbled out of her mouth. Josie felt like a giant weight had been lifted off her shoulders. She felt a little like she had betrayed Marco, but it was his idea that they all work together. John needed to know.

"What?" John's question bellowed through the restaurant. People were staring, and Josie buried her face in her hands. Quieter, John blurted, "What the—" Josie clamped her hand over his mouth to stop him from dropping the f-bomb.

The surprise on John's face didn't seem to be fading. Josie's hand was still on his mouth, and their eyes locked on one another.

"Josie, you're not joking?"

"No, John, I wish I were. But it's the truth. It's been going on for a while."

"What's a while?"

"It's been a few years, for sure."

"So that's why you've been talking to him? I just couldn't figure out what you were doing or why." John regretted saying that as soon as it came out of his mouth.

"Yes. Again, like I said before, there is nothing going on, but we have been in touch." Josie was not going to elaborate. She was still feeling things out with her and John.

"You don't have to explain yourself to me, Josie."

She wasn't sure how to play this without being obvious, but she wanted to let him know ultimately, she was single, without actually coming out and saying it.

She very shyly said, "I know. I agreed to meet you tonight because I wanted to spend some time with you. I haven't spoken to or texted Marco since I came back to the city." *Too obvious*, she thought.

John's eyebrows raised slightly with hope at what Josie was telling him; there might be a chance. Hope was a big word for John. John, deciding not to dwell on her comment, smiled coyly at Josie, saying, "That's good to know."

As much as John wanted to see how far he could take this part of the conversation, they couldn't avoid the original reason for dinner.

"Do you want to talk about . . ." Josie held her hand up, indicating that she didn't want John to repeat Anthony's name out loud.

"I don't want to talk about it, but now is as good a time as any," Josie said.

"You don't have to if you don't want to," said John.

"I know, but ironically, Louisa and I were talking about it at the viewing."

"Why?" John asked with a very concerned expression on his face.

"We were talking about the Paretti family in general. How the years have not been good to them. How even when they try to do the right thing, a disaster seems to ensue."

John didn't say anything. He knew she wasn't defending them. He knew that Josie was well aware that most of the bad that followed the Parettis was brought on by them. He patiently waited to see where she would take this conversation, just happy that she was sharing it with him and not someone else.

Josie continued, "I know they aren't innocent whatsoever." John nodded his head in relief.

"I know we never really talked about what happened, so here it goes." Josie felt anxiety twist in her stomach like a knot.

"Josie, I already know what happened."

"No, John, you don't really know the truth." John stiffened. What he did know was awful. How much worse could it get? Maybe it was not as bad as what he thought. He hoped so, for Josie's sake, anyway.

"Antho—" Josie stopped herself, dropping off the rest of his name. She took a deep breath and relayed to John how Anthony, or the devil, as she liked to call him, was trying to extort money from her father's business. He threatened her parents endlessly until her father refused to take it any longer. He was at his wit's end and ready to give in when somehow Mr. Paretti got involved. Her father still said he had no idea how Mr. P knew what was going on, but he approached her father, saying he'd noticed that her father just wasn't himself lately and wanted to know what was happening. Her father, of course, didn't want to get him involved. He thought he could handle it on his own, but most importantly, he didn't want to owe Mr. P anything. He wasn't sure what would be worse.

John stared at Josie in awe. He had no idea all of this had happened. This was not the story he had heard.

"Mr. P suspected what was happening, and basically called my dad out on it and promised my dad that he would never ask for anything in return. My father asked what he was going to do, and Mr. P said it was better if he didn't know."

"Josie, this is some scary stuff. Why do you think Mr. P didn't want anything in return?"

"He told my father that since they grew up together and he was such a good man, he just wanted to help him. My dad was very skeptical, of course, but what else was he going to do? And my dad and Mr. Paretti were very good friends at one point."

"It didn't stop there," Josie continued. "It got much worse. Something obviously had happened with Mr. P and Anthony years prior, because Mr. P not only got Anthony off my father's back, but got Anthony's wife to leave him and take all of his money in the divorce."

"Oh my God, Josie, is that why . . ." John stopped. He could not say it out loud. Not if he didn't think Josie was OK with it.

"It's OK, John. We're talking about this, so you can say it." He was astonished that she knew what he was thinking.

John continued, "That's why Anthony spent all that time tormenting you?"

"Yes," Josie said.

John explained, "I was always so angry at Marco's family. I blamed them for you getting caught up with Anthony. Meanwhile, it was your dad. Not that it was his fault, but it was more related to him than the Parettis."

John was completely stunned. He never knew anything about what Anthony was doing to Josie's parents. He realized he'd just been a stupid kid caught up in the rumors. He had obviously gone about it all wrong back then when he tried to talk to Josie when it was all going on. She didn't want to talk about any of it, and now he understood why.

And he now realized why the Parettis were involved. It was a positive thing that they had done for Josie's parents. They weren't trying to hurt them. They were helping them.

"Josie, I am so sorry about this. I wish there was something I could do. I'm sorry for being such a childish ass back then."

"John, you didn't understand, and I didn't try to make you understand. You can help now though. Carmine would have had to know that someone was taking out an insurance policy on him, right?"

"Yes. That means Carmine knew that Lexi was first beneficiary!"

"And knew that Anthony had taken out the policy," Josie added.

Josie shivered. "What the hell is going on here? And what in God's name is Anthony's relationship to Carmine?"

Chapter 31

Mr. P sat on the other end of the line, waiting for Marco to say something. He had been dreading this conversation, but after all these years, he was happy to get it off his chest.

"Why are you having Josie followed?" Marco asked before it really sank in that she was out to dinner with John.

"Because I can. If Anthony is involved in the situation with Carmine, I needed to make sure she was safe. I knew that is what you would want, so I took the liberty of doing so."

"So, I'm putting some pieces together in my head and recapping all the things that I've seen over the years. It's not adding up, and I don't like what I'm starting to believe is true," Marco said, sounding disgusted. "Were you actually a pharma rep like you lead all of us to believe?"

"Yes, I was. However, that's not all I was."

Marco's heart started pounding. He got up and started pacing. *This is not happening*, he thought. *What kind of danger are we in as a family? What has happened over the years that is going to come back to haunt us?*

"It's not what you think. Your mother and I—" Marco cut him off.

"Mom? She's involved, too?"

"Would you just listen to me? Your mother and I have been working on fixing things that have happened in the past. Not things that we have done, but things that others have done."

Marco was confused. He wasn't quite picking up what his father was putting down. It wasn't making any sense, and with as close as he was to his mother, why wasn't she the one telling him this? How could she have kept this from him all these years?

In response to Marco's silence, his father continued, "You asked me if I was having Josie followed. I am, and for good reason."

Marco was unaware of all the details of what happened with his father and Josie's father all those years ago. Mr. P went on to explain all of that to him, and what he had done to fix the situation for Josie's father.

Marco was silent, wondering why Josie didn't tell him what was going on at the time. Why didn't she confide in him?

"So, you are fixers? Like undercover cops?" Marco asked.

"Well, I wouldn't go that far. Some of the things that we do aren't always good. I won't elaborate on that, but we are no saints."

"So, what does all this mean?"

"Well, nothing for right now. I just need you to know that whatever happens going forward, your mother and I will always be here for you kids and you don't need to worry about anything."

Marco had no idea what that meant, and at this point, he was afraid to ask.

"I have to go, son. And listen, I'm sorry." Mr. P hung up without giving Marco the chance to say a word.

I'm sorry? Marco thought. *What the hell is that supposed to mean? Sorry for the past? Or the future?*

Chapter 32

Josie rolled over and looked at the clock on her nightstand. It was 5:27 AM. Her alarm would be going off in three minutes. She was wide awake, so she leaned over and turned the alarm off before it had the chance to sound on its own.

As she walked towards the bathroom, she recalled her night with John. Josie had closed the door to her past and was working hard to open new doors. In the last few days, it had become very evident that she needed to reopen that door to the past and deal with what she left behind. *But, really*, she thought, *I haven't left anything behind. It's all still there.*

Her thoughts drifted back to John and how he was so nice and polite. He genuinely seemed to want to help. He didn't need to get involved, but he was choosing to anyway.

Now he had all the details of what was happening. He could put all the pieces together and truly understand what had happened all those years ago.

Last night, they discussed Anthony and how he had made inappropriate advances on Josie when she was barely eighteen. John was so angry back then, but there was nothing he could do about it. He always told Anthony how it was not right, and he should stop. Josie certainly did not accept his advances, but she never reported him to the authorities, either. She was too embarrassed. Looking back on it as an adult, she should have told her parents, at the very least.

In such a short period of time, things had changed enough to give her the confidence to speak out about Anthony's assault on her. She recalled all the times that he taunted her and how she didn't realize at the time that it was not OK. She kept saying to herself that it was harmless, he'd never do anything, it was no big deal. Now, she realized how wrong her thought process was. It wasn't harmless, and he did do something, and it was a big deal. She repeatedly shot down his advances, but never thought that he would physically attack her; and that's exactly what he did.

She was drawn out of her thoughts from a text message alert. She looked down; it was John.

John: Thank you for last night. I had a great time, all things considered. I would love to see you again.

Josie wanted to reply right away. No reason to play games.

Josie: Thank you for dinner, John. It was very nice, and I would love to get together soon.

John replied with the smiley face emoji with the hearts for eyes and Josie replied with the laughing face.

She felt good about their conversation and she looked forward to seeing him again.

After she showered and got ready for the day, she sat down at her desk to write. It kept gnawing at her that she had missed calls and missed texts from Marco. Often, she found that her thoughts seemed to lead back to Marco. The more she tried to put him out of her head, the more she thought about him. She really did still love him. Much more than she wanted to, given the situation.

She did need to focus on herself right now, though. Marco needed to work out his life and figure out what he was going to do with Lexi. She could not move on until he sorted that out.

This was the most important time of her career to this point, and she needed to focus for her future. If Marco figured things out with Lexi and decided to leave her, then Josie would cross that bridge; but for now, it was all about Josie . . . and maybe John. She would forget about her confusion on either one of them. She was just going to let the cards fall where they may.

Before she knew it, it was midmorning. She decided to take a break.

Chapter 33

Marco was up and had already eaten breakfast by the time the sun had fully risen. He was wondering how much longer Lexi was going to sleep. He certainly didn't want to talk to her, so he just left her alone.

He finished up some work and decided to go out to grab some coffee. Maybe it would help him focus on something other than Josie.

He kept thinking about Josie and everything his father told him last night. Even though he didn't know all the details of what happened, he was sad for Josie. He just wanted to hear her voice, but clearly, she was not taking his phone calls and she wouldn't even reply via text. He thought maybe if he could at least tell her that he and Lexi talked about divorce, she would be more willing to talk to him, and maybe even let him come and visit her in the city.

Heading back from the coffee shop, he picked up the phone and dialed her number.

It was ringing. He figured it was a good sign that she didn't just push him to voicemail. *Although*, he thought, *if she is writing, her phone probably isn't even in the same room and she doesn't even know I'm calling.*

"Hi, Marco," she answered.

Marco was so caught off guard that he stumbled over his words, finally managing to say, "Hi! I thought for sure you wouldn't take my call." He had to be very careful not to say anything about John. He did not want her to know that his father had her followed. *How absurd*, he thought. *Why are we in this situation and how are we going to get out of it? Do we even have a future together?*

"Well, I did," Josie said.

"I'm glad! How are you?"

Josie was glad to hear his voice, but she kept her feelings distant. "I'm good. Just working. Trying to hit my deadline. I'm pretty focused, so I'm on a roll today."

"That's great. I'm glad to hear that. I'm sorry if I am bothering you," Marco replied, a hint of hesitation in his voice.

"No, it's OK. I just got up to take a break. It's like you were spying on me or something." Josie had softened her tone.

Marco swallowed hard. This was so unfair to her, not to mention that someone was, in fact, spying on her. She was already in a bad enough situation with him and Lexi, and now she had his dad having someone follow her and she didn't even know it was happening. Or why it was happening. Hell, he didn't even know why.

"That's good. I'm glad to hear that. I know this is weird with me just calling you and telling you this, but I didn't know when I would see you again and I wanted to tell you right away. That's why I was calling yesterday. I'm sorry for all the messages and texts, but I was just so excited to tell you."

"Out with it already, Marco."

"Lexi and I are getting a divorce." Josie was silent. She never thought he would have that conversation with Lexi. Not now, anyway. She wanted in her heart for him to do it, but she never thought he would.

"Are you still there?" Marco asked.

"Oh, yes! Sorry Marco, I just didn't . . . I mean I never thought . . . I just . . ." Josie gathered her thoughts. "I thought you would eventually do it, I just never thought it would be now."

Marco was not surprised by Josie's response. He wanted to prove how much he loved her, and this would make them both happy together.

Josie knew her reply was halting partly because she had a great night with John, and since she decided to put Marco on the back burner for now, she thought things were moving in a positive direction for her. It also just occurred to her that she would now be stuck in the same love triangle she was in back in high school. It wasn't like it was front page news, but she never even considered anything with her and John until after she saw him at the viewing.

"Well, are you happy?" Marco questioned.

Josie had no idea how to answer this question. She did know that it was something she was going to have to process. She was caught so off guard that she didn't know what to say.

"Yes, Marco, I am happy for you that your life will be moving in a better direction."

"Is that all you have to say? I thought you'd be happy. Josie, is this because of John?" Marco just threw it right out there. He wasn't pulling any punches, and he wanted her to know that he wasn't stupid. Meanwhile, it never would have crossed his mind if his father hadn't told him.

"Marco, I am not seeing John." While this was true, it did not mean that she did not *want* to be seeing him.

She continued, "We had dinner last night to discuss the situation with Carmine. You asked us to look into some things and we decided to talk about it and get a game plan together."

"Were you going to fill me in?"

"We didn't get too far yet, but if we come up with something, we'll let you know." Marco noted that Josie kept referring to her and John as *we*. He was not OK with that.

"Look, I know you're busy, so I'll let you go. Why don't you call me when you get a chance? I would love to see you sometime soon," Marco said.

"I will call you the first chance I get. After my deadline. OK?"

"Do I have a choice?"

"No, Marco, not really."

"OK, then. I miss you, and I'll wait for your call."

"Miss you too. Talk to you soon."

Josie hung up. Marco just sat there, staring at the phone. He wanted to throw it out the window of his car. It was his fault that they were getting so chummy, Josie and John. He asked them to work together. He put them together. He had dragged his feet with leaving Lexi and now he might be losing Josie for good.

He was going to wake up Lexi as soon as he got home so he could be one step closer to getting her out of his life once and for all.

He walked up the stairs and into the room he put her in. As soon as he entered the room, he knew something was not quite right. He had a bad feeling.

She looked very odd laying there; so still. He got closer to her. Her chest didn't move. Marco thought it looked like she was not breathing. He poked at her shoulder. He called her name. "Lexi, wake up. Lexi!"

She did not move. He checked her pulse, and he could not find it.

He started to panic. He raced downstairs to get his phone to call 911.

He got to the bottom of the stairs and the doorbell rang. "Who the hell could that be?" he whispered in a panic.

He opened the front door and there stood his mother and father.

"Sorry, son, did we catch you at a bad time?" his mother asked, eyebrow raised.

Chapter 34

Marco was fairly panicked now. "I think Lexi is dead," he blurted out. If it had been anyone else at his door, he would have sent them on their way, but it was his parents.

Mrs. P said, "Well, she was already dead when I brought her home last night."

Marco felt the floor disappearing beneath his feet. He was pretty sure he heard what his mother said, but he was not quite comprehending.

His mother could not have killed his wife. It just was not possible. He was not going to give her the satisfaction of losing his shit. His eyes shifted to his father's.

Mr. P said, "It's not what you think it is. This is far bigger than you could ever want to understand."

Marco stood there, staring at his parents as though they were strangers. Afraid to ask what the hell they were talking about. He thought his heart was going to beat out of his chest.

As he replayed the prior evening in his head, he couldn't shake how calm his mother was. The reality didn't seem to shake her one bit. *What about Jackie? Did she even know?*

Mrs. P gently said, "Maybe you should take a ride."

Marco stood there unable to move a muscle. He didn't even know what to say, or if he should say anything. Should he protest? Did he even really care what they were going to do with her?

Without saying a word, he grabbed his keys and walked out the door. His mother and father needed to take care of Lexi.

Josie was sitting at her desk and thinking about Marco. It was beginning to finally sink in that Marco told Lexi he was leaving her. She was starting to feel a flutter in her stomach. The old feelings were coming back. She had been in love with Marco ever since they were teenagers. Now it sounded like they would actually get to be together, once and for all.

She blew him off because she was having a difficult time processing that he told her they were getting a divorce. She had waited too long to hear those words, and he just blurted it out on the phone at her. She was hoping for it to be a much more intimate moment. The more she thought about the possibility of them being together, the more excited she got.

Josie's phone began ringing and she was ripped from her thoughts of Marco and their future together.

"Hello?" Josie said.

Marco was stunned that she answered. He thought for sure she was going to blow him off again. Even though he did what she wanted, she always seemed somewhat displeased with him lately.

Now that she answered, what was he going to say to her? *My parents are murderers?* His parents were hit men . . . man . . . and woman? What the hell was he going to say to her? Maybe he would just let her lead the conversation. That was probably not going to work, as he was unsure if she answered just to tell him he was an ass. He should have thought twice before calling her.

"Hello? Marco, are you there?"

"Oh, yes, sorry, I'm here. I just, I was just . . ." He paused again. He was at a loss.

"Marco, listen, I need to talk to you about something. So many things actually. I'm so glad you called." Josie went on to tell him everything that she and John spoke about at dinner. Well maybe not everything, but everything related to his family and the insurance policy.

She gave him all the details that John shared with her about Anthony and Mrs. Paretti. The policy and the stipulations and beneficiaries.

Marco was still silent. His palms were starting to sweat, and he wanted to put his fist through the car window. He was so angry in his late teens, but he had mellowed out significantly in his adulthood. He felt that anger creeping back up inside him again.

Josie could hear him breathing heavily on the other end. "Marco, what's wrong with you? You call me and then you just sit on the other end of the phone angry. Did you call to say something?" Josie was getting frustrated and raising her voice. "And you were supposed to be waiting for me to call you. Did you even hear a word I said?"

Despite her evident anger with Marco, her voice pulled Marco out of his state of rage.

"Josie, I'm sorry."

"I know, Marco, you already said that. What's going on? I know what I just told you is a lot to take in, but you were acting like this before I told you."

"Yeah, Josie, I know. I called to tell you that Lexi . . . Lexi is dead."

Chapter 35

Jimmy took a train into the city for a few days. Partly, he wanted to get away and clear his head; however, he did have one thing he needed to address.

He arrived at John's building and waited for him to come down.

"Hey, buddy," John said.

"Hey, man," Jimmy replied. They did their man hug and held each other for an extra second. They were about to do something that neither one of them was looking forward to. Jimmy wasn't quite sure how they got to this point, but they got into this together and they were going to end it together.

They walked for a while and made small talk. Jimmy asked about John's dinner with Josie, and John told him how great it was, how he felt like she was letting down her guard a little, maybe even moving on from the past.

Jimmy was happy to hear this. He loved Josie. Everyone did. He wanted her to be happy, but he didn't think she could be happy with Marco. Even though Marco still cared deeply for her, the situation with Marco was much bigger and he was going to have to figure it all out before Josie would even entertain spending time with him again. *John is the better choice*, Jimmy thought.

Jimmy and John arrived at their destination. They looked at each other with confidence before heading inside. They had one another's backs, no matter what happened. They'd been friends for a long time, and they weren't going to let each other down now.

Before they went inside, John turned to Jimmy and, very seriously, said, "I am going to stand my ground and hold his old ass accountable. I am not backing down no matter what he says, especially if he starts threatening. He doesn't have a leg to stand on here and he knows it."

Jimmy replied, "I totally agree. I know we talked about this already, but my stance has not changed, and I'm with you. No matter what he says, I'm not backing down either."

John gave a reassuring pat on Jimmy's shoulder. Jimmy nodded at him, a sign to get in there and get this done, once and for all.

They checked in at the front desk and headed toward the elevator.

As the floor numbers lit up and they crawled upward, the adrenalin started to rush for both John and Jimmy. This was it.

They walked up to the door and John knocked.

The door opened and a very shady, very sleazy Anthony Scarano greeted them. "Hello, fellas."

Chapter 36

Josie was silent. Her brain was mush. Her whole body was cold. Fear was the only thing she felt in that moment. She had so much to say, and nothing at all to say, at the same time.

"Josie, are you there?"

"I'm here, Marco."

Josie thought about hanging up. This was too much. *I don't need this on my plate right now*, she thought. *With the book deadline and the movie premiere, this is the last thing I want to deal with.* She left home with Marco in the rearview mirror, so to speak. And things had changed a little since then—he'd called her saying he and Lexi were getting a divorce—but why the hell was she dead?

Did he kill her? If he did, why? Is he that attached to his money that he would rather her be dead instead of losing half of what he worked so hard for? This cannot be happening. How much more is this family going to endure . . . or maybe cause? She started to get dizzy. She leaned up against the door jam. It was the closest thing she could lean on. She would be a hypocrite to tell him that she did not need this right now when she had just given him an ultimatum.

"Josie, are you OK?"

"As OK as I can be at this moment."

"I didn't think you would be excited, but I thought you would be relieved, maybe."

"Marco, are you joking?"

"Josie, I don't even know what I'm saying right now. I don't even know what to do."

Josie's disbelief quickly turned to anger. Why did Marco call her? Where was the body, why wasn't he talking to the police?

"Marco, where is she?"

"I don't really have an answer for that right now."

Marco knew how pissed she must be. He had done nothing but drag her through the wake of his family's disasters and pain. She didn't deserve this. And he knew she sure as hell didn't want to be part of it. She didn't even know the half of what was happening. He couldn't tell her; and if he did tell her, it would have to be in person. It could not be over the phone.

"Can I come see you, Josie?"

She was silent again. She really didn't want his black cloud following her home. She didn't want him infiltrating her normalcy. She was thriving. Marco would only cloud her focus.

"That's probably not a good idea. Why would you be coming here? Don't you have enough to deal with at home? Your wife is dead, for God's sake."

He could hear the anger in her voice. He figured he would just leave it alone.

"Josie, I know this is a lot to take in right now. Just call me when you are ready to talk."

In reality, Josie wanted to see him so badly, but there was so much she needed to get done. She felt like this was something that he needed to deal with. The more she mulled over the situation in her head, the more she realized that she was just trying to be polite and do the right thing. The man she loved, who she had been longing to be with, just lost his wife. She felt it was completely distasteful to revel in this new situation. How vile could she be? She was becoming disgusted with herself.

She had been trying to keep her head down and get her work done and bury herself into John so she didn't have to feel the pain of Marco not leaving his wife. Now, not only had he told her he was leaving, but she was dead!

Call ended, the phone chirped in Marco's ear. Maybe he would just have to tell her what was happening. He knew he could trust Josie, but he didn't want to push her away. She was already more than pissed, and she had good reason to be. He completely understood that.

Now, what was he going to do about his dead wife?

Chapter 37

John and Jimmy walked into Anthony's penthouse suite. Before Anthony could say anything, John said, "We aren't staying long, and you are going to listen to everything we have to say and then we are all going to move on."

John could lose his job for this, but he had to believe it would all be worth it in the end. After all, was it really so bad that he talked about the policy to someone who was named on the policy? He decided to take the chance anyway. There was too much at stake, and way too much going on for him to just let it go. He knew Anthony would be furious, but it wasn't his fault that those documents just happened to come across John's desk.

"Is there anyone else in the apartment?" asked John. Anthony waved his hand, insinuating there was nothing to worry about. John let it go, but Jimmy had a bad feeling. He could sense something wasn't quite right, but he kept quiet about it.

"I'm pretty sure I know why you're both here," said Anthony. "You want to make sure I don't give you up to the feds if they come after me."

"No, you old coot. We're not here about something that happened over ten years ago. You can't be that stupid to think that the feds would give a crap about us running some bets for you before we could drive," said John.

Anthony childishly and arrogantly laughed. He knew John was right.

"Get on with it, then," Anthony said.

"I'm sure you are very well aware of what I do for a living." John bit his tongue instead of pointing out that he had a real job like an adult, much unlike Anthony.

"Yes," said Anthony reluctantly. He kept calm, but he knew what was coming.

"A file came across my desk a few days ago. I know you know what I'm talking about. I don't want to hear a bull crap excuse about it not being you, or you having nothing to do with it . . . blah, blah, blah."

"Yeah, and what's your point?" said Anthony, sounding a bit defensive.

John was not prepared for that answer. He was prepared for Anthony to deny, deny, deny, like he usually would. Anthony wasn't the type of guy to own up to his shady dealings.

Very calm and collected, John said, "Well, what the hell is going on?"

"Why do you think I would tell you anything about that? What would I have to gain in telling you that?" said Anthony, smiling deviously.

"Why does everything always have to be about you? Have you ever done anything for anyone other than yourself?" Jimmy asked.

"I don't think I need to answer that."

Before John could say a word, a voice from behind them said, "I can answer it, though."

Jimmy's heart dropped. Fear struck John's whole body. It couldn't be. They turned around, and strolling into the room was Carmine.

Chapter 38

Josie needed to focus on her work. Everything was working out as planned. The movie launch was in just a few days and she was pretty much ready. There were a few loose ends that needed tying up, and then everything would be complete.

She wanted to take some time to write today, but she was waiting for a phone call. She knew it would be coming today, but didn't know when, and she didn't have the time to sit around and wait for the phone to ring. She figured she would just get to work and when it came, it came.

She was making great headway on the new book and was letting that distract her from what was happening in her life. She couldn't wait until this was over and she would be able to put it all behind her and move on for good. No looking back. No looking in the rearview mirror. Her family could finally be free. Whether she ended up with Marco or not.

The phone was sitting on the desk, right next to her computer. She saw it light up and knew this was the call she was waiting for.

She heard the comforting voice on the other end of the phone, and she knew it would all be OK. "Lexi is gone. No more worries for my dear Josie."

Josie, almost breathless, whispered into the phone, "Thank you." Mrs. P was gone in a second and Josie was overwhelmed with relief.

Anthony Scarano would never see it coming. He would never see Mrs. P coming! He would never know who was behind it all.

Chapter 39

Anthony opened his mouth to speak, but John said to him, "If you even think about uttering a word out of that old, useless mouth of yours, I will kill you myself."

Anthony left the room, knowing he was clearly not welcome, even in his own apartment.

The three men stood there staring at one another. No one said a word for quite a few moments.

Out of nowhere, Jimmy developed an overwhelming feeling to hug his brother. He was so angry at him. He did not understand why he would want to hug him. He resisted the urge.

John was completely disgusted by Carmine. He just couldn't understand how someone could be so selfish and horrible. After the things that Josie told him about Carmine, he had more hatred for Carmine than ever before. John typically was a gentle and caring kind of guy. He was raised right, and his parents were still always watching out for him. However, when it came to Carmine, he got angry. There was no good reason for this privileged brat to be acting so stupid.

"Carmine, you are a total piece of shit. I'm sure you already know that," John said. Carmine didn't seem to care much about what John was saying.

"Yes, John, I know. You don't do the things I've done to my family and think you are a good person."

John was shocked to hear Carmine admitting his faults.

"Carmine, do you have any idea what you are going to do now?"

"I'm not going to hurt anyone anymore. My only plan is to get as far away from everyone I've hurt as soon as I can."

"What about your children?"

"John, please just leave it alone. Don't worry about me. What you really should be worrying about is your precious Josie."

John gritted his teeth. "And what exactly is that supposed to mean, Carmine?"

Carmine nodded his head in Anthony's direction. John and Jimmy could hear him scurrying around somewhere at the back of the hallway, like the little rat that he was.

John tamped down the shiver creeping up his spine. He was seriously questioning his existing efforts to protect Josie. He was more than certain that Anthony, or maybe even Carmine, was plotting something awful.

How stupid was John to believe Carmine, after all this?

"Why should I believe you, Carmine?"

"You shouldn't. You have no reason to trust me, but you and Marco have never done anything to hurt me, and I know how much both of you care for her, so this is your heads-up. I don't really want to keep talking about it." Carmine gave John and Jimmy something that resembled his old warm, genuine, crooked smile and told them it was probably time they leave.

"We would love to go, but sadly, we need to speak with Anthony. That's why we came here in the first place," said John.

"Why would you possibly need to speak with Anthony?"

Jimmy finally piped up and said, "It's really none of your business."

Just then Anthony found his way back in the room. He told Carmine not to worry about what they wanted with him. Anthony looked back and forth between John and Jimmy and said, “It will be taken care of. No questions.”

John and Jimmy looked at one another and back at Anthony.

In unison, they said, “Thank you,” and left.

Jimmy was shocked that Anthony just let them go with no questions and agreed to their request. Without them even saying anything, he knew what they wanted. Given the situation with Carmine, he figured he should just leave it in the past.

Jimmy and John got in the elevator and didn’t say a word until they got outside. “Do you believe that he will leave this alone?” Jimmy asked John.

“Jimmy, I think we are making a bigger deal out of this than we need to. He only asked us to do some research. I know it’s concerning because we’re dealing with Anthony, but even if he decided to use this research against us, there is nothing he can do. We didn’t make what he wanted. We didn’t hurt anyone with it. We don’t even know what he used it for.”

“Yeah, I hear what you are saying, but I can’t help but worry about it.”

“I know, but don’t worry. He said it’s done, and he really doesn’t have much of a choice but to leave it at that. You heard the words from the medical examiner—Carmine died from a heart attack. Carmine looks completely fine to me. We have far too much information and evidence on Anthony for the authorities to give a crap about some little research project we did for him,” John said reassuringly.

“Now that you put it like that, I’m far less worried. What do you think he was going to do with that research?” Jimmy asked.

“I don’t know. Honestly, I’ve been trying not to ask myself that question since he approached us with the project.” John shook his head quickly, as if he could shake the whole thing away.

Chapter 40

Antonia and James sat in silence in Antonia's car, Lexi's body sprawled across the back seat. They were both wondering how in the world they let it get to this point. Their lives were not the most honest, but they never thought they would have to do something like this, especially not in their own family.

James thought back to when he and Antonia first got married. They vowed to make this life they were going to share work, no matter the cost or the consequence. There had been enough consequences over the years. They fought more than they got along, but he never thought they would never be together. She was the only woman for him. Just as ruthless, and she never complained about the work away from work. Everyone needed a front. When you did what they did, you needed the money to come from a legal source. You needed to make sure the IRS wasn't sniffing around to find things you didn't want them to find. He made more money working in pharmaceuticals, but his real joy was what he did working with Antonia.

He took the risk of putting his hand on Antonia's while she was driving. If she pulled away, then she pulled away, but he was not going to stop trying to get her back. This latest job they were doing was more for them and the future of their family than any other job had been. Maybe this would be the last one. Maybe they could agree on retiring, together.

Antonia saw James moving his hand closer to hers. For a split second, she thought about pulling away before he even got close enough to touch her. They weren't getting any younger, and she thought they would always be together, but that was a long time ago. Maybe this could be it for them. Maybe they could move on from here, together. She would not dare say how she was feeling. If that's what he wanted, then he could come to her with the madness of it all. She did not move her hand. She left it there for his bear paw to engulf her hand until she could not see it anymore.

They both opened their mouths at the exact same time to say something, and then both closed them. Stopped at a light, they looked over at each other. Almost in unison, they sighed. They each knew this would all end OK. There was just one problem to solve.

Anthony.

Chapter 41

Josie's mom and dad were sitting on the front porch, relaxing and feeling grateful for what they had in their lives. Josie, even though she rarely traveled home, was successful and the fairly quick trip to the city allowed her parents to see her often.

Joe and Kate had always supported each other. It was another thing to be grateful for. No matter how the coming events unfolded, they were ready to support each other with whatever the other needed.

The Parettis pulled up in front of the house and got out of the car. The men shook hands, and the ladies gave each other a warm, reassuring hug. When they released from their embrace, Antonia didn't say a word, but she nodded and winked at Kate.

Joe waved his hand toward the house, "Let's go inside to talk."

Inside, the table was set with food and drinks for their visit.

Joe had a very playful smile on his face as he sat down at the table. "It's good to see the two of you getting along nicely these days," he said, trying to keep things light. "It reminds me of how things were in the good old days. Our friendship may have faded a bit over the years, but I'm sure we can pick right back up where we left off."

James glanced around the room, looking for something specific. His eyes gripped a briefcase on the desk in the corner. Joe followed his gaze, locking in on the briefcase as well. He looked back at James and nodded, confirming that the ammunition they needed to share with the right people was inside. Anthony did not stand a chance.

James got down to business, as he usually did when there was business to be done. "As nice as it is being together like this again, let's discuss our goals and concerns."

Each one threw out their concerns and what they were looking to accomplish. No one had any stipulation that was unmeetable. No one was asking for anything impossible. Everyone was honest, and for the most part, all had the same goal in mind.

At one point, Antonia, touching Kate's hand to address her, said, "We pulled off putting Anthony's life on hold once before. This time we are going to ruin him for good."

Kate gave Antonia a sly smile and said, "I don't feel the smallest remorse for doing this. I have had it with this vile, disgusting man. He needs to be stopped. He came after this guy"—she pointed to her husband—"and bringing the kids into his nonsense was inexcusable. If we all work together, we can get this done."

"Ladies, there is something very exciting about you taking the bull by the horns on this project," said James.

The ladies raised their eyebrows at James.

Antonia questioned, "Project? Is that what we are calling it?" They all had a nice chuckle at her question.

"You know what I mean, dear." The word *dear* slipped right off his tongue like it was part of his daily vocabulary. She waved him off like she was tired of hearing his voice.

They began mapping out the details and next steps, making sure everyone knew what their role would be and how it was all going to shake out.

Kate, needing confirmation, asked, "Just so we are completely clear, Josie does not know or need to be involved until it's all over?"

"Yes!" Antonia confirmed. Perhaps a little too quickly. "No need for her to know the details until you want her to. I have been keeping her in the loop, though."

"Keeping her in the loop?" Kate questioned with worry in her voice.

"No details were shared, just that we were working on something that would get him out of the picture."

Kate trusted her dear old friend; however, anxiety was creeping into her gut.

The group looked from one to the other and nodded, showing that they were all in on this project, as James had called it. They also looked frighteningly excited to be able to witness the mayhem unfold. After all this time, they would get their revenge.

Chapter 42

John and Jimmy continued walking down the street in silence. John had talked Jimmy into having lunch before he headed home. Of course, he wanted to spend more time with Jimmy, but lunch would have to be enough. Not that either of them would be able to actually eat after what just happened.

John chose a place close to his apartment. He wanted to make sure they went somewhere good, but more importantly, quiet and not too busy.

Jimmy looked defeated and sad. So many thoughts were flying around in his head. *How could Carmine be so awful? How could he do this to his family? His children? What was he thinking?*

John could see it on Jimmy's face that he was distraught. "Do you want to talk about it?"

Jimmy was silent for a few moments while he very visibly tried to find the right words to answer John. "I really don't know what to say. There's nothing we can really do, and I guess it's just a waiting game to see what happens. How could I face Jackie ever again? What would I possibly say to her?"

John felt for Jimmy. He hadn't considered the fact that Jimmy would have to see Jackie eventually. He was her children's uncle, for God's sake. Jimmy would be seeing her forever.

John had no answer. He just shook his head, his shoulders slumped. There was nothing he could say to make the situation better. He certainly was in no mood to answer Jimmy on the fly or give him empty words of comfort. He couldn't come up with something good if he tried.

The two men sat there in silence, poking at their food, knowing there was nothing they could do; knowing that they wouldn't speak a word of this day ever again.

Chapter 43

Josie was so excited. She was calm and proud. Her parents had arrived last night in time for a wonderful dinner and some drinks. John was able to meet them as they were being seated. It was a wonderful evening before the biggest night of her life.

Louisa and her husband were driving in today for all the festivities. Josie put all the drama from her hometown out of her mind for now. Even if it was just for tonight. She was not going to let anyone take this away from her.

The doorbell rang. She was expecting John. She was dressed and ready to go. She opened the door and found a very handsome-looking John standing in the hallway.

John was speechless at the sight of Josie. Her long black hair was pulled back on one side with a sweeping bundle of curls on the other. She had a beautiful pin pulling it back. Her dress was all black with a band of shiny beading around the waist. She looked like she should be in the movie they were heading to see.

"Hi, John," beamed Josie.

"Josie, you look wonderful!" John blurted out at her.

"Thank you! Are you ready to go?"

Josie's mom and dad eyed John very approvingly. As close and as far back as their relationship was with the Parettis, they weren't sure that Marco was the best fit for Josie. They were going to treat this evening like the beginning of Josie's promising future and be thankful that John was back in Josie's life again.

"Yep! Let's get this night started," said John.

They arrived at the premiere and mingled with some of the cast whom Josie was fortunate enough to get to know quite well. It didn't always work like that in the business, so Josie was very happy to have these new friends.

They also spotted Louisa and her husband, just arriving. They made their way over and they all hugged and kissed. Louisa eyed up John, thankful for the possibility that he might be back Josie's life again.

Mrs. P had called Josie to decline the invitation to her premiere. She just wouldn't be able to make it, but she had sent Josie a beautiful vase full of exotic flowers and a very expensive, very unnecessary monogrammed pen. The note in the card caused tears to prick the corners of Josie's eyes. She recouped quickly. She wanted to focus on the evening and not worry about the future.

They made their way into the theatre and took their seats. Everyone was telling Josie how proud they were of her and how happy they were to be able to spend this evening with her, when her dad suddenly raised a concerned and obvious eyebrow at Josie.

He did not make a scene about it, but instead leaned in close to Josie. "Don't turn around and give him the satisfaction of being noticed. Anthony is here. Listen to me. Regardless of his being here tonight, you need to remember that no one is going to take away the wonderful name you have made for yourself. Your hard work has paid off, giving you the chance to do something you love every day. You should be very proud of yourself. Just as I am proud of you. Don't let him ruin this for you."

Josie was comforted by her father's words. She was going to enjoy the evening, no matter what.

Chapter 44

Carmine woke with a start. He was not sure what he was hearing, and he was very groggy from the night before. He'd had too much to drink. He stayed put. He did not get up. He had a horrible feeling in his gut about how much he disappointed everyone in his life. The disdain for himself was starting to settle in. He was beginning to realize how alone he actually was.

Faking his death. Leaving his wife and children to think he was gone forever. His mother orchestrating the whole plan to get him away from everyone he crapped on for good . . . including her and his father. Even his own brothers were not very fond of him. He certainly couldn't blame Marco, even though he wasn't sure if Marco knew that he was having an affair with Lexi.

Who does that to their own brother? he questioned himself. *What narcissistic jerkface does that?* He didn't even deserve to still be alive.

Who leaves their children the way he did? If he did not do this, he would be in jail for a very long time. That's what his mother promised, anyway.

His thoughts drifted to Lexi and how she was just as immature and ridiculous as he was. She was to blame in all of this, just as much as he was, but with all that said he was completely in love with her. There was no question about that. Maybe because they were both so ruthless and selfish. Maybe he made her that way? Maybe she was just fine until he forced his nonsense on her? He didn't want to think of that now. After all, he was never going to see her again. Everyone in his life who he treated like garbage, but he truly loved inside his heart, he would never see again. Lexi and his kids. Jackie was his last thought. She had been a convenience, like a mother, instead of spouse or life partner. He thought he may have loved her once, but he got so caught up in himself that his love and respect for her just fell away. He was not as remorseful for that as for the other things he had done.

The bedroom door opened, and Anthony came strolling in. He opened the curtains to let the sunshine in, bright and blinding, to Carmine's eyes. "Wake up!" said Anthony, with a hint of human decency in his voice.

Carmine just rolled over.

"What do you want?" Carmine eventually slurred out of his tired and miserable mouth.

"I think it's time we talk," said Anthony.

"What could we possibly have to talk about?" asked Carmine.

"Since you are such a piece of crap, it's time you figure out if you want Marco to be happy or not."

"What are you getting at, old man? And why are you bothering me with this so early in the morning?" Carmine asked.

"We all know how hung up your brother is on Josie, and word has it she is getting pretty cozy with John these days."

"Yeah, so?" asked Carmine. "Did you forget that my brother is still married to my mistress?"

With a very sinister and questionable laugh, Anthony said, "Oh yeah, I guess I must have forgotten that small detail. How much longer do you think Lexi will be in the picture? Or even alive, for that matter?"

Carmine thought he was going to be sick. No one ever discussed anything bad happening to Lexi. He was beginning to panic. His mother was in control, but how far would she possibly go?

Anthony could see fear on Carmine's face. "What's the matter? Never thought that something bad might happen to Lexi? What did you think? You would disappear and Lexi would just get away with the things that she has done?"

Carmine closed his eyes and said, "Just leave me be for a while. At least give me that?"

Anthony got up to leave Carmine. "Don't make me put you on suicide watch. I'm not footing the bill for twenty-four-hour surveillance. It's bad enough I have to stay here most of the time."

Anthony walked out, locking Carmine in his room with his thoughts, which hadn't been suicidal until Anthony brought it up.

Chapter 45

Josie's mom and dad were getting ready to head back home. They had spent a few days in the city with Josie after the premiere. Since Louisa and her husband spent a few days in town seeing the sights, they had met up for dinner here and there. Josie didn't invite John, as she just wanted to enjoy the time with her parents and her longtime friend.

When everyone was gone, Josie took some time to get caught up on emails and call her agent. As soon as she finished, she told herself she was going to go for a walk.

She had a sinking feeling in her stomach; she should really get back to Marco. It had been days since they spoke or even exchanged texts, and she had said she would be in touch when the premiere festivities came to a close.

She figured today was as good a time as any to reach out, but she wanted to be prepared for whatever he was going to say. She wanted to be prepared with whatever she was going to say as well. While she sat there with her phone in hand, she just kept thinking that she didn't really have anything to say.

She knew he would ask about John. What would she say? She figured telling the truth was the best thing to do.

She decided to just skip the call and go for a walk to clear her head. She headed up to the park. It was crowded today, and that was OK with her. People watching would be great for new writing inspiration.

While she was walking, she felt a shift in her surroundings. Like she was being watched. It was probably nothing, but given the events of the last few weeks, anything was possible. Her eyes started playing tricks on her. Why would anyone need to follow her? It's not like they were going to catch her doing anything wrong. Her life was pretty simple these days. Her love life, not so much, but everything else was sort of boring.

In the not so far distance, she saw Anthony walking towards her. He was wearing a hideous velour tracksuit. Maroon, no less. He was not going to get the best of her; she walked past him without so much as a sideways glance.

"Josie?"

"What, Anthony?" As she turned around, she made eye contact with a friendly looking man whom she did not recognize. He nodded at her as if to say, "If anything happens, I'm right here." This threw her off briefly, but she regrouped even quicker.

Anthony blurted out, "Don't believe everything you hear, Josie." He looked concerned, but didn't show much emotion other than in his eyes.

"What is that supposed to mean? Why in the world would I believe a word out of your criminally twisted mouth?" Josie was instantly angry.

Anthony answered, "I'm not claiming innocence; I'm just simply saying that not everything is what it seems." He took a step towards her, and it confirmed that the man she made eye contact with had absolutely been following her, but to protect her and not to hurt her. He stepped closer to her when Anthony did.

Anthony continued, "I don't expect you to believe anything I say, but I can at least hope you find out for sure what's really going on. There is always more to a story than what's on the surface."

Josie puffed out an, "Ugh," in disgust and just kept walking.

My God, she thought. *What was that about?* Why would she ever believe him? She was tired of the games, but his words sparked her curiosity, and this made her uneasy. Maybe she should talk to Mr. Paretti instead of putting all her faith in Mrs. P.

When she got back to her apartment, she pulled out her phone to call Marco and saw that she had a missed call from John. She must have bumped her ringer to off in her pocket.

She put off talking to John until she got ahold of Marco.

She realized that once she walked away from Anthony, her mystery man had vanished. Maybe she needed to speak with Mr. P after all. That episode had his name written all over it.

Chapter 46

Marco was lying in his hammock, staring at nothing. How did he get here? How did his life implode so quickly? The more he thought about it, the more he realized it wasn't quickly at all. It was slow and evident. Part of this was his fault . . . maybe all of it was his fault. If he hadn't let Josie get away in the first place, his life would be different.

She was too strong-willed to let him dictate what she was going to do. He could have at least not been a little shit and tried harder.

What was he going to do now? He needed to talk to her. Why was she so standoffish when they spoke last? She wanted him to leave Lexi. That's what he did. He at least did that before . . . how could he possibly be thinking about Josie when Lexi was . . . He rubbed his forehead with the tips of his fingers, hoping to rub away the headache that was brewing.

This was too much to handle. As tough a man as he believed he was, he wasn't handling this very well. This just could not be happening. How were the cops not beating down his door? How was Lexi gone, and no one even cared? His thoughts were beginning to get out of hand. It just happened yesterday, and he hadn't called the police, so how would anyone ever know?

He could feel his heart beginning to race. He was getting anxious.

His phone rang and he nearly fell out of his hammock.

He glanced at the phone, afraid of who might be bothering him during the onset of a possible heart attack.

With pure relief, he saw Josie's name on the screen.

He stabbed at the answer button and nothing happened. *Is the screen really freezing now?* he thought. *Now, of all times!* He needed Josie, and his phone wouldn't even work properly.

Finally, he was able to answer the call. "Hi!" he yelled into the phone. "Hi," he said again, trying to sound far less frazzled.

"Marco, what is it? What's wrong?" Josie asked, knowing full well what was wrong.

"Josie," Marco started, but then fell silent.

"I just had a run-in with Anthony in the park," said Josie.

Marco's brain was hurting. How could he help her when he was hours away from her and his brain was ready to burst?

"Josie, what do you need me to do? Can I help?"

Josie didn't know how to reply to this. She didn't want him to suspect that she might know what was going on.

"No, no, I just wanted to tell you."

"Oh, OK, well thanks, I guess. If there's anything . . ." Marco trailed off.

"Marco?"

"Yeah, Josie?"

"Do you think you might want to come here so we can talk and spend some time together?"

Marco was shocked. He was under the impression that she was no longer interested in any type of relationship with him. Never mind the fact that she seemed to be getting pretty close to John. Something that Marco was still pretty pissed about.

"Um, Josie, what's going on with you and John?" He didn't even think before he blurted out the question. She might be pissed, but it was too late now.

Josie was silent and Marco was waiting for her to freak out, but she didn't.

"Marco, I'm sorry about everything that's been happening."

"Josie, I don't blame you. Well, I blame you for John, but not the rest of this," Marco said playfully.

Josie laughed, and at that moment, she knew everything was going to be OK. "Well, are you coming or not?"

"Sure. When?"

"Tonight, tomorrow. Whenever you want."

"I'm on my way."

They got off the phone and Josie smiled. She felt in her heart that this was the right thing to do. She just needed to be very careful.

Chapter 47

Anthony was walking down the streets of New York City without a care in the world. Not a care that he ruined his family's lives over the years. Not a care that his kids hated him. Not a care that he had tormented families that never did anything to hurt him. He was a horrible human being. He knew it and didn't care.

What bothered him the most, though, was that he continued to be unsuccessful at almost everything he did. He just wasn't good enough at being horrible.

He headed into a coffee shop that he'd been given directions to for a chat. Not much was going through his narcissistic head. He made decisions on the fly, but it never occurred to him that it might be the reason why he never really did anything right. Well, he sold drugs well, and he killed people very well, but those were only useful in the criminal word.

He saw the woman he was there to meet with and recoiled. She was not alone, and Anthony began to panic. Not visibly, but inside, he was worried. She promised she would never do this, so there must be a good reason for her to be with this man again. As arrogant as Anthony was, he knew he needed to play nice, or this could be the end of him.

Mrs. Paretti greeted Anthony with a squint of her eyes and a tilted head. This woman frightened him sometimes. She might be more ruthless than him.

"Hello," said Anthony. "James," he said, nodding in his direction. They both knew the last place Anthony wanted to be was here talking to him.

James, while putting his hand on Antonia's, said, "I'm only here because of her. She will be speaking, and I will only speak if I have something to say." James could see the smug look on Anthony's face, and he said, "You know how we work. She is my equal. You are the only old school moron at this table with the thought that she is beneath me. If you treat her as such, you will be sorry."

Anthony's smirk faded and he did as James had suggested and listened.

"You are helping us with Carmine as a favor. A favor due to your completely useless life. We will not owe you anything, and you will not try to cross us. We have eyes on you everywhere and we will not let anything slide, so do not be so stupid as to get yourself killed. Not that anyone would care. If I find out that you are treating him poorly, I will not hesitate to end your sorry life," she said.

Anthony felt a very small pang on the one possible heart string he may have left. Maybe he was getting soft in his old age? He brushed it off.

With his sad and ridiculous smirk, he decided to test the waters. "Carmine is fine, and I haven't done anything that I'm not supposed to do. If anything, I have been a little more lenient than you both would like, but not much." He directed a question to Mrs. P. "Do you have to call me Anthony?"

"Do not even start this again with me. I will not cater to your needs. Not now and not ever. Don't even think about it, and don't ever ask me again," she said.

He put both hands in front of his chest, waving her answer off, surrendering. "OK, OK. A man can try. You know, Elizabeth says it sometimes."

"Please! My sister hardly knows her own name sometimes. Do you expect me to really believe she would utter those three letters?" Antonia rolled her eyes.

Anthony's heart was feeling the insult again, and he didn't like it one bit. "So why are we here today?" asked Anthony.

"We are here today to tell you that you will be receiving a package tomorrow afternoon, and you need to keep your mouth shut and do as we tell you," said Antonia.

"What is it? What am I supposed to do with it?"

"Leave that to us. We will be delivering it ourselves, and we will tell you what to do with it once we bring it to you. This package is not particularly important to you, so it won't matter once you have it. You will not be able to use it for leverage for whatever bullshit you might try to pull. No one will be looking for this, and no one will want it. You will not be in any danger."

Anthony was becoming very wary of this whole situation. Maybe he didn't want to be involved at all. Who was he kidding? He really didn't have much of a choice. He was nothing, and he knew it. He would never be able to pull one over on these two. He wasn't even going to try.

"What time shall I be expecting you?"

"We'll call you in the morning to confirm."

As Anthony strolled out of the coffee shop like he was just some old, retired man waiting to die, he was thinking about how the reunion was going to be with Carmine and his parents. They could kill each other for all he cared, but he was very excited to see what would happen and what the package was. And he would see, soon enough.

Chapter 48

Josie was getting ready for Marco. He would be rolling into town any minute and she wanted to be completely ready when he got there. She knew this would be a long night. She would let him stay over on the couch instead of making him get a hotel room for the night. Who knew, maybe they would be up all night talking anyway.

She set special ring tones for her mom and dad, and her agent. There was no bothering them tonight.

Her stomach performed an unexpected flip when she thought of the two of them in her apartment together. It had been a while since they had been in a good place emotionally. She understood that she was going to need to give him some space after what happened to Lexi. She was even open to the idea of letting him talk and vent and even cry about her, if he needed to. It was going to be a long road ahead of them toward their future. If there was a future.

Either way, they needed to clear the air once and for all and whatever came out of this night would have to work for the both of them.

She heard the buzz of the door. Her stomach clenched. She buzzed him up and her butterflies came back again, full speed ahead. She could do this; it would all be OK.

He knocked on the door and she ran two quick hands over her dress and checked her face in the mirror right by the door. She was ready and looked perfect.

Josie opened the door and was stunned. She was shocked at how great Marco looked, given the circumstances. His broad shoulders filled out his button-down shirt amazingly. His clean-shaven face looked soft, but still masculine. Even though Josie was in three-inch heels, he towered over her. Standing only a few inches apart, he grabbed her in his signature bear hug, meant only for her . . . always.

He didn't say a word, and neither did she. She just let him hold her. His face was buried in her long black hair. She could stay there forever.

Just as quickly as John flooded into her thoughts, he flooded right back out. That's how she knew it was time to let go of the thought of being with John. Even when she was with John, Marco was always on her mind. This is where she belonged. Right here with Marco.

She could feel Marco loosening his grip slightly. He pulled away from her hair and put his giant hands on her face. "Hi." He said it in almost a whisper.

Her stomach clenched. His deep voice excited her so much. Just as it had when they were young. Her cheeks flushed and he knew she was happy to be with him again.

"Hi," Josie managed to unsteadily get out. She felt like a schoolgirl again.

"What is that amazing smell?" asked Marco. "Did you make my favorite?"

"Yes. I thought this night called for us to have something comforting and filling. Something tells me we'll be up for a while. Of course, I also got us ice cream."

"Josie, you really didn't have to go to all this trouble," Marco muttered, embarrassed.

"Marco, please. I don't want to waste time going out, and I wanted this to be relaxing. I know some things we are going to talk about aren't going to be easy, so better to be in a nice environment with good food and, well, ice cream."

He smiled and kissed her forehead. He was so much in love with her.

Chapter 49

"Thank you for the support with Anthony. I appreciate the fact that you think of me as your equal," Antonia said to James. She was beginning to soften the more time they spent together. This man had put her through hell, but the more she thought about it, maybe she was no picnic either. *We tend to remember what we want to remember*, she thought. *Usually it's more of what fits our own narrative.*

"Of course. I really feel that way, and you scare me sometimes, so it's a no-brainer for me. Just go with your flow and everyone will be happier," said James.

She smiled and let out a breathy laugh. She looked up at him and he winked at her. She hadn't seen that wink in what felt like a lifetime. It hit her unexpectedly.

"I can't believe I am going to say this—" Antonia started, but James cut her off.

"That you are having a good time working together like this again?"

She smiled again at him. "How did you know I was going to say that?"

"I still know you well, and I feel the same way. I was hoping you would be the one to say it first," James said with a proud smile.

"That is nothing to be proud of. You are a coward, and technically you said it first," Antonia said, smiling back at him.

They laughed together and held their gaze a little longer than Antonia would have liked. Even worse, she didn't want to admit how handsome he still was after all this time.

"Would you like to come to my house for a drink?" asked Antonia.

"Are you sure?" James questioned warily.

"I wouldn't have asked if I wasn't sure."

"Then yes, I would like that very much," he replied. "What time will everything be ready for us to head over to Anthony's?"

"It should be all set for midmorning. Does that work for you?" Antonia asked.

"Yes, that's fine. I was just wondering if you had an idea. Do you think this will be the end of all that?"

"I'm going to make sure it is. There should be no reason why it would not be. I have everything in place and my . . ." She cleared her throat and James raised his eyebrows in obvious shock.

They looked at one another in silence and uneasiness. He wasn't going to dare say a word. This was up to her to verbally address, if she chose to do so.

"I . . . I don't know why I almost said it."

James was going to tread lightly on this matter, but they'd been together for so long that he knew how much he could push her, if need be.

"It's just fresh in your head from the conversation with him today. That's all. Nothing more." This would confirm that she was in control, and he thought she might need the reassurance. If she didn't, he was screwed. She'd be yelling and screaming before he could even mutter, "I'm sorry."

"I really have pure disdain for that man," she said, "I can't believe that he threw Elizabeth in my face like that. Where does he get the nerve? And he can't *really* believe she actually cares for him. Do you think he believes that?"

James was uneasy with this whole thing. They were having what seemed to be a very nice evening. Now her mood had changed, and he was worried that the evening would be lost if they continued down this road. He spent many years trying to say the right thing, and screwed up royally a number of times, but also saved them a time or two. He very carefully considered what and how he was going to respond to another loaded question.

"I don't believe there is any way for us to ever know what he actually thinks. He's such a jackass that maybe he needs to believe it, so he doesn't kill himself."

By the look on her face, he had managed to say the right thing. Maybe even right enough that she would drop it and they could continue on with their pleasant evening.

They pulled into Antonia's garage. James was hoping getting out of the car and heading into the house would be distraction enough for Antonia from their conversation. He was also hoping for a stiff drink, if the conversation was going to continue for a while.

Now she was talking, but she was more muttering to herself in anger and disgust. He knew just to let her natter on; senselessly or not, at least she was getting it out. He caught a word or two here and there and just let her continue. She was like the energizer bunny. She just kept going and going.

She looked at him with a familiar smile. "Thank you for letting me go on like that."

"We've been apart now for a while, but we were together much longer than we have been apart. I still know what you need, and in that moment, you just needed to be left alone."

She finally brought up the point she'd been tiptoeing around for the last fifteen minutes. "Can you believe that asshole wants me to call him Dad?"

Chapter 50

Marco and Josie made some small talk to ease into the conversation and to acclimate themselves to each other again. They were both feeling a little wary of the other one, and of how this would all play out. Josie was fully aware that Marco knew she pushed him away to see if she had any feelings left for John. But she had been fed up with Marco and his promises. Now, she felt bad for even thinking this way, but she had made her feelings very clear to Marco so he understood that there was a chance he could lose her. He pulled through, though. He kept his promise and now she didn't have to worry about it. Whatever happened with them, at least they could both say they gave it an honest try.

"Marco, as selfish as I would like to be right now, I want you to know that we can talk about whatever you want to tonight. This evening can be whatever you want it to be."

This was why Marco loved Josie so much. Marco believed she'd made her decision to be with him and not John, and this conversation should be about her, but she was making it about him, given the circumstances.

"Thank you, Josie. Always thinking about someone other than yourself. I really don't know what to say. I'm sort of still in shock. So my trip doesn't end up being wasted on me being stupid, why don't you tell me what's on your mind? We can be adults about this, and I have things I want to discuss, too. I also feel like it's not the best time, but maybe it's just because I don't feel right talking about us, after what just happened."

"Marco, if you feel like you should go, I completely understand."

"No, Josie, I want to stay. What time were you thinking we would eat?"

"Dinner should be ready in half an hour. We could have a drink now, and just chat."

"That would be nice. Oh! How was opening night?" Marco asked. Maybe this would help them both relax.

Josie tried to prevent her face from turning red. She had spent that evening with John, and she felt bad. Bad for John, because she knew what he felt for her, and bad for Marco, because he was not able to spend that evening with her. For such a long time, whether something good or bad happened, she always wanted Marco to be a part of it.

"Marco, it was wonderful. I can't tell you how well everything turned out. My mom and dad were here, of course. Louisa and her husband came, and they stayed to do some tourist things. It was very nice."

Marco's face fell and Josie noticed. "What's the matter?" she asked.

"I'm sorry that I couldn't be there with you to share the night."

"Marco, don't be silly. It won't be the last."

Marco's eye widened. "Does that mean?"

"Yep! I got a movie deal for another book!" Josie screeched.

"I'm so proud of you, Josie. I can't believe . . . well, I can believe it. This is so great for you. Congratulations again. You really deserve this."

They both raised their cocktail glasses and Marco toasted to Josie and her success. She was flattered by the wonderful things that he said. She knew he meant them.

He smiled shyly at her, and she blushed a little.

"Would it be OK if I came around the island and hugged you, Josie?" Of course she was OK with it, especially because the look on his face said he really wanted to come around and kiss her. She was leaving it up to him to decide what he would and wouldn't be ready for.

"Yes, please," she said, smiling.

Chapter 51

Antonia kept right on talking. "After all this time and after everything he did to us? After disappearing, oh wait sorry, *dying*,"—she made quotes with her fingers—"he has the nerve to say something so ridiculous to me? And Elizabeth! That is truly a whole other story. She's really struggling, and for him to even bring her up is just distasteful. He doesn't care about her and he certainly doesn't care about me."

While she was venting, she headed over to the bar and pulled out two tumblers from the cabinet. She filled them with ice and poured herself a bourbon, then poured James the best scotch she had in the house. She didn't bother asking what he'd like. She already knew what he wanted.

James smiled to himself. He was glad to have this time with her, but at the same time, he felt like such a shit. How could tonight be so easy? He began recalling the last forty years of their lives and wondered, *Where in the world did we go wrong? How did we let it all fall apart?*

She could see his eyes were a little distant. "Are you listening to me?"

"Yes, of course I am. I just . . . " He stopped. He was trying his hardest to keep the positive momentum of this night. Maybe he was kidding himself, by the sound of her rant.

"OK, just checking." She continued, "After tomorrow morning, there will be one last step or two, and this will all be over."

"What will be over?" James asked.

"Are you joking?"

Recover! Recover, you idiot. "I mean, I was hoping you didn't mean us spending time together was over."

Antonia was dumbfounded. She was not expecting James to make that comment. Wait, yes, she was. Who was she kidding? He'd been awfully friendly lately.

"What are you saying?"

"I'm not jumping the gun on anything here, but it's been nice. Us working together again. Maybe we could see where this can go. Maybe work another job? Maybe just date?" James said.

Now she was laughing, and laughing at him no less. "Those are two very different things," she said to him.

"I know," he said, but he didn't really know what else to say. He was thinking with his emotions and his heart. He wasn't thinking from a rational point of view.

"Maybe you've had enough to drink." She wanted to reach for his glass and take it away, but she left it on the table.

He laughed. "I've had two sips. If I'm drunk, you may as well just call the nursing home and get me a room."

She laughed, more than she would have liked to. There was far too much to consider off the cuff like this.

"Maybe that's something we can discuss. I thought we were retiring after this job." She playfully smiled at him.

"We did say that, didn't we?"

"Yes, we did." She gave him a confirming nod.

Proudly and with a confident tone, he said, "Well then, maybe this will have to be the second option."

She smirked at him. "I will have to seriously consider that."

Chapter 52

Marco was holding Josie. She felt so safe and loved. He was playing with a curl of her hair, like he used to when they were younger.

She was afraid to look up at him. She didn't want him to think she was looking for a kiss. He was a step ahead of her though. He backed away just enough for her to look up at him, wondering what he was doing. He put his hands on her face again and looked into her eyes.

"The question has been rolling through my head all day, and it's much stronger now. Am I here with you for comfort, or am I here because I belong here with you? Grief, if that's what I'm supposed to call this, is something I've never really dealt with before, so I'm not sure how to feel, or how to separate it all," Marco said.

Inside, her heart fell, but she kept strong for him on the outside.

"Josie, to be honest, I don't feel sad at all. I know that sounds pretty heartless, but I just don't care. I'm more shaken about the how, rather than the what. Since I told Lexi that it was best for the both of us just to divorce, I've felt like a huge weight has been lifted off my shoulders. My heart belongs to you, and it has for a very long time."

She smiled at him, still being careful not to be too dramatic. She wanted him to move at his own pace tonight.

"Josie, please say something," Marco urged.

She tried to choose the right words. "Marco, you are here tonight because you are ready for us. I just want to make sure you have enough time to process all of this and you don't jump into something if you're not ready."

"That's what I'm trying to say. I think I'm ready, and I really appreciate you for being so understanding. I also know that, before we move on, there is a lot for us to talk about. I want to hash out the past. I can't speak for you, but I know I'm in a good enough spot to take the blame for things that happened. I don't think we will be able to move on together if we don't take the time to clear the air."

With a giant sigh of relief, Josie said, "You have no idea how happy it makes me to hear you say that. I agree with you, one hundred percent. I'm ready when you are."

With a slight hint of aggravation in Marco's voice, he blurted out, "Josie, I know you are worried about me, but you have to let it go. I want to do this, and I want to talk about it."

"OK, jeez. Then let's get right into it, since you are so ready."

He brushed a curl out of her eyes again and pulled her forehead against his. "I'm sorry, I didn't mean to sound aggravated. I just don't want my messy life getting in the way of what you want any longer. I'm supposed to make your life easier, not harder, and up until this very moment, I have been failing miserably."

Josie was completely relieved to hear this from Marco. His statement would make this conversation a whole lot easier. She was willing to take blame for the things she had done in the past, but she also needed him to know how hard it was, being a part of his life.

"I can see those wheels turning, Josie. If you don't slow down, you'll burn out and then we'll have to cut the evening short," he playfully teased, trying to keep things light. He didn't want their heated personalities to ruin this crucial conversation. At times, their personalities clashed like oil and water.

Josie smiled brightly at Marco. He still knew her well. She could only hope that after all this time, they were mature enough to not let childish emotions get in the way.

Marco said, "There's not much I can say, and I know that even if I apologize, it won't be enough. Our biggest fight, and what I believe we never recovered from, was my fault. I obviously take the blame. I would be very stupid to deflect all of the blame to you. I was such a stupid kid back then. I was a spoiled brat. You know how I was back then. Once I got something, I was bored and moved onto something else. I mean, how many cars did I have while we were together, five?" He tried to make a joke. He didn't want it to sound like he was bored with Josie; he just wanted to reiterate that he was a spoiled brat back then.

But Josie stared at him, wondering what he was going to say next. She was thankful he was telling the truth, but on the other hand, this was a perfect example of how the truth hurts.

"So, what you are saying is that I was a conquest. You got me, and then you wanted to move on." She didn't even ask it in question form. She knew that was where he was headed with this.

"Josie, when you say it out loud like that, it sounds so horrible."

"That's because it is horrible, Marco." Her voice was flat, as she tried not to sound dramatic or too hurt.

"Josie, please know I just want to be honest, and we need to get all this out in the open. Even if it breaks us this time, we need to get it all out there."

"I agree, Marco. Even though it's hard to hear, I have to be honest in saying that hearing it said out loud makes it real."

Now Marco was nervous. He didn't want to lose her again, not over his childish ways from back then.

She continued, "What I mean is that I need an explanation. Why was I not important enough? Better yet, when did you realize that you actually were in love with me and you were just a stupid kid, as you put it?"

"I loved you the whole time. I just wanted more. I thought I could have my cake and eat it too. I was greedy. That's why I didn't break up with you. I thought I could stay with you and see what else was out there. It's awful, I know, but again, I was just a stupid kid and a boy, no less. I know it's not acceptable, but that's what I was doing."

"Marco, that sucks."

"Josie, I know. I was a total ass. Childish and spoiled."

"Marco, I expected far more from you at the time than you were willing to give me. Plus, I was a year older than you, and from senior year to junior year is a decent difference, with maturity especially."

Marco was thankful the conversation was moving on, but he thought he knew what she was going to say next.

Josie continued, "There was so much going on and I was going away to school and you never wanted to even talk about that."

Marco cut in. "I was so afraid of losing you by then that I didn't want to talk about it. I just wanted to forget you were even leaving. I never thought we would last after you left for school."

"You lost me anyway, and then as I recall, moved on not too long after I left."

"Josie, that's not fair. I think you might be leaving out a pretty big detail," said Marco.

"John is on the list of things I wanted to discuss. Actually, let's just bring it up now. Why wait? For me, it just comes down to the fact that I was with John before you and I got together, so I really don't feel like you have much of a leg to stand on with complaining about him," she said.

"Josie, you have to be kidding."

"Marco, I'm not kidding. You did what you did months earlier. I pretty much forgave you and we tried to move on. I did the same thing to you and you broke up with me. And John was someone I had already dated and had deep feelings for at one point."

"Well, it's not exactly what I did to you." Marco was trying to make her see the difference without seriously making her angry.

She stared blankly at him. She was trying to process the implications of what he said.

"I do understand where you are coming from, but when I found out you had feelings for another girl, I was crushed. That happened months before my one night with John. You weren't just trying to be with her physically, you actually had feelings for her," Josie said.

"To be fair, you did get physically close to John while we were together," Marco pointed out.

"I know, and like you, I am trying to explain why I did what I did. You were so distant, and had been for weeks. You refused to talk about me going away to college. You didn't even want to iron out all the other issues we were having aside from me leaving. Our relationship was a complete mess and you refused to talk about it. Yes, what I did with John was wrong, but he was in the same position I was in, and it was comfortable with him. I didn't exactly have the feelings for him that I once had. Also, you and I had broken up and gotten back together so many times just in one year. I felt like we were doomed at that point."

"You talked to him about us?"

"He brought it up to me and simply said if I wanted to talk about it, he'd listen. No strings attached. The strings were my idea. He was a perfect gentleman. It was me that made a move."

That was the last thing Marco wanted to hear. He wanted to think that John was a hormonal teenager that seduced his girlfriend. Obviously, that was not what happened.

"OK, enough. I don't need to hear the details," Marco said. He smiled at Josie to make sure she understood that this was maybe too much.

"I'm sorry. I'm not trying to hurt you. Maybe we should keep some of the truth hidden," said Josie. She didn't really mean it though. If they were going to make it, there couldn't be secrets about their past, and there couldn't be anything left unsaid. It was now or never for them, and they both knew it.

She said, "Marco, I know this really sucks for the both of us."

"So you want to stop talking then?" Marco joked.

Josie smiled at him. "I wish, but you know we're not done."

"I think I'm done," he said, hoping that there wasn't anything else she wanted to talk about. She pretty much covered everything that made him look like a dirtbag from their past. "I do have to admit that when I found out about you and John, it broke my heart. And after you left, I knew one hundred percent that I was in love with you. The pain was so awful that it was more than obvious that I was in love with you." Josie grabbed Marco's hand.

"There is one more thing, Marco," Josie said with tears welling in her eyes. "I'm not sure how to say this."

Her tears broke his heart all over again.

He moved closer to hold her, but she put her hands up to stop him. "I need to get this out, and I can't do that with you hugging me, Marco."

"Josie, what is it? What's the matter?"

"Marco, I had a miscarriage."

He stared blankly at her. He was so stunned that he couldn't feel anything in the moment. He didn't know if he was sad or angry. Was it John's? Or his? He didn't want to make this about him, so he didn't bother to ask. He was speechless.

"Marco, you look like you might throw up, or maybe put your fist through a wall." Josie's voice brought him out of his stupor.

"Josie, why didn't you tell me?" he said.

"Marco, I didn't really understand that's what actually happened until later."

"Forgive my ignorance, Josie, but how did you not know?"

"Marco, I never knew I was pregnant. I must have only been pregnant for six or seven weeks. I missed my period, but didn't realize it. I was so wrapped up into being accepted into college, finishing the school year, the spring sport season, and our dating turmoil that I didn't even realize I missed it, not until about two weeks after I was supposed to get my period. I didn't panic because I was really stressed and thought that was why. I had been late before."

Marco cut her off. "You had been late before?" he sternly questioned.

"Only a week or so, and my schedule was never really right on, so I didn't think anything of it."

"How did you end up figuring out that's what happened?"

"I started going to a gynecologist for yearly exams and one of the questions she asked was if I had ever been pregnant. I said no right away, but then explained what happened. She said that, without testing the tissue, she couldn't say for sure, but she thought it was most likely a miscarriage. She said that ten to twenty-five percent of first pregnancies end in miscarriages."

"So, you don't know for sure?"

"No, not one hundred percent for sure, but it was pretty awful, and the doc said every symptom I had and everything that I explained to her lead her to believe that I definitely had a miscarriage."

Josie saw his wheels spinning and the panic on his face. She needed to confirm for him. "Listen, Marco, it was definitely yours. I'm not sure if that makes you feel better or not, but it was yours."

"How can you be so sure?"

"It was at least three months before John and I . . ." she trailed off.

Marco pushed away the anger that had settled in his gut at the thought of the baby being John's, making way for an unexpected feeling of sadness.

"I'm not really sure what I am supposed to do with this information."

"Don't do anything with it, Marco. You don't need to feel sad, angry, surprised, upset. You don't really need to feel anything. If you feel something that's OK, but if not, that's OK, too."

"Well then, why did you tell me?" Marco looked at her begrudgingly.

"Because, this conversation is about throwing everything out there from our past, so we aren't hiding anything. You don't need to feel anything. I know you've always wanted children and it doesn't mean we can't have them. This won't affect our future. It's in the past," she said.

"What?" Marco asked in surprise.

"Just, if you were wondering if this affects my ability to have children, it doesn't. There should be no issues going forward."

He was so relieved that she knew exactly what he was thinking. Happy that it sounded like she wanted kids, which is what he wanted too.

Chapter 53

Joe was enjoying the night air, waiting for his wife to join him in their backyard oasis. He was recalling the last thirty years of his life in quick succession. He'd had a really great life, considering some of the setbacks, which were horribly out of his control.

He was so proud of Josie and the woman she had become. He was also so grateful for his wife. How would he have gotten through any of this without her love and support?

He had always tried to teach Josie that every time you fall, you have to get right back up and hit the ground running. Don't let the bastards get you down, he'd said. She wasn't aware of everything that he had been through, but enough for her to know that his advice came from experience.

Joe had been free of Anthony's torment and misery for a while now, and it felt good. He'd never thought he would be involved with that wretched man again, but it would all be OK. He would be lying to himself if he said he was not worried. But after all, offering his help to the Parettis didn't mean he was involved again. It was the least he could do to repay his old friends.

In a way, he felt bad for Anthony. He used to be somebody important. Not important for any good reason, but important, nonetheless. Every bad thing that had ever happened to Anthony, he brought on himself, with all those mobsters he surrounded himself with.

Joe thought of James. Of all James had done to help him. After all these years, he could repay James with just one phone call. One phone call, and it would all be over. He was almost giddy about it. And then the Parettis would handle things from there.

His lovely wife came outside to join him, and seeing the smile on his face, asked, "What are you smiling about?" Kate smiled, unable to keep a straight face herself.

"Oh, you know, this whole thing with our old friends is making me happy. It's like the nail in the coffin." As the words tumbled out of his mouth, he felt sorry. "I can't believe I just said that."

"Why? It's not like Carmine is actually dead," Kate said.

"I know, but the whole thing is just strange."

"Yes, but like you said before, it will be over, once and for all. I know we thought it was over before, and technically it was, but there was always that looming concern that he would pop up again and try something else to hurt us. It might not be over for others, but it will be for us."

"It's such a relief that karma will finally get that rotten—"

"Now, now, dear, let's be happy for where we are and enjoy retirement," she gently reprimanded.

"Well, I won't complain there." He took her hand and gave it a squeeze.

He'd checked the box about a hundred times today, just to make sure it was safe and sound. That briefcase held all the proof they need to be free.

Chapter 54

James and Antonia sat in silence for a while, sipping their drinks. The silence was comfortable. It came naturally to them. Antonia was not quite sure how, since they'd spent the last few years of their marriage screaming at each other.

"We have a big day ahead of us tomorrow," Antonia said. She needed to be very careful what she said and how she said it. She didn't want to give him any ideas. "I should probably take you home."

He didn't react. "Whatever you want is fine with me."

"I'd offer for you to stay here, but I'm not sure I trust you."

He laughed, knowing that she still knew him all too well. "That's probably a good call on your part. I wouldn't trust me either." His facial expression was uncontrollable this time. The old, but very familiar look he used to give her slowly crept onto his face.

"Don't even think about it. That is not happening; not tonight anyway."

"A man can try," he managed to say after realizing from her comment what the future could hold.

"Man?" she questioned.

He laughed at her. He had not realized how much he missed her. Most of the things they used to fight about were nonissues at this point in their lives. They had more money than they could have imagined, and their children needed them now more than ever, and they were in a place to help them. Together.

Antonia realized that it was no longer a question of who was taking which kid to what sporting event, or if James would even be home to attend the school play or a parent teacher conference.

The issues they had now were if their knees would hurt when they got out of bed in the morning and then, of course, the business of if they should keep working together.

"Whatever is rolling around in that head of yours, maybe it's time to put it aside and take me home."

"OK, there, big guy. Let's go."

He smiled at her, wondering if she realized what she said. She used to call him that all the time when they were together.

She smiled at him, knowing full well what he was thinking. It was not planned. It just tumbled out.

She dropped off her ex-husband and decided now was as good a time as any to reach out to John. She needed to clue him in so he didn't start nosing around where he didn't belong. She already knew he'd seen the insurance policy. She wasn't afraid that he would cause issues, she just didn't want him to carry the burden of this.

It was late, so she was prepared to leave him a message, but she was still hoping he would answer.

"Hello?"

"Hello, John."

John froze. He knew that voice anywhere. What could she possibly want?

He steadied his voice. "Hello, Mrs. Paretti. How are you this evening?"

John was polite and always seemed to know the right thing to say. He was genuine, though. He didn't have time to lie and cheat his way through conversations. He was too intelligent for that. Plus, he never seemed to have anything to hide. She wanted to use him as more of an ally rather than treating him like an enemy.

"I'm doing just fine, John. How are you?"

"I'm well. What can I help you with this evening?" he asked.

"I'm not going to beat round the bush, so I'll get right to it. I'm sure you've seen the insurance policy I took out on Carmine." She didn't say this as a question. She just threw it out there. If he didn't know the cat was out of the bag, this was a risk she was willing to take.

"Yes, I have. I'm not going to lie, it flipped me out when it first came across my computer screen."

She was pleased that he was willing to engage in an open conversation. She continued, "I'm sure you are asking who takes out an insurance policy on their own child."

"As a matter of fact, I have been asking that question since I read through the policy. What's the deal?"

He wasn't afraid of her, and that made her even more pleased. She didn't want him to be afraid. She wanted him to trust her so he would share information if she was in need.

"I took it out knowing that at some point in his life, something like this would happen, and I wanted to make sure that the kids would be taken care of. I wasn't worried about Jackie. She gives her whole life to those kids, so I knew they would be in good hands."

John knew it would be in his best interest to tread lightly in this conversation; however, Mrs. Paretti called him, so she was either fishing for what he knew, or wanting to make sure he would keep his trap shut about it.

"Mrs. Paretti, I know you know that I cannot discuss the policy and what I know with anyone outside of those named in the policy. I can discuss it with you because it is official that I will be handling it. It seems pretty straightforward, so there is no conflict of interest at the moment."

"At the moment?"

"Yes, at the moment. I don't have any familial connection to you, and there is no legal issue at hand. There are obviously procedures so this will just move along once all the pieces are put in place and the funds will be released to Jackie." John paused before continuing. "I do want to be very clear. We both know how the policy reads." Again he stopped to choose the right words. "You said Jackie would take care of the kids. We are both fully aware that Lexi is the primary beneficiary. I would hope you are not trying to tell me something here, Mrs. Paretti."

"No, John, of course not. I just have a sneaking suspicion that Lexi is going to end up doing the right thing in the long run."

At the sound of her tone, John got a shiver up his back. This woman was not to be messed with.

"Mrs. Paretti, since we seem to be speaking freely tonight, what is the reasoning for Lexi being on that policy in the first place?" John needed to know. He's been dying for the answer since he read it. It didn't make any sense.

She knew she needed to tell him the truth, so she took her time before she answered. "This was my desperate attempt to get her out of the family once and for all if anything ever happened to Carmine."

"So, because she wouldn't need Marco's money, you thought she'd just leave him and move on?"

"That's the hope."

He was on a roll now and he wasn't stopping.

"What in the world does Anthony have to do with the situation?" John asked.

"That conversation is for another time. For right now, just know that he is part of my past."

John was speechless. Completely and totally at a loss for words. He had thought that Anthony was just a worthless old man. Anthony had been worthless for as long as John had known him. *What could a lady like Mrs. Paretti want or need from that jerk? Maybe she didn't need anything. Maybe it's him that needed something from her? But what?*

"John, thank you for the chat," Mrs. P said.

"What is it that you actually wanted?"

She was careful now too. “I just wanted to make sure you believe this will all go very smoothly for us.”

“I can only do my job. Whatever it is you are expecting from Lexi is on you,” John said.

“I am fully aware of that, John, and I appreciate you speaking with me this evening.”

As soon as they hung up, John dialed Josie. He wanted to tell her what was going on.

He just didn’t understand why Mrs. Paretti thought the kids would get the money if Lexi was on the policy before Jackie. It was not adding up. Mrs. Paretti had said not to worry about Lexi, but how could he not?

Chapter 55

Josie's phone was ringing, and she checked it just to make sure it wasn't her mom or dad, even though she'd set the special alert for them. Other than them, she didn't care who it was.

She saw that it was John. She would have to speak with him sooner or later, but right now, she was planning the rest of her life.

"Marco, I need to ask you something."

"Isn't that why I'm here?" he joked.

"When did you realize you loved me again?"

"Again? I never stopped loving you, Josie. I was never not in love with you. Like I said, when I found out about you and John, I was crushed. That's how I knew I loved you, and I never stopped."

"Then why didn't you fight for us?" Josie asked. This may not have been a very fair question, but even after everything happened, he had still refused to talk to her. It felt like he gave up.

"You mean before or after you left me for John?"

"Not fair, Marco. I did not leave you for John."

"You pretty much did."

"I fully understand that was how it looked, Marco, but you were checked out long before that, and John and I never got back together."

"I may have been, but it didn't mean that I didn't love you, and it definitely didn't mean that I didn't want to be with you anymore, Josie." He paused. "When did you realize you still loved me?"

She smiled at him. "Still? You assumed I stopped?"

Marco's face fell. "Did you stop loving me?"

"No, not really."

"Not really? Seriously, Josie?"

"Marco, I was so angry at you. I was angry for all the reasons we talked about tonight, but I was mostly angry that you just moved on. You moved on without me. You didn't try to talk about it, you never reached out, you just moved on."

Josie felt the tears coming. Talking about it brought back the pain. She wasn't sure how she was going to trust that, if they found themselves hitting a bad patch, he would fight for them instead of just giving up.

"Marco, how do I know that you will fight for us if we run into hard times in the future?"

He smiled, trying to reassure her. "It will be completely different if that happens. I'm going to try my hardest to not let that happen, but if it does, I will do whatever I can to make it right. I'm not going to make the same mistake again with us. I know it's just words now, but I think I've proven to be much more grown up and responsible these days."

He got up to hug her. Josie welcomed it. She was drained. She didn't want to talk anymore, unless there was something else he wanted to say. It was getting late.

His arms were around her waist and her hands were gripped right above his elbows. His arms were bigger than she remembered. He was so handsome. He was looking down at her with so much love in his eyes and hope in his smile.

"It's getting late, Marco." She gave him a few seconds to reply and then asked, "Do you want to stay?"

"I thought you'd never ask."

She giggled and broke from his embrace, and, taking him by the hand, led him to her bedroom.

Chapter 56

Antonia was up and ready for the day. She had a feeling today was going to be a little rough, but she was ready for it. Oddly, she took comfort in knowing that James would be there. It was a good feeling to know that he would support her no matter what happened. He was in her corner, and she wouldn't have it any other way. Especially today.

She made herself a cup of coffee and sat on her back patio, hoping to relax a bit and get her head in the right place. She was not crazy about driving in the city, but she'd done the drive so many times that she could do it with her eyes closed. There was no good reason for her to worry.

She watched as two squirrels chased each other through the backyard, playing and having a grand old time. James used to chase her like that.

She recalled the day he proposed to her. When James came home from college, he moved back with his parents for a few months before he started his first job. She was playing with the dog in his parents' backyard and as he began walking over to her, she started to playfully skip away from him. He chased after her. He had caught her wrist and he brought her in close as if to dip her, and he put his foot out so she would fall into him. They floated to the ground, laughing and holding each other.

He was holding her head in his hand so it wouldn't touch the grass. "I love you," he'd said.

"I love you too," she happily squealed, out of breath.

"Maybe you could be my wife one day."

"Maybe," she'd replied, raising an eyebrow at him, knowing what was coming later on that night. He then took her to the most beautiful restaurant in the city. They ate and drank and planned their future together. He proposed on the terrace overlooking the water. It was the most wonderful night of her life.

She snapped out of her memory and looked at her watch. She gave herself plenty of time to get the package ready to deliver to Anthony. She wasn't sure how smoothly it would go, and she didn't want to be late. "It's go time," she muttered out loud to no one but the squirrels.

She got the package loaded and headed over to pick up James. As she turned the corner onto his street, Antonia passed a woman she would recognize anywhere. The two women locked eyes over their steering wheels, the woman smirking at Antonia.

Antonia was furious. She looked in the rearview mirror with her eyes squinting in anger. *She couldn't be coming from his house this early in the morning*, Antonia thought. *Unless . . . no way did she stay the night?* She didn't need to be dealing with this shit at her age. The feeling of dread began to creep up from her gut. There was no way she was going to let him do this to her again.

She pulled herself together. They had a job to do today, and that's what they were going to do.

She pulled up in front of his house and James came dancing down the steps, happy as could be.

She was fuming.

He opened the car door. "Good morning, sunshine. I made you coffee. I'm sure you've already had some, but, in this mug,"—he pointed to the name brand on the side of the mug, indicating that it would stay hot all day for her—"it will be ready when you are."

She was completely thrown by this. A woman, his second ex-wife no less, was just coming from his house, and he was acting like nothing happened. *What an ass*, she fumed.

She mustered a thank you, not sounding very enthused. Seeing that woman had her thoughts rolling around in her head. She felt dazed. She recalled a conversation that she had with Jimmy. He said they had reconciled, sort of, and were trying to give their relationship another go, but a few months had passed and they were on the rocks again. They were barely speaking. That was the only reason she even considered spending personal time with him again. She thought he was done with that woman.

James could sense Antonia's coldness. He cocked his head to the side in confusion. He rubbed the top of her hand quickly but softly with the tips of his fingers and smiled brightly at her.

She eyed him cautiously. *Something isn't right*, she thought. *Why is he acting like this when he most likely just had someone else over for the night?*

She was standoffish, not wanting him to see how much she was hurt. She refused to let him catch her being so vulnerable.

She saw him peek in the back of the car to check on the package. He looked back at Antonia and rolled his eyes.

"How did it go this morning? Did you have any issues?" James asked, bobbing his head in the direction of the back seat.

She glanced at him, seeing the concern on his face, and very flatly said, "No, everything was fine. No issues at all."

James was confused. He thought they'd had a great day yesterday, and last night was so natural. He was afraid to ask. He didn't want to even think that they might not be OK. He was hoping for something to come out of last night, but now he was not very confident.

Chapter 57

The sun was peeking in the window as Marco slowly began to wake up. It took him a minute or two to get acclimated to his surroundings. He rolled over to find Josie sleeping peacefully next to him. He didn't want to wake her, so he lay there a few moments longer, hoping she'd wake up on her own.

He recalled last night and believed they talked everything through. He smiled.

His thoughts become strained at the thought of Lexi and what was going to happen with her. He was not so sure he cared at this point, but he knew he would have to address it with his insane parents. He wished he could just put it out of his mind, but he was not that heartless. Not as heartless as his parents were, apparently.

What would possess them to do such a thing? He had so many questions for them. Most of them he didn't want the answers to, but sooner or later, he would be forced to learn the truth about them and their past.

He felt Josie begin to stir. He was so happy to be there with her. She was facing him, so when she opened her eyes, he was the first thing she saw. "Hi," she sleepily said with a slight smile.

"Hi." He rolled closer to her so he could engulf her in his giant bear hug.

"Have you been up for a while?" she asked.

"No, not long at all. Maybe ten minutes or so."

"You weren't staring at me the whole time, were you?"

He huffed out a small laugh, "No. Not the whole time. Maybe nine minutes and fifty-nine seconds."

She looked up at him and smiled. She nudged him with her elbow.

He wanted to stay there with her forever. He dreaded the thought of going back home, knowing what was there for him to deal with and also knowing that she wouldn't be able to go back with him. Well, maybe she could. She could work from anywhere, after all. It was worth asking, anyway.

Josie rolled out of his hug so she could see him face to face.

"I know it's early for me to be blurting this out at you, but I don't plan on playing any games and I'm not going to be worried every minute about what you are thinking. Our lives are very different with me living in the city and you living back home. I think it's important to share most of what's on each other's minds so we can move forward . . . together," Josie said.

He sat there staring at her. He didn't quite know what to say. Relief washed over him. "How do you do it?" he asked her.

"What?"

"How is it that I'm thinking something, and you come right out and say it?"

"Marco, do you remember when we used to finish each other's sentences? Do you remember when people used to ask me what you were thinking and you what I was thinking?"

It was like a light bulb went off in his head. "I haven't thought about that in—"

"Years," she finished.

Marco smiled at her. "That was an easy one. Josie, I was just thinking about today and the rest of the weekend. I don't really want to go home."

"So don't. Just stay here with me."

"I would love to, but I think I really need to go home and deal with Lexi. I don't know what I'm going to do, but I should probably do something."

"It's not like you can file a missing person report."

"That's what I was going to do, but now that you say that, it doesn't make any sense at all."

"Yeah, I would just wait to see what happens. How did you leave it with your mom?"

Marco just rolled his eyes. He couldn't believe they were even having this ridiculous conversation.

"She just told me not to worry about it. But I feel like I should. Shouldn't we hold a funeral or something?" he said. Marco sighed, wanting to change the subject. "Would you come home with me?"

"When? Like today?"

"Yeah, today, until maybe Monday?"

She reached for her phone on the nightstand to check her calendar for Monday. "Sure, I can do that. I don't have anything scheduled for Monday, and if something comes up, I can do a phone call from anywhere."

Marco was so happy. This would make things a lot easier for him. His mother would be happy too. He was always thinking about her. This put him in a sour mood, suddenly.

There was one detail that he was going to have to share with Josie, and last night he was just too much of a coward to tell her. He would have to spill sooner or later, but he was putting it off as long as he could. He was terrified of what she might do when she found out.

Chapter 58

James continued to eye Antonia cautiously. He wanted to say something, but figured it was best if he waited until after they left Anthony's. It was eating at him though, and he was not sure what to do.

As they approached Anthony's building, Antonia very tersely said, "I'll be glad when this is over with." Her emotions were swirling around in her head.

James knew how all this was going to end, so he was a little taken aback. *What is going on with her?* He was struggling to understand what happened in such a short period of time for her to have become so standoffish and angry.

She pulled into the parking garage and found a spot closest to the elevators. That would be the best way of getting the package into Anthony's apartment.

Antonia looked in the back seat, eyeing up the package, making sure there would be no issues getting it inside. She was hoping for full cooperation.

They got out of the car and Antonia opened the door to the back seat on the driver's side. She put one hand on the package, guiding it out of the car and inside the elevator.

James followed closely behind Antonia and the package, in his own world, just dying to say something, but he kept quiet. It was really eating at him now. He could not recall caring this much about something in quite a while, and he was completely uncomfortable with that feeling.

Anthony was waiting for them outside of the elevator. He looked surprised when he saw the package they had brought with them.

As they entered the apartment all together, Carmine was in the front room, standing around like a lost puppy. James and Antonia didn't react. They barely acknowledged him. They weren't there to see him.

But Carmine, seeing the package, took one step closer and stopped. He didn't want to make a scene, but he could hardly contain himself. James moved out of the way, and Lexi ran into Carmine's arms.

"Carmine! What? How?" Lexi was crying uncontrollably. She never expected him to be here. She was certain he was gone. The small bit of hope she had held onto now came back in full force.

"Hi, sweetheart," he murmured into her ear as he hugged her. He had no idea she was going to show up like this. "It's OK, it is all going to be OK." Tears welled in Carmine's eyes. He knew things were far from OK, and judging by the fear in her eyes, Carmine knew that Lexi knew it too.

Antonia and James rolled their eyes at each other. They both found Lexi and Carmine's affection for one another disgusting. If Lexi wasn't married to Carmine's own brother, it would be a great love story; but this? This was just pure shit.

Carmine and Lexi separated themselves from the others, leaving the room to catch up without being judged any more than they already were.

"Carmine, I can't. . . I can't believe you are here, and you're alive!"

Carmine pulled her in for another hug to hide his sadness. Lexi was talking like they were going to live happily ever after, and Carmine knew that was the furthest thing from the truth.

He didn't bring it up now, but soon he knew he would have to tell her what was actually going to happen. He wanted her to be happy, if only for a few days.

As they turned to leave the apartment, Antonia looked at James and was put off by the moment she shared with him. She was not happy with him, but she couldn't help but feel herself still drawn to him.

Anthony eyed everyone with what seemed to him to be guilt. But why?

Chapter 59

"Marco, can I ask you something? You might not even remember if it wasn't important to you at the time, but do you remember when your mother called you, the day we were at my parents' house, the day before the viewing?"

Oh no, why was she asking him this? Why did she care? He was just going to have to lie. There was no way he was telling her now. He could tell her the truth about the conversation, but he would not tell her what they talked about when he'd gotten to his mother's house.

"Yes, I remember."

"What did she want? You ran off pretty urgently."

He wanted so badly just to tell her it was none of her business and she shouldn't be sticking her nose where it didn't belong. She knew so much already that even if he did say that, it really wouldn't make much sense. He just wasn't ready to talk about it. He was being completely irrational in blaming her for asking. Total transparency, they said.

"She called me and asked me if I could go over to her house." He tried not to make eye contact with her. He wasn't in the mood to fake his facial expression, too. "It seems like an eternity that she asked me to go over there."

Marco kissed her on the forehead and snuggled her, hoping that she would just drop it, and she did. He was so grateful.

"When are you going to talk to John?" Marco asked. This wasn't even really on his mind, but he thought about it and it just came out.

"I don't know. Probably later this week after I get back here, when you and I have a better idea of what's going on."

"That's good."

Marco was way off in the distance.

Josie didn't want to disturb his thoughts, even though she was a little worried about him. He certainly had enough on his plate right now. He was talking to her, but she could tell his brain was somewhere else.

"Shall I make us some breakfast?"

"That would be great, Josie. Your famous pancakes?"

She laughed and kissed him. "They aren't famous to anyone but you."

"That may be true, but they should be famous to everyone. Let's just run away and open a diner somewhere in the Midwest."

She smiled a genuine smile at Marco. She threw on his t-shirt and walked out to the kitchen.

Marco was glad to have some time to himself, even for only just a few moments. His mind was reeling. He was happy, sad, angry, and a few other things. He was all over the place. He just wanted all of this to be over. He wanted his parents to be normal and leave him out of whatever they were doing. This was the last thing he wanted to deal with right now. He seemed to be thinking that a lot lately.

His phone began buzzing on the table. Marco gently tapped the headboard with the back of his head and whispered, "What now?"

Chapter 60

Anthony's daughter and ex-son-in-law had just left, and Anthony couldn't help but notice his overwhelming feeling of disgust.

His daughter had barely looked at him when she left. Not that he expected her to, but since he'd started seeing her more often, he had noticed that each time she left him, or they hung up the phone, he was hoping for something. He couldn't quite pinpoint what he was wanting, but he knew it was something other than parting ways.

He sat down in his old rocking chair, the one from his great-grandfather. It was the only piece of furniture that made its way through the generations. There was a small, oblong chip taken out of one of the arms. He ran his finger over the chip, and for the first time noticed that the top had smoothed over from rubbing his arm over it all these years.

He laughed, remembering how the chip got there in the first place.

He and his brother had gotten in so much trouble that day. He threw something across the room and almost hit his brother right in the face. He hit the chair instead. He saw what it did to the chair, and he was instantly thankful it didn't hit his brother as he'd intended.

As he recalled the memories he had of his younger brother, he smiled, thinking about the thirteen-month age difference between them. His mother was a saint to deal with the two of them and their other four siblings.

He thought he might be having a breakdown. It was ingrained in his head from such a young age that boys didn't cry. They didn't show their feelings no matter what. This was all he knew. Whatever his father and his uncles taught him. A horrible realization was rising up from his gut. From birth, he was groomed for the business which he was eventually forced into against his will.

What had he done? How could he have spent all these years being such a horrible person and not even realizing it? When did he become such a monster?

He really could not recall. There was no defining moment that he remembered that made him angry, and arrogant, and down-right nasty. This was not the way he wanted to live the rest of his life. Maybe he still had a chance to make things right?

It would be a long road, and knowing his age wouldn't allow it, he began thinking of ways he could make things better quickly. It could be as easy as a conversation. He would have to say the right things and act the right way. Could he really pull it off? It would be genuine, so he would be speaking from the heart. Would his family believe him?

He sat there not knowing what was coming over him. He was so emotional that he almost began to cry.

He heard Lexi laugh from the other room and it only reinforced his thoughts. He needed to make all this right again. There was so much to fix. So much to be done.

He knew it would virtually take a miracle. But he must try. He better get to it before he keeled over.

Chapter 61

As they walked out of the apartment and into the elevator, James looked over at Antonia, still wondering what could have happened between last night to this morning that had her so displeased with him.

He was just going to come right out and ask her. "You seem to be peeved with me today. Did something happen since last evening? I thought we had a nice time."

Antonia didn't want to respond right away. She didn't want to give him the satisfaction of knowing how upset she was that he had that woman at his house, and overnight no less. She was getting angry again. She wanted to calm down so there wouldn't be so much emotion in her answer.

"I saw"—she couldn't even bear to say her name. She refused to say her name—"that *woman*. I saw that *woman* driving away from your house. Some people never change."

They were now walking through the parking garage and she looked across the row of cars, noticing an unmarked car that looked an awful lot like a law enforcement vehicle.

She didn't acknowledge that she saw it, and she didn't mention it to James. She kept her cool.

Her thoughts veered from the supposed cops as she heard James say, "It is not what you think," bringing her back to the conversation.

"Why would I possibly believe you?"

He tilted his head and looked at her with a straight face, as if to suggest that he didn't want her bringing up the past. He was hoping they could start fresh. It is never easy to forget the past, and he understood that, but in this case, it would be the only way they could make it.

"I thought you went home after you dropped me off?" He raised his eyebrows in question.

"What are you talking about? I did go home after I dropped you off."

James was very confused. As he looked at her with a scrunched-up face, wondering what she was talking about, the question he just posed registered in her head.

"I saw her this morning. What does last night and me going home have to do with seeing her?"

He looked at her, stunned. *Shit*, he thought. Now he was busted for sure.

"When did you see her?" James asked.

"Are you serious? After you just admitted to her being there last night, are you going to try to lie and say she wasn't there?" Antonia said.

"No, no, I'm not going to lie. I was just confused as to when you saw her. She did not stay the night, so I don't understand why you saw her this morning. I am confused."

She bit her tongue. "Why should I believe you?"

"You should believe me because it's true. Where did you actually see her?"

"I saw her coming through the stop sign as I was approaching the turn to get onto your street."

"Oh, well that could explain it. Her daughter lives not far from me. Maybe she was just visiting her, or maybe she stayed with her daughter last night when she left me. She was pretty upset when she left. She just happened to call me after you dropped me off and asked if she could come over because she wanted to talk. As you would say, the coward in me thought she was going to break it off with me. I was relieved, because then I wouldn't have to be the one to do it."

Antonia was listening, but she didn't have enough information to believe or not believe him. She was already leery about going down this road again with him, and now she was even more uneasy about it.

She stayed silent, so he continued. "When she got to my house, she gave me a non-lingering hug, so I thought this solidified my guess that she was going to break it off once and for all. We sat in the living room. I didn't offer her anything because I assumed she wasn't going to stay long, and to be honest, I didn't want her to. She began the conversation dramatically, by saying that we have been through a lot and our kids have grown close. These things, as you know, are not true at all. We haven't been through much of anything, and our children"—he shuffled his hands back and forth with his pointer fingers waving between himself and Antonia—"can't stand her children."

"I wasn't sure where she was going with all of it, so I very nicely asked if she could get to the point. She was struggling, and it was beginning to make me uncomfortable. She said that she wanted to be together again and take our relationship to the next step. I was stunned. I didn't know what to say. Here I thought she was going to tell me that she was done with it all, and she goes and says the opposite. We hadn't spoken in weeks. We texted pleasantries here and there, but I had not spoken to her and certainly had not seen her."

Antonia was still staring at him blankly. They had gotten to the car, but were standing outside it. She wanted to just let herself in, lock the car doors, and leave him standing there in the parking garage.

He kept his tone even and truthful. He did not want to screw this up if he could help it. "So, I took her hands in mine and I told her that I enjoyed the good times we spent together, that she was a nice lady, and that she would make someone else very happy, but it just wasn't going to be me. She was at my house for about a half hour and then she left. Where she went after that, I don't know, but that's what happened, and she was not at my house when you saw her."

"So, she didn't spend the night?" Antonia confirmed.

"No, not at all. And as I said, she was only there maybe a half hour."

"Well then. Get in the car and let's get out of here. Those cops over there are probably wondering what the hell we are doing, and there's a good chance they are going to follow us."

His mouth gaped open. James did as she said, and they drove away like nothing ever happened. He was not quite sure where they stood.

Chapter 62

Marco picked up his phone from the nightstand and saw that Jimmy was calling. He let it go to voicemail. Josie should be done with breakfast shortly and he didn't really want to be tied up on the phone with Jimmy.

He could hear her singing out in the kitchen, and felt so grateful to have her back in his life. His mind wandered off to the nightmare of what was ahead for them. He didn't know how they could possibly make it through all this unscathed. What his mother told him on the phone that day at Josie's house could possibly shatter any hope they had of building a life together.

He again considered just telling her everything, but he wanted to prolong the time they had together as long as he could. She'd be seriously pissed at him when she found out. He just needed to make sure he told her before anyone else did. That would be disastrous.

He heard the alert that Jimmy left a voicemail. Against his better judgment, he listened to the message. Jimmy's voice said he had something urgent to share with Marco.

Why? Why now? Why today, when he was supposed to be spending time with Josie? Couldn't he get one day of no drama and nonsense? Jimmy was not usually one for drama, but the urgency of his voicemail left Marco wondering.

He decided to call Jimmy back. Maybe it would be quick. *Yeah, right*, he thought.

"Jimmy, I'm with Josie, so I just wanted to call you back really quickly to make sure nothing was wrong."

"Um, well, I'm not sure what I would call it."

"What does that mean? Oh wait, hold on. Someone is calling me." Marco pulled the phone away to look at the number. He froze. From the phone, he could hear Jimmy yelling, "No, wait. Don't answer it." But he did anyway.

"Uh, hello?" Marco whispered into the phone.

"Hey," the voice on the other end whispered back, just loud enough to make out who it was.

Marco did not say a word. He remembered that he left Jimmy hanging on the other line. He didn't even know if he was still there or not.

"Hold on, Jimmy is on the other line." Marco stabbed at the phone impatiently, trying to get back to Jimmy. "What the F#(%!" Marco screamed at Jimmy.

"What? What's wrong?"

Marco again was at a loss for words. They both were silent until Jimmy finally broke in. "Is that Carmine on the other line?"

"Why would you ask me that? Did you know?"

"That is why I was calling you. Go back to him and call me when you hang up. Or at least when you have a break from Josie. Whatever, just call me back."

Marco hung up with Jimmy, wishing he could just go back to bed. Hit the restart button on this miserable day. He'd been feeling that a lot lately.

"Carmine, what the hell do you want? Why are you calling me?"

"Don't be so happy to hear from me. Why don't you sound surprised that I'm calling you? Surprised I'm not dead?"

"I'm more surprised that you are calling me than the fact that you are alive. You're an asshole," Marco said.

"Thanks for that. Why aren't you surprised that I'm alive?"

Marco wanted to reach through the phone and choke him. Or maybe just hang up on him; but he didn't. "I'm not surprised that you are actually alive because mom was asking far too many questions and the extended autopsy situation just didn't make any sense. I don't think she cared any more than I did that you might actually be dead."

"That's harsh, Marco." Marco rolled his eyes. Carmine was such a pompous ass.

"The icing on the cake for me was when my wife, you know, your mistress, ended up . . ." Marco trailed off. Right at that moment, Marco realized that Lexi was most likely not dead either. He was beyond angry.

Marco kept his composure. "Look, I'm at Josie's and I really do not have time for your shit today. What do you want?"

"I know all you want is to tell me to go to hell, but I need to ask you a favor."

"A favor? Are you serious?" Marco's voice thundered through the phone.

"Yes. Listen, I know you hate me and I would never try to convince you to feel otherwise, but I need you or Jimmy, whichever one of you hates me less, to watch over the kids and Jackie. Please make sure that you stay in their lives and if Jackie ever needs anything, please make sure you help her. If she moves on and meets someone and brings them into my children's lives, please make sure he's not an asshole like me."

"Carmine, what are you talking about? You are *not* dead, so why are you asking me this? Unless you are planning on running away with my wife and abandoning your family. If that's the case, you really are a piece of shit!" Marco yelled in the phone. "You really are a jackass! Your kids are better off without you. At least they have Jimmy and me." And with that, Marco hung up on Carmine.

Marco swung his legs off the side of the bed, put his elbows on his knees, and put his face in his hands. He heard Josie call for him that breakfast was ready. He would have to muster up an appetite after she just made her awesome breakfast that he pretty much asked for. He would need to eat every bite. But he wasn't hungry. Not after that.

My God. He not only had to tell her about Carmine, he now needed to tell her about Lexi. He forgot all about the conversation that he had with his mother on the phone while he was at Josie's parents' house. She was going to keep on him about that one, too. Maybe not for a while, after he told her about Lexi and Carmine. Marco sighed. Just when he thought his life was going to move on, he kept moving backwards, further and further into the past.

Chapter 63

Carmine put the phone down. Those were some pretty awful things that Marco said, but he really couldn't blame him. How could he? Look what Carmine had done to Marco.

Carmine was always ready to pass the blame. He was like a child who never took personal responsibility. He knew this about himself, but whenever he wanted to change, he was too much of a coward to do it. He didn't want anyone to know he was wrong. He believed that not admitting fault would make him less wrong.

Carmine's heart began to race. His hands were slightly shaking. He looked around the room and wondered how he got himself in the situation that he was in. He knew that the only person who was wrong was himself. He only had himself to blame for all of this.

Everyone thought Anthony was horrible, but as Carmine sat there and replayed the things that Marco said to him in his head, he realized how awful he really was.

Carmine blamed his cheating on Jackie because she was boring. He blamed Lexi's cheating on Marco on him not paying enough attention to her and still being in love with Josie. He even blamed his parents for his illegal actions throughout the years. He said they didn't pay enough attention to him, even though his mother was practically up his rear end making sure he had everything he needed and wanted. Although his father was working most of the time, as Carmine thought back, he always tried to be around as much as possible, and Carmine saw that now, too.

The way he approached all these situations and how he blamed everyone else were playing in his head. He was looking at everyone in his life and how, at one time, they truly cared for him. Now they despised him. Even his own parents. There was no way to make this better, and even if he thought there might be, he had already made his decision.

"Carmine?" Lexi was watching him. She could see he was seriously deep in thought. She was hoping they could spend some time together and that he could put all of his demons aside for now. They made a perfect couple. This time should revolve around them, not just him.

"Yes, Lexi? What is it?" Carmine was annoyed, not with her, but he tried to hide it in his tone. He didn't want to take his personal frustrations out on her.

"I was just wondering what the rules are here with Anthony. Are we allowed to do anything? Watch TV? Go out?" she asked.

His heart sank. They had discussed this numerous times and now, based on what she had asked, Carmine realized that every time they spoke about this, he was much too vague. Each time they talked, he always had something else going on, something more important on his mind. He made her think he was fully tuned in to what she was saying. He was deceptive that way.

He now realized that Lexi had no idea what was really going on here. His vagueness and short attention span left her completely in the dark. Once again, it was no one's fault but his.

Chapter 64

Marco decided to put off calling back Jimmy until he had talked to Josie. He was not going to keep this from her.

"Marco, were you on the phone?"

"I was." He just stood there, looking at her. He opened his mouth to talk, but nothing came out. His emotions were so intense that he wanted to throw something across the room. He didn't, of course. He didn't want to scare Josie.

"Speak, man!" Josie joked. It was an inside joke from when they were dating.

She has no idea how amazing she is, he thought. He almost laughed. She calmed him down in seconds, and she didn't even know what was wrong yet.

Josie was busying herself with breakfast, getting everything on the plates and putting dirty dishes in the sink. Amid her clattering, she heard Marco say, "I was on the phone with Carmine."

She fumbled with the dishes, almost dropping everything on the floor. *The train is really off the tracks now*, she thought. *It's going to be a free-for-all.*

He rushed closer to her, seeing her fumbling. "Easy there. You good?"

"Yeah, I'm good. I'm pretty sure I just heard you say that you just got off the phone with Carmine," Josie said.

"Yes, that's what I said." Josie didn't appear to be shocked at all. *What does she know?* Marco thought.

"I knew it! I just knew it! The whole thing seemed ridiculous. Your mother with the extended autopsy and the insurance policy." Realizing she was rambling, she quickly stopped, looking at Marco. He was smiling at her.

"I thought you might be a little more shocked," he said.

"Oh, I was shocked alright. Initially. For about a second. But it does not surprise me one bit. Not even a little bit. Well, do you want to talk it through?" she asked.

"Yes, I think I do. He asked me for a favor."

She puffed out a large exhale. "That figures."

"Yeah, right? The nerve of him. He asked me or Jimmy, whichever one hates him less, to watch over the kids and Jackie."

Josie smirked at this. Even during all this, Carmine was trying to make light of the situation. At least he knew that everyone was pissed.

"Did you talk to Jimmy yet?"

Marco considered her question. It occurred to him that Jimmy knew about Carmine, even before Marco got the call. How did he know? And why didn't Jimmy tell him?

"Not yet. Carmine actually called me in the middle of speaking with Jimmy. I think I'm done talking about this."

Josie laughed. "Already?"

"Yeah." He eyed her cautiously, then moved closer to her and wrapped an arm around her waist. He kissed her, deeply but controlled. "Let's eat. That will get my mind off of this for a little while anyway."

After breakfast, they headed to the living room with their coffees. They wrapped themselves around each other on the couch and looked out the giant windows to the city below. Josie draped a blanket on her feet.

Thoughts of Carmine and Lexi were rolling around in her head, and she was wondering what was going to happen next. The only piece that

Josie knew was that Lexi was taken care of. Mrs. Paretti had assured her of that. At that time, she didn't know what that meant, but she was now guessing it was not what most people would have thought. She felt less of a chill now than when Mrs. P had uttered those words to her over the phone.

"Oh, so you asked me what was so urgent about my mother needing to talk to me when we were at your parents' house the day before the viewing," said Marco. "Full disclosure this weekend, so I'm just going to come right out with it."

Josie tensed. She wasn't sure she wanted to hear anymore. Not after Carmine. Although, she pretty much already knew about him.

"Oh yeah. I didn't forget, but I was certainly not thinking about it now." Josie's eyes got very big, and she slowly looked toward the window, away from Marco. He laughed at her facial expression. She could be quite the comedian at times.

"This may come as a surprise to you, and you might want to throw me out, but like I said, full disclosure this weekend, so . . ."

"Out with it already!" Josie couldn't take not knowing.

"Anthony is my grandfather."

Josie recoiled, pulling away from him. She did not see that one coming.

"What are you talking about, Marco?"

He remained calm, hoping he was prepared for whatever happened next. He didn't want to lose her, but he couldn't live knowing this about Anthony and keeping it from Josie. It would eat at him forever, and he would live in constant fear that she would find out and leave him anyway.

"Like I said, my mother called me that day and asked me to go to her house. We sat down at the kitchen table and she told me that Anthony is her father."

Chapter 65

John was set up in his home office reviewing the policy on Carmine's life. He needed to get himself out of this situation. There was no way he was going to take part in committing any type of insurance fraud. Especially for this family.

He had just gotten off the phone with Jimmy, who was still freaking out about Carmine. John had tried to talk him off the ledge. He didn't do a great job, but got him to calm down, for the time being. Jimmy didn't know anything about the policy, and John was going to keep it that way. He didn't want anyone any more involved in this than they needed to be. He would lose his job if he shared the policy information with Jimmy and someone found out, so that was off the table.

John decided he was just going to tell his boss that he knew these people personally and he wanted out. This would be enough to get him off the account, and he could forget he knew anything about it. It would be harder than that, he knew, but he would do his best to stay out of it.

His phone was buzzing on the desk. The caller ID said Antonia Paretti. He was definitely not answering it.

He was scrolling through his emails, trying to get caught up on some things that he'd missed, when the phone buzzed again. He didn't want to be bothered, but he saw that it was Mrs. Paretti a second time, and this time, he felt like he needed to answer. He knew she'd keep bugging him until he did.

"Hello?"

"Hello, John." The sound of her voice, even though he knew it was her, went through him like a snake bite. Not that he had ever been bitten by a snake, but he imagined it would be comparable. He willed himself to get back on track and focus on what she had to say.

"Hi, Mrs. Paretti. What can I help you with?"

"I just wanted to make sure we are on the same page about Jimmy. I assume you want to keep him out of this, as do I. Are we in agreement?"

"Yes, of course."

"OK, talk to you soon, John."

"Wait! Are you still there?"

"Yes. John, is something the matter?"

John didn't know how to say this, but the more he realized that she was at the root of the chaos that was unfolding, the more he felt that she needed to know what he and Jimmy had done for Anthony. She might be able to shed some light on the subject. At this point really, he didn't care what was going on in the big picture, but he wanted to know about his part.

"Mrs. Paretti, I need to tell you something."

Mrs. P sounded concerned. "What is it, John? Is everything alright?"

"Yes, everything is fine, but I need to come clean about something that happened a few years ago." Mrs. Paretti let him talk. "Jimmy and I did something really stupid for Anthony when we were in high school to earn a little extra money. We ran some bets for him, and I know it was stupid, but I'm learning how stupid I actually was as a kid."

Mrs. Paretti interrupted. "John, while I am very displeased to hear this, it is not that big of a deal compared to what you could have been doing with Anthony. With all his connections and the other things he was involved in, it could have been far worse."

"Sure, I understand that, but there's more." Mrs. P braced herself.

"Anthony tried to blackmail us. He was in need of some information, which we only really needed to research on the internet, but since he doesn't use a computer, he wanted us to do it for him. We just assumed that he didn't want anyone to be able to trace this research back to the people that were closest to him, so we did it."

"What did he give you in return for this research?" Mrs. P asked.

"He promised that he wouldn't ever say anything about the bets and that he would destroy any evidence of us being involved."

"What was it that he wanted you to research?"

"Medications that can cause memory loss. He didn't tell us why he wanted this information, and we didn't ask. It was so ridiculous that he basically just needed us to google something that we just said sure. We thought it was a small price to pay to be disconnected from him forever."

Mrs. P stiffened. Her heart was racing so fast that she thought she might pass out. Her hands began to shake. She steadied herself, holding tightly to the phone.

"Thank you for telling me. I have to go now." She hung up before John could say another word.

Just like that, she was gone. *Did she really have to call and tell me that?* John thought. She should know by now that John followed the rules, and he would lose his job, or worse, if he discussed the information with anyone not directly involved with the policy. Why did he have to keep having this conversation with her, and with himself? Maybe she would leave him alone now. He could only hope. He was glad he'd gotten his dealings with Anthony off his chest. He thought she should know. He was almost sorry he didn't have any more information for her, but now he could just forget about it

He continued to leaf through the paperwork, when suddenly he stumbled upon something he seemed to have missed earlier. He stared at the pages. His thoughts were spinning. Maybe he was making a big deal out of nothing.

He stepped away from the paperwork for a while and tried to get his mind off everything, but the more he tried not to think about it, the more he just could not leave it alone.

Maybe it was not a coincidence that Mrs. Paretti's first name was Antonia, and, well, Anthony was Anthony. Maybe there was something there? Maybe they were connected in some way? But then John thought maybe he was just stupid and was making something from nothing at all.

He began doing some research on Mrs. Paretti. He dug through her Facebook page, which was completely useless. He was able to find her maiden name in a photo of an old newspaper article that one of her friends tagged her in, but it was not the same as Anthony's. There was nothing else in there that would even remotely connect her to Anthony.

He stumbled on a very small story on Mrs. P's Facebook page that revealed that she had a sister named Elizabeth, but Elizabeth's Facebook page was also very sparse. He sat for a moment and pondered that Mrs. P had a sister. He never knew she had a sister. Why didn't he know this? It appeared that she didn't live in the US any longer, but she was certainly born here.

From what he could see, it appeared that she hadn't lived here in quite some time. It also looked like she was significantly younger than Mrs. P. *What was going on with these people?* he thought. He decided to google Elizabeth.

He used the same maiden name as Mrs. Paretti. He thought his search would be a long shot, but he wanted better information. His search came up with a few hits.

The first was the face of an old woman, and connected to it was an obituary. She had died twenty-five years ago when she was in her eighties. That was definitely not her.

The second was a young African American female biochemist who was far too young to be Mrs. P's sister.

The third was a ten-year-old girl who was kidnapped and sold to a sex trafficker. Though he was relieved to read that she was found and safely returned to her mother and father, she was also not the person he was looking for.

He kept scrolling through some hits that didn't connect with anything he had searched. He ran his hands through his hair in frustration. He was about ready to begin another search or just give up entirely when he stumbled on a fourth lead; the woman was an environmental scientist living in California. His eyes widened and he moved his head closer to the screen, as if that would get him closer to finding her. He kept clicking for more information until he came across a photo of her. He closed his eyes and hung his head after he saw that she was of Asian descent, and almost the exact same age as Mrs. P.

After reading about the scientist, he looked at the google search bar, realizing his thoughts completely drifted off course. After his search came up with nothing useful, he decided to dig deeper into Elizabeth's Facebook, hoping there was something on her friends' pages that would lead him to something more helpful.

As he continued to scroll through her page, he realized there was much more to this woman than was publicly able to be viewed. Maybe Elizabeth was someone famous? If she was, he did not recognize her from the very few and much younger photos of her that were posted.

Who *was* this woman? John realized that he had thrown himself completely down a rabbit hole that really had nothing to do with Anthony or Carmine's life insurance policy.

He needed a break. He needed to talk to Josie.

Chapter 66

The car was stopped at a light and Antonia's brain was reeling from what John had just told her. She glanced at the time. She had somewhere she needed to be, and this time she was taking the mister with her. They were in this together now, and she was not going to leave him out of anything unless she had to. She was keeping him involved, just in case all of this blew up in her face. He was the only one who could pick up the pieces with her if it all went sideways.

She just couldn't believe what John had shared. She was trying not to fidget. It was a matter of minutes, she worried, until James noticed.

"Do you have somewhere you have to be?" he asked.

"I do, as a matter of fact, and so do you."

"Oh God, here it comes. Are you going to drive me to some warehouse full of goons so they can kill me, and you can leave me for dead?"

She was amused by this. She laughed out loud at him, much to her dismay. It also made her feel a little better.

"If I wanted you dead, I would have done it myself, years ago." She smirked at him, knowing the mood needed to be significantly lightened up.

He squinted his eyes at her, showing that the dig was received, and his silence showed that he couldn't blame her for the rude comment.

He sat in the passenger seat and watched the buildings go by, and hoped whatever she had up her sleeve next was going to get them closer to all of this being over.

He noticed that she was pondering something, and deeply at that.

"Are you OK?" he questioned with much concern.

She looked over at him quickly, trying not to crash the car. "No, actually, I'm not."

"Is it about the phone call you just had?"

"Yes, it is." She went on to tell him what John just told her. She kept rolling it all around in her head. Her eyebrows were knitted with questions.

He looked at her in disbelief. Trying to put the pieces together himself. "You don't think . . ."

"I'm afraid to say it, but yes, I do think Anthony is somehow making Elizabeth sick on purpose."

James sat there in shock. "But why? What is his motivation for that? How does that help him? We all know full well that Anthony doesn't do anything for anyone but himself. If that is the case, he has put us in quite the predicament."

"I really don't know what to say. I'm shocked and obviously angry. I know she and I aren't the closest, but I don't wish her any harm. There has to be a reason for this madness."

They looked at each other simultaneously. Antonia blurted out what James was already thinking. "We need to tell Fitz. It's a good thing that's who we are meeting with."

She pulled over at the curb of a busy street, right in town. There were people outside, eating and running in and out of local shops. She parked and turned off the car. She walked around to the passenger side and James extended his arm and hand, suggesting that she lead the way.

They walked a few storefronts down and entered the coffee shop. Antonia walked up to the counter and ordered a coffee, black. James ordered a latte.

She couldn't help herself. "A latte, really?"

"Stop, I already had two cups this morning. I'll have a heart attack if I drink any more," James said with a hint of a smile.

"We should all be so lucky." She quickly raised an eyebrow so he immediately knew she was joking.

They chose a table and he reached around to pull her chair out for her. There was a much younger couple sitting next to them, and the guy laughed. The girl was so amused. James and Antonia overheard the girl say, "Why don't you do that for me?"

They looked at each other and smiled. "Kids," they huffed in sync.

The bell on the door of the coffee shop pinged. The very handsome, dark-haired younger man from Carmine's viewing waltzed in the coffee shop. He commanded the room and was heading in their direction.

James noticed this younger man and at that moment, came to the realization of what was about to happen. He had left the details up to Antonia, so he figured that this was another piece of the puzzle.

The man arrived at the table and Antonia stood up to greet him. "Here's my favorite nephew."

He smiled sheepishly. "Hello, Auntie."

He shook James's hand. "It's nice to see you again, sir."

James went on to tell him that it was nice of him to come to the viewing. He was not expected to, but it was nice that he did. They all shared an eye roll.

James had met his ex-wife's nephew a few times, but they never spent an extended period of time with one another, so he didn't really know him that well.

"So, Stephen—" Antonia began, but he interrupted.

"Just call me Fitz, Auntie."

"Alright, Fitz, if you insist," Antonia said with a smile.

"I do." Fitz smiled back. "I just want to say that this isn't hard for me at all. This man, my grandfather, means nothing to me at all. I can guess that you feel the same way I do, but I don't want you to think that all of this will be difficult for me."

"I'm glad to hear that, but I wasn't worried about that. I'm more worried about how this is all going to be resolved." Antonia clasped her hands together on the table to show that she was serious.

"If I know you at all, Auntie, I assume you have some plans of your own, and I don't want to know anything about them. I'll do my best to keep you both hidden from the law. The things you have done are not necessarily right, but I know you are doing them for a good reason. I have always turned my head, but I do have to say this: if you ever do something that I am not comfortable with, I will have to take legal action. I hate even saying it, but we need to keep this honest as best as we can."

James and Antonia glanced at each other, knowing that they would never want to put Fitz in a bad spot, or worse, be the cause of him losing his job.

James chimed in. "We fully understand, and we wouldn't want anything to happen to you or your career. We know how much you love your job, and we would not want to jeopardize your professional career in any way. Who wouldn't want to be a federal agent!" James was a little jealous.

"Great!" said Fitz. "Now can we all agree that we will take care of our piece of this and stay out of each other's way?" Fitz was hopeful that they would agree.

Antonia bobbed her head in agreement, and James followed her lead.

"I know you can't tell me what's going to happen, but can you at least give us a heads-up as to when it will happen?" Antonia asked Fitz.

"I think that is definitely something I can do for you."

Antonia and James shared a glance, suggesting this would be a good time to bring up her conversation with John.

"There is one more thing that we need to share with you, actually, about your mom." Fitz slightly jerked back, worry crossing his face.

"Is she OK?" he asked.

"Well, yes." Antonia answered. "This is a little confusing, but I will try to keep it short and on point. John, an old friend of Jimmy's, happens to have been involved with Anthony." Fitz's eyes were widening. "He visited Anthony on another matter and saw Carmine there. We were talking just now and he confessed that he was working something out with Anthony from a while back and Anthony attempted to blackmail him unless he did some research for him. That's all he wanted, was for John and Jimmy to google some things. Odd, we know, but the kicker here is that he wanted them to research drugs that cause memory loss."

Fitz understood instantly. "What the hell? How can that be though? Someone would have to be giving it to her. She wouldn't be taking it on her own."

"I don't really have any more information than what John shared with me. I'm sorry."

"Don't worry about it, Auntie. I'll work on it. I'll see what I can find out."

Antonia thanked Fitz and they continued to make small talk. She didn't want to let him go. She enjoyed hearing his stories and was excited to hear the news that he was going to be marrying one of his fellow police officers. His face lit up when he talked about her. Antonia was so happy for him; he was able to have a good life and turn out well, despite their family. It gave her hope.

"I better head out. I need to get back to work," Fitz finally said.

"One more thing before you go. Do you still have someone watching Josie?" asked James.

"Yes, we do. Do you want me to have them stop?"

"No, no, I was just making sure we were still on her."

"Yep, all good there." Fitz stood up and stuck out his hand to James for a shake, and Antonia stood up to hug him. He towered over her, and she felt protected.

They hugged and said their goodbyes, and Fitz told them he would be in touch within a few days.

Antonia could barely contain her uneasiness. Fitz could see it on her face. "It will be OK, Auntie. This needs to happen. And once it's over, you will be at peace." All three of them knew that there was a great possibility that this was going to snowball into a whole new set of troubles, but they would be ready for it.

"I know," she said, and patted his arm.

Fitz left and James and Antonia sat back down to order some lunch.

Chapter 67

Josie suddenly realized she was no longer sitting on the couch. She was standing, staring at Marco. She felt frozen in time, paralyzed. Her mind was reeling. Her heart was racing. She felt betrayed. She had believed that Mrs. Paretti was being totally honest with her through all of this. *I guess she was*, Josie thought, *but maybe only with what concerned me. She probably didn't want to get me all riled up about Anthony.*

Anger was rising in her, but she knew she couldn't take it out on Marco. Even if she did, it would be stupid. It wasn't his fault. He hadn't known till recently. But why didn't he tell her sooner? She questioned this, but then realized they hadn't really been talking until now, so why would he tell her? He owed her nothing, and it was his family secret that he was now dealing with. She realized that she was being selfish.

"Josie, please say something."

She reluctantly snapped out of her daze. Still not knowing how to respond, she just stood there. Finally, she looked at Marco, and all that came out when she opened her mouth was, "What?" Her eyes looked catatonic and her tone was emotionless.

She was hoping that Marco would have more to say. All she wanted was silence when he first broke the news, but now the silence was killing her.

"Yeah, so apparently, Anthony is my grandfather. He's my mom's dad. Oh, and also I have an aunt."

"I know, Marco, I've met her."

"No, Josie, not her. Apparently I have an Aunt Elizabeth and some cousins."

Josie remained stunned. She was struggling to put it all together. It did not make any sense. The timeline was way off for Anthony to be Antonia's father. And where had this aunt been that Marco was talking about?

"I don't understand," Josie said.

"I didn't either. I'm still sort of lost. I don't think I was listening to everything my mother was telling me. After the Anthony part, I sort of lost focus. I heard bits and pieces. The more I try to recall the conversation with her, the more I'm starting to make sense of it."

Josie was pacing around the room. She thought to herself, *How can this be? How could I possibly be in love with someone who shares DNA with that awful human being?* What was she going to do? What was Marco going to do? She needed more information.

"So, what is your mother going to do?"

"What do you mean? About Anthony?"

"Yes, Marco!" Josie was letting her emotions get the better of her. She was angry.

"Josie, I am not going to tell you to calm down, but what I can tell you is that my mother does not care. She is not going to have a relationship with him and certainly is not going to force me to. She made it sound like she just wanted me to know and that was that. I think she was afraid I was going to find out on my own and then blame her for not telling me. My mother doesn't seem to give a crap about him at all."

Josie felt her muscles begin to loosen up. *Mrs. P could certainly take care of herself. How did this all come about? Had she known for a long time that he was her father? Why wait until now to say anything about it, and why bother Marco with it?*

"Well?" Josie said. "So? I don't . . ." She was looking at Marco, and clearly not able to form a sentence. She was beginning to think he might not have all the answers that she was looking for.

"It's OK, Josie. Just say whatever is on your mind."

She could see the pleading look in Marco's eyes that said he didn't want this to change anything between them.

"I don't know why, but the only thing that keeps coming to me is to ask who the man is that raised your mother."

"Apparently, my grandmother got pregnant with my mom, but she and Anthony weren't actually dating. They had gotten together"—Marco said it in quotes and they both shuddered at the thought—"but my grandmother was actually seeing someone else at the time. The grandfather I knew didn't care that my mom wasn't his."

"Holy shit, Marco!"

"Yeah, and the crazy part—" Josie cut him off.

"The crazy part?!"

Marco laughed at her facial expression. He sensed that she was beginning to tease him again and make light of this awful situation.

"Are you being funny, Josie?"

Her eyes widened and she looked to the side without moving her head and Marco started laughing at her. She was clearly being funny.

"I don't want to interrupt you, Marco, but I am much calmer now. This really has nothing to do with our relationship, so I don't want to get so caught up in it that it affects us and our future together."

He was thrilled to hear her say this. This was a big deal for him to tell Josie, and he just realized that if she had not asked him about the conversation that he had with his mom that day, he may never have brought it up.

He was not hiding it from her, but it wasn't top of the list of things to talk about. He knew how hard it was going to be to tell her. But everything was all out in the open now and there was nothing else to hide. He was beyond relieved.

"I'm really glad to hear you say that, Josie. I'm still trying to process it myself, and as you can see, I don't really know much about what happened."

"You seem to have enough information." She quickly moved on to more questions. "So, who is this aunt, and what happened to Anthony for all those years?"

"I don't really know. She lives in Italy somewhere. Apparently, she had triplets with her husband and then split right after Anthony disappeared, or died, or something. I don't know."

"What the hell? Why did Anthony disappear? Where did he go?"

"Oh, yes! That's the crazy part. I think my mom said something about him needing to skip town and faking his death."

"What? Marco, this is ridiculous. What is it with you people faking deaths?"

"Josie, we're talking about Anthony. Did you expect anything different?" Marco was not being rude, but he realized his tone was condescending. "I'm sorry, I didn't mean to sound like an ass."

"No, no, don't worry about it. You're right. I don't know why I would have expected normalcy with that retched excuse for a human being." Right at that moment, it dawned on Josie what could possibly have been happening. She recalled that day she heard Anthony talking in the back of her father's store. The hairs on the back of her neck began to stand up. She was beginning to figure out how much more horrible Anthony really was.

"Marco, I need to tell you something. Well, a few things, actually."

Chapter 68

"That nephew of yours really is a great kid. He's clearly worked his butt off to get where he is," James said.

"Yes, I am proud of him. It's too bad we couldn't have spent more time with the triplets."

"You can't blame yourself. You tried. It's too bad that everything had to happen the way it did with them. That jackass of a husband that your sister had, or has, or whatever they are, certainly didn't help matters at the time."

"No, but he was out of the picture long enough for me to try to reconnect and have a relationship with my sister," Antonia said.

"Sure, but you knew what a mess everything was, and you wanted no part of it then, so don't beat yourself up about it."

"I guess you're right."

"WHOA!" Antonia looked around in alarm. "Was anyone recording that?" asked James.

"Very funny," said Antonia dryly.

As she thought more about it, there really wasn't anything she could have done. She often questioned her decision to keep it from her children that they had more family and cousins out there somewhere, but James was right. She made the decision at the time to protect her family and keep them far away from the life that Anthony was living. Why put them in jeopardy for a man she didn't even know, and who certainly couldn't have cared less about her?

Even though she knew that Anthony didn't really know about her for sure, she used to hold on to this hatred for him, that he didn't want her, but her mother never would have allowed Anthony to be a part of her life anyway. It had all worked out for the best, in the end.

When she approached Carmine about the relationship he had with Anthony, the only thing he said was, "Anthony treats me like family, and he barely knows me." That's when it hit her that Anthony was trying to weasel his way into their lives, even if it was only with Carmine. Carmine didn't make it sound like Anthony told him anything about being related, but he did make it sound like Anthony was fawning over him. Creating this family-like relationship with him to make Carmine feel wanted and special. Carmine still didn't know the truth. At least, she didn't think he knew. Her mother's intuition—or daughter's intuition—made her think he would never know.

It would be OK with her if Carmine never knew. What would it matter? Nothing. Carmine was already in too deep with Anthony and his horrible life.

When she gained the knowledge that Anthony was such a horrible man, she couldn't bear the thought of ever having any relationship with him. When she learned of Carmine's connection with him, she nearly tore down the house in anger.

When Anthony "died," she thought it was the end. She hoped she would never see him again, but when he resurfaced, Carmine got mixed up with him. Even though Anthony kept an extremely low profile when he did come back, he somehow was able to sink his claws into Carmine. Once he got ahold of him, there was no turning back for Carmine.

"Penny for your thoughts?" James said.

"Oh, sorry, I was just thinking about Carmine and Anthony. There are so many reasons to hate Anthony. I know hate is a strong word, but he's just awful. I can never forgive him for what he's done to our family."

"I know, but Carmine is a grown man. I know he doesn't act like it, and I guess that's what got him in the position he's currently in, but there is only so much we could have done when we didn't even know that Anthony had come back."

Antonia sat there pondering what James had said, and again thought he was right. She was beginning to lose her edge in this whole thing. She must not blame herself in this. She had to stay positive.

James continued, "Not to mention what the SOB did to our dear friends. The Altieris are the nicest people we know, and look at how he terrorized them."

"Yes, that's true, and it's a good thing he came to you about it, or else we never would have known, and who knows what would have happened to them and their business. I am glad I made the decision to reach out to Fitz. I was even happier to know that he, as well as the FBI, was completely aware that Anthony was back."

"Don't you mean not actually dead?" James raised an eyebrow.

She huffed in disgust and shook her head at the thought of Anthony faking his own death to escape the feds and his crime-infested world.

Chapter 69

Marco looked at Josie skeptically, wondering what she was going to say to add to this already terrible conversation.

"One day when I was working at my father's store, I heard Anthony on the phone yelling at someone. I swear he mentioned Carmine's name. I only heard bits and pieces of it; it was like Anthony was talking to Carmine on the phone. Then he was yelling about some guy named Carl. It sounded like they were really arguing about something, and then I heard him say, 'Just kill him if you have to.'"

Marco was terrified for Josie. He couldn't imagine what it was like to overhear something like that as a teenager.

"I'm sorry you had to hear all that," Marco said.

"Why are you apologizing? It wasn't your fault."

"No, but I'm sure that's part of all this hate that you have been carrying around for Anthony all these years."

Josie took a deep breath and shook her head. She put her face in her hands and rubbed her forehead.

Marco said, "My mother mentioned something briefly about Carmine being mixed up with Anthony and I just let her talk. I didn't ask any questions, but I figured as much this whole time. Anthony is one of the most corrupt men I know, and my brother is always involved in an insane business deal of some sort; however, he doesn't really have an actual job that we know of. I've always wondered where he got all that money that he has."

Josie shifted topics again. "So, where does your aunt fall into the mix here?"

"She apparently is much younger than my mom. They have different mothers, obviously, so Anthony actually raised my aunt with her own mother. I believe she is gone now, but they raised her as a family. The old lady passed away, and then all that mess went down with Anthony."

"What mess?"

"The story goes that my aunt's husband, who was sort of involved with Anthony, helped him fake his death."

Josie started laughing. Hysterically. Marco just sat there staring at her. He thought she had finally cracked. As amusing as it was to see her laugh, he was afraid she might get angry with him if he laughed too.

She kept on laughing, so he smiled at her to test the waters. He started laughing with her. It was quite ludicrous. He thought the family that he knew was messed up. Little did he know his extended family was way worse.

Josie finally calmed down and asked, "Any idea who this Carl guy is?"

"I think it might be my aunt's husband. Or ex-husband? I'm not sure what is going on with them."

"So, let me try to understand what we know so far. Anthony has your mom with your grandmother, who he's not even dating. She marries the man you know as your grandfather. Then years later, Anthony gets married and has your aunt. Then maybe twenty-some years after that, he fakes his death. Then he resurfaces just to throw things upside down again. Is that the gist of it all?" summed Josie.

"Yeah, that seems to be right so far. That's pretty much all I got from my mom. Oh! Except that I didn't need to worry about anything because she and my dad were taking care of things." Josie went still. She had a feeling she knew what that meant, and although it didn't mean Mrs. Paretti was going to kill Anthony, she was sure it meant something awful. Marco continued, "She was so nonchalant, like my parents just needed to figure out how they were going to make a mortgage payment."

"Well, Marco, one good thing in all this is that, even though you are connected to it, you aren't exactly involved in it, so at this point there is really nothing for us to worry about. Right?"

Marco wished he could say yes to her, but he really didn't know that answer. The most he could give her was, "Yeah, so far."

She shivered and he walked over to hug her.

While he was hugging her, she pulled away and looked him in the eye. "Marco, there is something else I need to tell you."

Marco hung his head, wondering what else she could have possibly been through. "OK." He touched her shoulders to let her know whatever she had to say, he would be there to listen.

"Because we were on the rocks and not exactly communicating like we should have been at the time, I didn't get into this with you, but he . . . he . . . it seemed harmless. He would say inappropriate things and make disgusting gestures at me, and . . ." She stopped to compose herself so she could finish.

"What is it, Josie?"

"It had been going on for weeks and I just kept blowing it off as Anthony just being a creep. I ignored it because I never thought he would act on it." Marco stiffened. Just by the words she was using, Marco knew what was coming next. He knew what she was going to say. Beads of sweat were appearing on his forehead.

"Josie, my God. What did he do?" Marco was getting agitated in anticipation of her saying it out loud. He was beginning to get choked up.

"Marco," Josie's voice broke slightly, "Anthony sexually assaulted me."

Chapter 70

It was a beautiful day and the kids were running around the backyard while Jackie was reading a magazine. She was sitting on a chair in the lawn. She didn't want to be too far away. She sipped her sweet coffee and angled her tired face towards the sun.

"Mommy, Mommy, watch!"

She watched her little girl twirl around the yard like a ballerina. She thought how odd it was that kids dealt with grief so differently than adults, but then again, some adults dealt with it very differently from one another.

Maybe she would meet a nice, normal man at some point, and the kids would have some idea of what family was supposed to mean. He'd be kindhearted and maybe even love them as his own. She knew she was getting way ahead of herself. But if she thought happy thoughts and looked to the future, positive things would start falling into place for her.

She thought she would have been missing Carmine a little more than she did, but just as her heart suspected, she didn't miss Carmine at all. She had never felt so free. She had never imagined she'd feel so liberated by the fact that she didn't have to worry about making a huge meal for dinner every night. She could finally eat healthier and make sure the kids got enough exercise. She was able to plan better and have enough time to relax and do something she wanted to do. Once the kids were in bed, she could read a book or binge watch whatever she wanted.

She feared this feeling would fade and she would feel lonely but so far, she was loving every minute of it all. She had already lost a few pounds, and she was thinking about sprucing up her wardrobe. She had always wanted smart clothing that kept her in check for her age but didn't make her look homeless. She certainly always had the money to do it, but Carmine never wanted her to look too good. He thought other men would start looking at her.

"Phew," she puffed out loud. *What an ass*, she thought. She had devoted every minute of her day to that man and all he could do was have an affair with his brother's wife. She was beginning to get angry, and she had promised herself that she would try to focus only on the things that she was now able to do for her own sanity and to make herself happy. She took a few deep breaths and talked herself out of her anger. There was so much to be happy and thankful for.

Her children still came first, and she was OK with that. Without Carmine tying up her day, she could devote as much time to the kids as she wanted and make sure there was plenty of time left for her.

The kids came running over to her. "Mommy, is it time for lunch yet? I'm starving to death," her little girl whined in her singsongy, super cute little voice.

Jackie picked her up and plopped her on her lap, pulled her little shirt up just higher than her belly button and blew out a raspberry right on her belly. "Mommy, that tickles," she screeched. When Jackie stopped, both kids were rolling around in the grass laughing.

She couldn't help the thoughts drifting in and out of her head. She wanted to use every bad memory from Carmine that made her angry to make her happy now. Carmine would be yelling that the kids were too loud and now the sound of them carrying on made her so happy that tears pricked the sides of her eyes. She wanted to hide it from the kids. She didn't want to have to explain that she was happy that their father was gone. If she did, would they agree?

She began thinking that the kids were sociopaths, but then took a step back to realize that they felt less stressed too, and happy. She hadn't heard them laugh this much ever.

She was taking in the moment and watching them rolling around when they both jumped up. Waving to their grandparents, they yelled in sync, "Nonno! Nonna!"

Jackie glanced behind her and saw her in-laws walking across the lawn, uninvited. She rolled her eyes and mumbled under her breath, "Good God, what do they want now?" Jackie was not in the mood for them today.

Chapter 71

"My God, Josie." He hugged her tight. Not because it would take away what happened, but he didn't know what else to do. All he wanted was to find Anthony and strangle him to death. Marco tried to keep his cool. This conversation wasn't about his feelings; it was about Josie's.

"Marco, I know that I didn't do anything to provoke it. I know that it wasn't my fault that Anthony did that to me, so you don't have to tell me that." She smiled at him.

"Josie, why are you worried about me and how I am reacting? You should be thinking about yourself."

"Marco, as scary and hurtful as it all was at the time, I have moved past it, and like I said, I know I didn't do anything to cause it. Anthony is just a load of shit, so I still get choked up about it, but I don't blame myself for what he did."

"Josie, I love you so much and I wish you would have told me sooner." Marco thought about how he would have reacted back then.

Josie could see in his eyes that he was thinking about what he would have done to Anthony. "Marco, it's just as well that I didn't tell you. You were full of anger and craziness back then. Who knows what you would have done."

"That's exactly what I was just thinking."

"I know, that's why I said it. I'd know that face anywhere. I knew what you were thinking."

Marco smiled at Josie and took her in his arms. He held her for a while and they sat in silence.

"Josie, I should call Jimmy back. Do you mind if I give him a call now?" Josie nodded, and just as he got up, Josie's phone started to ring.

Josie rolled her eyes. "Looks like we both have some things to take care of. It's John."

"Let him down easy," Marco said, winking at her as he walked away.

Josie waved him away and tried to cover the phone so John couldn't hear Marco.

"Hi, John."

"Hey! I'm glad you answered." He sounded frazzled. Josie was a little worried.

"John, are you alright?"

"Yeah, I'm fine. I just . . . I'm just going to say this. Is Marco there?"

For a split-second, Josie thought he was picking a fight and that he was upset because he thought she and Marco were getting back together. She had known John a long time and she could tell that something else was bothering him.

Not that he could see her, but she held her head up with confidence, and said, "Yes, he is. What's up?"

"Maybe you should check with him, but I'd like to stop by and talk to you both. Do you think I could drop by this afternoon sometime?"

Josie wasn't sure what to say. She could tell in his voice that he wasn't angry or combative. Either way, she was dreading how awkward it would be.

"It's OK with me. Let me just check with Marco and I'll text you and let you know. Does that work?"

"Yes, Josie, that's fine with me. I just want you to know that whatever makes you happy, makes me happy."

She was ridiculously relieved to hear him say that.

"I appreciate you saying that, John. So this doesn't have anything to do with us?"

Through the phone, she could hear his smile when he said, "Don't flatter yourself there, missy."

She laughed.

"Just send me a text then, OK?" John said.

"OK." Josie hung up and went to track down Marco.

He was sitting on the edge of the bed with his forehead in his hand and his elbow on his knee. He was okaying and yessing, so Josie knew that Jimmy was talking. She had no idea what about, but Marco didn't seem very thrilled about what he had to say.

He heard her walk into the room and he looked up. He patted his knee for her to come and sit down.

She padded across the floor to fulfill his request.

Marco covered the phone with his hand, whispering, "He hasn't stopped talking since I told him I know about Anthony and Carmine. He's angry, to say the least."

Josie's eyes narrowed, and she tilted her head. The sides of her mouth drooped with sadness.

Jimmy went on and on, yelling into the phone about their mother and how she kept it from them that Anthony was their grandfather. Josie could hear him and the phone wasn't even on speaker.

"Jimmy, you should probably calm down," Marco said.

"How can I calm down? Our brother isn't really dead and one of the most hated men we've ever known is really our grandfather and Carmine is with him? Does Carmine even know?"

The thought hadn't even occurred to Marco.

"I don't know. I would think so, but then again, it wouldn't really surprise me if he didn't."

Jimmy started yelling again, and Josie told Marco that she was getting in the shower. Marco raised an eyebrow and went to grab for her waist. "Behave," she said, and slapped his hand away.

Josie was just getting out of the shower as Marco hung up with Jimmy.

"I thought he would never stop yelling," Marco said.

"Well, at least he wasn't yelling *at* you."

"I wasn't yelling, so he wasn't yelling *with* me." Marco smirked.

Josie laughed.

"Did you talk to John?"

"I did, and he wants to stop by this afternoon."

Marco's eyes widened. "He doesn't want to fight me, does he?" Marco's laugh was almost childlike, and Josie liked when he let his guard down. She felt that he was at peace when they were together.

"Don't flatter yourself." She didn't know why she said it. Maybe subconsciously, she felt guilty for sharing that flirtatious moment with John moments ago.

"He sounded frazzled when I spoke with him, so maybe he has some info on the insurance policy . . . or maybe he knows something about Anthony or Carmine."

"Oh! He definitely knows about Carmine. Jimmy told me. He and John went to Anthony's, and that's when they saw Carmine."

Josie was silent.

Marco watched her cautiously, waiting for her to say something, but she didn't.

"So, you're good with John stopping by, maybe midafternoon?"

"That's it? That's all you have to say?"

"What can I say? This gets more ridiculous with each new piece of info."

"Then let him know midafternoon is good."

"OK." Josie clearly considered that this might be the worst idea of the century. *We are all adults*, she thought. *We can all act like adults.*

"It will all be OK," she whispered.

She would have to be honest with John, and judging by their short conversation, he must have figured out that she already made her decision.

Chapter 72

Walking through his giant apartment, Anthony realized just how lonely he really was. His grandson was just in the other room and Carmine did not even know him. Anthony hadn't watched him grow up, never attended a baseball game; hell, he didn't even know if Carmine played baseball as a child.

Anthony thought now would be as good a time as any to break the news to Carmine about their relationship to each other. He didn't want Lexi around for it. No telling how she was going to react, and he didn't feel like dealing with the drama.

How would he tell him? Would he just come right out and say, "Carmine, I am you grandfather?" He'd sound like Darth Vader. *This is a disaster*, Anthony thought. He didn't even know how to strike up a meaningful conversation with someone. Never mind flesh and blood.

He approached Carmine in the room he was staying in, "Carmine, can I speak with you for a minute? In my office."

Carmine eyed him very cautiously. Usually, Anthony would address him with some derogatory name or comment. Carmine got up and followed Anthony, leaving Lexi behind.

Carmine was nervous. *What could he possibly want now?* Carmine thought. Carmine wanted to enjoy the next few days. He wasn't sure where life was going to take him . . . or death, for that matter.

Anthony sat on a large leather sofa in his office and invited Carmine to sit beside him.

"Anthony, what's going on? You're acting like a decent human being, which, frankly, is strange for you." Carmine smirked slightly, trying to keep it light.

"That comment was mean, but understood." Anthony was trying to keep calm. He didn't want to have a heart attack before he could get out what he wanted to say.

Carmine sat there looking at Anthony. Waiting for him to speak. Sitting that close on the couch, Carmine could see the age more closely on Anthony's face. He had never really noticed how old Anthony looked before this moment.

"Carmine, I'm not really sure how to say this, but I want you to know . . ." He stopped, trying to find the best words.

Carmine was watching him intently now. Carmine was pretty sure that Anthony was unaware of what was going to unfold in the next day or so. He wasn't supposed to know, so Carmine continued to sit in silence.

"Carmine, you have been so loyal for all these years to me, and I've been such an asshole to you and everyone around me. I know there isn't much I can do to reverse that, but there is something I need to say."

"Talk, old man. I don't know what you are blabbering about."

Anthony laughed. His stomach was churning at the thought of what he needed to say. He had felt nerves like this before, but long ago, and only before he was going to do something really awful or illegal. Maybe he was a little human after all.

"Carmine, the man you know as you grandfather, your mother's dad, is her adoptive father."

Carmine did not want to show the shock he was feeling inside. He shook his head and put both hands in the air to show he didn't know what the hell Anthony was talking about.

"Your grandmother had gotten pregnant by an awful man who was not the greatest to her. She was dating your grandfather at the time. She explained what was going on with her and he stayed. He stayed, and they got married and he raised your mother as his own. This is how I understand it, anyway."

"Why are you telling me this? Does my mother know?" Carmine's head was spinning.

"She knows, but she doesn't seem to care."

"Well, why would she? My grandfather was a wonderful man. That's how my mother talks about him, and I remember him being pretty great. He left us kids a lot of money." Carmine thought it was an awful thing to say after it rolled out of his mouth.

Anthony was disgusted by Carmine's comment about the money. The man he knew as his grandfather was a far better man than Anthony would ever be. It wasn't right that Carmine was talking about him this way.

"Carmine, that awful man that treated your grandmother so poorly was me."

Carmine's eyes were wide with disbelief. "You can't be serious."

"I'm afraid I am. I didn't want to tell you, and I thought it should be your mother who told you, but since you've been staying here, and I've been seeing and talking to your mother more often, I thought you should know."

"You probably should have let my mother tell me."

"Maybe, Carmine, but if she hasn't told you by now, maybe she never would have."

"I'm not sure what to say, good old granddad. Is that why my mother hates you so much?"

"That's part of it. The obvious part is all those horrible things I did many, many years ago." Carmine shuddered. He knew exactly what

Anthony was referring to. Carmine might be a criminal, but he never had the stomach for the things that Anthony had done over the years.

"I need to process this. What were you expecting to get out of this?"

"Not much really. I don't know how much longer I'm going to live, and I was hoping that we could have some type of relationship before that happens, I guess."

Carmine was confused. "Don't we already? Would it be safe to say that you recruited me knowing that I was your grandson?"

Anthony never wanted to admit that he had recruited Carmine on purpose, but now that Carmine said it, he agreed that it must have been subconsciously on purpose.

With Anthony's silence, Carmine got up and walked out of the room. Anthony had no idea what was about to happen. If he was looking to reconcile with the family, that ship had sailed . . . especially with his mother. Carmine wasn't sure if he would able to reconcile with her. Anthony did not stand a chance.

Chapter 73

Jackie got up to greet Mr. and Mrs. P. "Hello," Jackie said, hugging her in-laws with hesitation. "Do you want to go inside?"

"No, no, we are fine out here, dear," Mrs. P insisted. "We won't be here too long. We just wanted to stop by for a quick visit."

Mr. P said, "We are sorry for not calling first. We just took a chance that you might be home. We didn't mean to barge in like this."

Jackie noticed that Mr. P, during the few times she had been in his company, was always apologizing for Mrs. P. She seemed so high and mighty all the time, but was always doing the opposite of what was proper. She would be the first to judge someone else for doing the same thing she was doing.

Jackie could feel her heartbeat escalating again for no reason.

"So, what brings you by?"

Mrs. P answered. "Nothing really, we just wanted to say hello and let you know that everything is working itself out. There is nothing to worry about anymore."

Jackie's heart, instead of speeding up, dropped into her stomach. She wasn't sure what was actually involved in "everything working itself out," but she knew it probably wasn't anything good. Good for her maybe, but good for others? Probably not.

Jackie wasn't sure she would be able to calm herself down, so she began reciting the Hail Mary in her head. That usually seemed to work when she felt her nerves acting up.

Once she was calm enough, she managed to croak out, "Well, that's good news, I suppose."

A quick glance was shared between Mr. and Mrs. P. He began to open his mouth, and Mrs. P touched his arm to shut him up.

"Dear, are you questioning all this?"

Jackie swallowed hard. She was quickly reminded of how much this striking, older woman could scare the complete crap out of her.

Jackie sunk slightly in her chair and cleared her throat. "No, not at all. I'm just glad it will be over soon."

"Yes, dear, we are too," said Mr. P.

Jackie shivered inside at the thought of what could possibly happen and how these two could be so calm. She was amazed at how they could be such normal people most of the time and have such a horrible dark side. There they were, just playing with the grandkids like normal people. Mrs. P pulled out some small gifts for the kids. Jackie hated when they spoiled them like that, but the trinkets they gave them weren't worth fighting over.

When this was all over, Jackie wondered if they would stay in her life or disappear into the night. The more she sat there and thought about it, the more courage she built up to just come right out and ask them.

"Do you plan on popping in like this often?" She smiled to imply that she was OK with them doing so. She wanted them to be a part of the kid's lives.

Mrs. P answered. "Yes, if that is OK with you. We want to be a bigger part of their lives." Mr. P added, "It's no secret that—" He stopped. He did not want the kids to hear him speak badly of Carmine. They all knew where he was going with his comment. "As long as you are OK with it, I would love to be a part of their lives from now on."

Jackie was pleased to hear this from them, but she needed to say something.

"That would make me very happy, and I know I might be out of line in saying this, but can you both consider leaving them out of the things that you may be involved in?"

Mr. and Mrs. P both huffed an uncomfortable laugh. Mr. P spoke for both of them this time. "There will be nothing to be involved with after this is over."

Jackie looked surprised. "What do you mean?"

"I mean," Mr. P continued, "that we are done. Let's say we are retiring."

Jackie was surprised, but extremely pleased, to hear this. Throughout this whole thing, Jackie had become hardened. She was much less skittish than she used to be, and she had grown a great amount of confidence that she never thought she would have.

"Wow! That is great news."

Mr. and Mrs. P glanced at each other.

"What?" Jackie questioned.

"We have one more thing to do, but it's not what you think. I need to track down my sister, Elizabeth, and let her know what's going on."

"Your sister?"

"Yes, I have a half-sister." Mr. P was taken aback. He didn't think that Mrs. P was going to share that with Jackie.

"Oh, I didn't know that. But then again, I'm not surprised." She rolled her eyes.

Mrs. P saw it and she thought Jackie was getting awfully comfortable with them. This was a good thing, though. She was happy that Jackie was coming out of her shell. Who knew this would make her stronger? Maybe she should have taken care of Carmine long ago, just so this woman could have a life of her own.

"Yes, well, Elizabeth and I share a father. It's Anthony."

Jackie felt like the very earth her lawn chair was sitting on was going to open and swallow them right up. She thought she might throw up all over her father-in-law's Ferragamo shoes. She'd kept her cool up until now but this was way more information than she was able to process without breaking down. Her children shared a bloodline with the most awful, most corrupt man she had ever met. It was bad enough her husband was part of this man's life, but to actually be related to him was more than she wanted to know.

As this concept was rolling around in her head, the kids' yelling brought her out of her daze. "Mommy, are you OK?"

She snapped out of it and realized she had slumped so far over in her chair that she fell right out of it and was sitting in the grass.

So much for keeping my cool, she thought.

Mr. P helped her to her feet and back in her chair.

As Jackie continued to process this news, she began to get angry. Finally she said, "Thank you for picking me up off of the lawn." They shared a laugh, and the kids were crawling all over her, scared that she was not OK.

"Did he know about Anthony?" Jackie refused to say her husband's name, still trying to hide it from the kids.

"We don't think so. If Anthony ever told him, he never mentioned it to me, and you know him. If he had a reason to bark and complain about something, he would," Mrs. P said.

The kids finally broke away and were now running around on the lawn.

Jackie laughed. "Yeah, that's for sure."

"Honey, why don't you lay down for a while. We can take the kids for some ice cream, if you want," Mr. P said.

"You know what? Why not. That sounds great. Thank you. Are you willing to share when it will all be final?"

Mrs. P hesitated, but answered, "Most likely by the end of the week."

Jackie felt faint again. The end of the week was sooner than she thought, but she knew how freeing it would be when it was all over.

"OK," Jackie muttered.

She hugged and kissed the kids, and off they went with Grandma and Grandpa Paretti.

Chapter 74

John left his apartment and began heading in the direction of Josie's building. He was not looking forward to seeing them together. By the way that Josie has been acting towards him and the fact that Marco was now with her in the city, it was evident to him that she had made her choice. He was upset, but like he had said, he wanted her to be happy. Marco was a good match for her. Crazy, but a good match.

John arrived at Josie's building and he suddenly felt like someone was watching him. He took his phone out of his pocket and leaned against the building. He lifted his head up, as if he were thinking, so he could scan his surroundings. He spotted Marco carrying three coffees and a bag of what he assumed were pastries. He let out a giant sigh of relief.

Marco approached John, and slightly bashful, said, "Hey, man, how's it goin'?" Marco went to raise his hand and awkwardly remembered that they were full. He stuck his elbow out, and John bumped his against Marco's.

"Hey, Marco." They stood there for a few seconds, staring at each other.

"Oh, here, I got you a latte." Marco didn't want to say this, but maybe it would ease the blow of all this for John. "Josie suggested what to get you, so that's what I got." He smiled a sideways, crooked smile.

John tried not to be cocky, but wanted it to sting a bit for Marco, so he smirked, saying, "Thank you. That's very nice of you."

It was well-received by Marco, and he chuckled. "Let's get up there. We don't want to keep her waiting."

"That's for sure," mused John.

They walked through Josie's apartment door. She'd planned on hugging John, trying to keep it from being uncomfortable, so she went in for the hug and John hugged her back, more tightly than he should have, but he didn't care.

"Come and sit at the island. Marco, break out those pastries, please." Josie was more nervous than she anticipated, and she found herself babbling.

Marco just sat back and let John steer the ship. He did not want to step on toes. He felt bad, but not terribly bad, about the situation with Josie. Even Marco could not have predicted that something that he had wanted for so long would really happen. He didn't know that he would eventually end up with Josie.

"So, I was looking through the paperwork," said John. "I know you have some details, and you understand I can't share much of anything at all with you about the policy. Whatever you know is for you to know and please don't share it with me." John took a breath. "I'm rambling now, so I'll get right to it. Marco, I think there is a connection between your mother and Anthony." Josie and Marco glanced at each other, and John realized that they knew something he did not.

Marco began, "So, here's the thing. I found out the day before Carmine's—whatever you want to call it—that Anthony is my mother's father."

"I knew it!" John slammed his hand into the top of the island. Shaking a small pain from his hand, he said, "I couldn't find anything to prove it, but the pieces were just fitting together too well for it not to be true."

"Yeah, it was a complete shock to me, as you can imagine," said Marco.

John turned his head toward Josie. "Did you take the news OK?"

"There's really nothing I can say. It's not like Anthony's been a part of their lives, or will be, so there really isn't anything I can say about it. After everything that has happened up until now, I'm sort of numb to the insanity."

"So, you won't be surprised when I tell you that your mother, Marco, has a sister that belongs to Anthony as well?"

"Nope, already knew that, too." Josie shook her head from side to side, laughing a bit.

Silence fell on them, and John thought it was great that they already knew. He didn't come here to gossip, and he definitely didn't want to get caught up in the drama.

"It's a relief that you guys already know this. I wasn't really down for a drama trip."

"So, John, why are you here then?" Marco asked.

"Well, I'm here to tell you those things, but also to tell you that I am extremely worried that something really awful is going to happen. I don't know what it is, but I have this horrible feeling that something dreadful is about to go down. I'm not sure with whom or what, but something. I'm sure you spoke with Jimmy, so you know that I know that Carmine is still with us." John rolled his eyes and twisted his mouth in disgust.

"Yes, I spoke with Jimmy earlier," Marco said.

"Do you plan on ever speaking to Carmine again?"

"I'm not sure. I know he still has his same phone number because he called me from it. I could always call him, but . . ." Marco trailed off. He was pretty sure John didn't know about Lexi. He was not so sure he should tell him. They all knew what was on that policy.

Josie nodded her head up and down, suggesting that Marco should tell John about Lexi. Marco looked at her and questioned, "What about the policy?"

John said, “You can say whatever you want about the policy. I just can’t say anything about it. There will be an investigation and death certificates will need to be provided for anyone to get paid out from the policy, so whatever you want to tell me, you can.”

Marco opened his mouth but closed it. He looked at Josie and bobbed his head in the direction of John.

Josie took over for Marco, “Lexi was supposed to be dead, but she’s still alive. We believe she’s with Carmine.”

John turned toward Marco. He wasn’t sure what to say, but he felt like he should say something. It was about time that someone addressed the elephant in the room.

“As screwed up as all of this is, you are better off, and your future has bigger and better things in store for you.” John put out each of his hands and laid one on Josie’s and one on Marco’s. There was a sigh of relief from all three of them. The feud with John and Marco was officially over, and in the moment, it was unspoken, but sealed for good.

“Not to mention what else Lexi would have done to Josie if she were still on the loose,” John added.

“So, John, what are you suggesting we do next?” asked Josie, hoping to deter Marco from catching on to what John just said about Lexi. Amid everything that was going on, she’d forgotten to tell Marco about the car chase.

Chapter 75

"OK, Mom. You take care, and I'll call you soon."

Fitz got off the phone with his mother and sat down to prepare himself for the events that would be unfolding in the next few days. He was sad when he hung up. He did not know how much longer she would even know who he was. He needed to get over there to see her soon.

He was scanning his large investigation board hanging on the wall. Some of the pieces of information, as well as the photos, went back before he was even born. He was reviewing all of the information the bureau was able to retrieve from the archives to make sure he had everything in order and that he hadn't missed anything.

He got lucky, because as he read through all the documents again, he came across something he hadn't noticed before. It was a photo, and what he saw in the background was unmistakable. How could he have missed it? There was a photo of Anthony in one of his legitimate businesses that he owned. A bar. *Shocking*, Fitz thought. Right there behind Anthony at the pool table was Fitz's father, Carl.

How could he have missed this? *That was a stupid question*, Fitz thought. He'd just recently met his father. As good as Fitz was at his job, it was altogether possible that he wouldn't be able to recognize what his father looked like thirty-some years ago.

At the thought of his father, Fitz remembered that he'd received something from his father in the mail. He'd forgotten all about it. It might have been a letter. Leave it to Carl to write a letter in this current age of technology. He was probably too stupid to figure out how to use email. He couldn't imagine what his mother saw in him all those years ago when they got married.

Even now, how could she stand him? She left him before he was born and now they were back together. His mind again drifted to his mother and that awful disease that she had. Alzheimer's was such a horrible, horrible thing. As much as he hated his father, he had to respect him for accepting such a huge undertaking with his mother.

He was digging through his piles of junk mail. "Where is it?" he said, talking to no one but himself. He finally tracked down the letter, ripped open the envelope, and unfolded the piece of college ruled paper, filled on both sides. He snapped his head back. "Good God, why did I even open this?"

He began reading: *Dear Son.* Fitz rolled his eyes. It's not that he was opposed to having a relationship with his father, but Carl wasn't the sharpest knife in the drawer. He acted like they had known each other forever when really, they just met.

He continued reading,

> I know you think it's archaic to write a letter, but I don't have time to figure out how to use the computer. Your mom can be a lot of work sometimes. I'm not complaining, I'm just telling you like it is. Anyway, I'm writing you today to say that I think it's a bad idea for you to take any legal action toward Anthony. It might not be in your best interest to do that to him. Of course, you know I can't tell you why, but please trust me on this. There are some things you will eventually understand.
>
> I want you to know that I have not done the horrible things that Anthony has done, but I was involved to some extent.

More importantly, I pledged an unwritten oath to him to protect and watch over him. I know you are thinking that I am a total idiot, and I couldn't be watching over him when I'm not even in the same country, but I have my ways and I have eyes and ears wherever he goes.

One more thing, I'm asking that you not take it out on me that your mother never told me you and your brothers existed. I don't want you to blame her, either, but if I had the chance to know you, I would have jumped at the opportunity to be the best dad I could be to you boys. I needed to say that, just so you know how I feel.

Please reconsider on Anthony.

Love,

Dad

Fitz put down the letter and rolled his eyes. He felt like he was getting a headache from all the eye rolling lately.

What was this nitwit talking about? He had no idea what was going on. But he did have Fitz thinking. Though it sounded like it was just his loyalty talking, what kind of connections could Anthony still have? Wouldn't he have burned every bridge after that stunt he pulled? Fitz knew he'd been working with a very small crew, including Carmine, but not a huge empire like back in the old days. Maybe it was Carl's connections, and not Anthony's at all?

He would have to do some digging, but time was running out and he needed to figure it out soon.

He picked up his phone to call Joey.

Chapter 76

Marco's wheels were turning. Josie could see it on his face. She crossed her fingers like a junior high school kid trying not to get caught in a stupid lie. She didn't keep the incident with Lexi from him on purpose; she just forgot to tell him, with everything that was happening.

John sensed it as soon as Marco looked at Josie and tilted his head.

"Oh!" Marco blurted in excitement. "That must be what my mom was talking about. I remember her blabbering about something on the phone one day when she was telling me about something that was going on with Carmine and the body and something or other. I don't think I was even listening." Marco wasn't really talking to anyone. He was just working something out of his head, but out loud.

Josie and John waited for his rant to be over. They didn't want to interrupt.

When Marco was finished, John waited a beat and added, "Well, maybe I'm not always late to the party." This was a feeble attempt to take the spotlight off Josie. He thought Marco would be peeved that she wasn't the one to tell him herself.

"Josie, why didn't you tell me?"

"We weren't really speaking at the time and we had just had that argument and by the time we connected again, everything else happened and I completely forgot about it. She wasn't really a worry any longer, so it just didn't matter anymore," Josie said apologetically.

Marco's face fell. He recalled the fight they had, when he thought he lost her forever. That's when he decided that he was going to leave Lexi and there was no going back. He knew then that Josie was the most important thing in the world to him. He wasn't going to argue now about it and he certainly wasn't going to let Lexi get in the way of them any longer.

"Fair enough, I don't want to waste any time arguing about her."

"I'm sorry, I didn't know you didn't know and . . ." John said.

"It's fine, John, don't worry about something so silly. We're good."

"OK, well, now that's settled, you guys might both think I'm completely insane, but I think we need to do something about Anthony. I think something seriously wrong is going to happen."

Josie shifted in her position around the island and was busying herself with something in the kitchen. She wanted nothing to do with whatever John was suggesting. John knew it too, so she was caught off guard that he would even suggest something like that.

"Why are you sticking up for him? Why would you want to protect him?" Josie threw her hands in the air, questioning John's proposal.

John wanted to be very careful how he worded this, because it really wasn't about Anthony, it was about Carmine. Not that he was any better than Anthony, but after everything that he'd done, for some reason Josie still valued the friendship they shared.

"No, I'm sorry. It's not really involving Anthony. It's my fear for Carmine," said John.

"Eff him!" Marco barked, realizing how angry he was. "Sorry, John."

"Yeah, I get it, but you both know there is an insurance policy and it's complicated, so I don't know what Carmine's intentions are, but I am going to ask to get this taken off my plate. I don't want any part of it, and honestly, I think there is something very bad that is about to happen. I can't put my finger on it, but something seems very off. It was off the day that Jimmy and I went to Anthony's and saw Carmine." John took a breath.

"I just want to say again that a death certificate will need to be made. Even though the pathologist faked the death report, I don't think he or the initial examiner would be willing to forfeit their medical licenses to forge a death certificate. Without that? No pay out."

"Yeah, I get that," said Josie. "Go back to what you were saying before. What do you mean by off?"

"It's hard to describe. Carmine was not his usual arrogant self. Anthony was, of course, but Carmine had a much different attitude."

"Maybe he finally realized that he's a piece of crap," Marco barked again.

This conversation took Josie back to the day in the park when she ran into Anthony. Her skin crawled just thinking about it. She had mentioned it to Marco, but hadn't told him the details. Maybe she should tell them now? Not that it would make a difference, but they should both know, just in case something did happen or they were pulled into the miserable vortex that Anthony seemed to create.

"Anthony must have tracked me in the park one day because I ran into him and—"

"What? How did you not tell us?" John looked at Marco as if they were a team. At this stage in the game, they sort of were. If one of them wasn't looking out for her, the other one was.

"Anthony kept saying that things aren't what they seem and he's not the man I think he is. Why would he say that? Do you think maybe he didn't really do all those horrible things we think he did?"

John couldn't believe what he was hearing. He needed to tell Josie what he overheard. That would make it real. That would show her that he really was the awful man they always thought he was. He needed to be firm, so she fully understood that what he was saying was the truth and Anthony really was, and always would be, a monster.

John took Josie's hand. "I never told you this before, but I don't want you even considering that Anthony might be a good person. When I worked for your father at the sporting goods store—" John broke off as Marco shifted in his seat. John didn't think what he was saying might be awkward. It was more important for Josie to be completely informed about Anthony.

"Just when I thought we were all getting along," Marco mused.

"No, Marco, it's not like that. I just need Josie to hear me out." John smiled at Marco to make it clear that he was getting down to business.

"No, I get it, I was just lightening the mood so Josie doesn't have to be uncomfortable. Not that you were doing that. I just wanted it to be OK. For the record, in all fairness, she was mine first." Marco grinned.

John rolled his eyes. Josie flushed.

"Can I go on?" John asked. He didn't bother to fight. They all knew John and Josie were together first.

Marco waved his hand, urging him to continue.

"I was working one day and that was the same day that . . ." John continued cautiously. "This was the day that Anthony was being inappropriate with you."

"You mean the day that you knocked an old man right on his ass?"

"That would be the day, Marco." Josie blushed.

Josie could hear John talking in the background while she was lost in her thoughts. She should have been paying attention to what he was saying, but she zoned out. That day, she was so angry when Anthony attempted to force himself on her. She was barely eighteen years old and he was such a scumbag. She was grateful for what John did, but certainly not enough to make it all go away. She would forever have that memory embedded in her head. She wondered now if things would have been different with her and John if she knew what he did at the time.

"Earth to Josie." John snapped his fingers in her direction.

"Oh sorry, that day flooded back to me so quickly, I couldn't shake it out of my head."

"I was telling Marco that I overheard Anthony on the phone that day. He said, 'Well, just kill him then.'"

"Weren't you afraid?"

"Obviously not at the time, because that was before I knocked him out. I was so angry for what he did to you and I had just put the pieces together of what he had done to your parents. Then I heard him on the phone and that was it. I just snapped. I was fearless in thinking that he wasn't going to do anything to me. I was just a stupid kid. He wasn't going to risk going to jail over something so stupid. There was no one in the store and no one ever saw what happened."

John looked at his watch. "I'm going to head out. I guess there's nothing else for me to do, but if either one of you needs anything, just give me a call."

John and Marco shook hands. John leaned in to hug Josie and she accepted it, even though she felt her body begin to shake. She was hoping that John wouldn't catch it, but she sensed that he did. As they pulled away from each other, his gaze caught her eyes. With his own eyes, he squinted at her. He knew she was not OK.

He pulled her in again and whispered in her ear, "Call me anytime."

Chapter 77

Sitting at the kitchen table with her cup of coffee, Antonia was thinking of the day before when she spent some much needed time with her grandchildren. When all this was over, she was looking forward to spending more time with them.

She heard James coming down the stairs and shuffling through the house. She used to hate his shuffling, but for some reason it didn't bother her so much anymore. It now provided a much needed comfort.

"Good morning, light of my life," James said.

Antonia rolled her eyes. "Good morning, old man."

"Ah, you were always great at finding the right term of endearment. As long as I'm your old man, I don't care what you call me," James said.

Antonia smiled. She didn't know what to say. She found herself at a loss for words more and more these days, and she felt oddly at peace with it.

"I know you are going to be on the phone quite a bit today, so I thought I would head home and get some of my things to bring over to keep here." James dropped that bomb on her unforgivingly.

She rolled her eyes again. "Whatever you want to do."

"Jeez, don't sound so excited."

She chuckled, "I am. I have to be honest in saying that I was really angry with you, and unsure of how I wanted all this to play out."

"I understand, but we got it all resolved, and I'm hoping we can move forward. Together. How does that sound to you?"

"It sounds pretty great," Antonia confessed.

He kissed her on the forehead. "I'll see you in a few hours."

Antonia's phone rang and she braced herself. James gave her a thumbs up as he made his way out the door.

"Hello," she said into the phone, then pulled it away to yell after James. "We are keeping our own houses!"

It was her nephew, Fitz. She was expecting his call. "Hello, honey."

She was twirling a pen on the table, which she recognized as a habit she had developed as she got older. She used to hang on every word of whomever she was talking to about the next job. Now she knew what to do and when to do it, so she sort of tuned in and out.

Fitz mentioned that he just ducked out of a meeting to give her a quick call. He went on to explain that her request was going to be tricky, but they were going to do their best to make it happen.

He also mentioned that his father, Carl, had written and mailed him a letter.

This snapped Antonia to attention.

"What? Did you just say your dad wrote you a letter?" Antonia was bothered by Carl's archaic way of communication. *He is so stupid*, she thought. She detested that man for so many reasons. Was it awful that she despised him mostly because he was stupid? "Are you having second thoughts?"

"No, not at all, and the issues don't have anything to do with my father, it's just a bureau issue in the investigation. We have come across a major problem that I already knew was going to happen, but I thought we would have worked it out by now. We are on the right track and it won't delay the timing or the outcome, but we do need to figure it out," Fitz said.

"As long as you are working it out, then I won't worry about it."

"All good. Talk to you soon."

Antonia had a very good feeling what this was all about, and she thought it might come to that. She also had confidence in Fitz that he would work out the details in time. They could not afford for this to blow up in their faces. She wanted it over and done with and behind them.

Behind them for a while, anyway. There were a number of other things to be sorted out, but that could be done later.

She had been trying to contact her sister, but was having no luck. Even Fitz told her that there was no return address on the letter, so there was no easy way to find her. She would have to get creative. She would wait until everything was done with and then she would try to track down Elizabeth.

Chapter 78

Marco walked in his front door, tossed his keys on the table, and leafed through the large pile of mail he'd pulled out of the mailbox. Josie would be arriving soon after him; he was excited to have her there.

He plopped down on the couch and grabbed for his computer bag. He dug out his computer and fired it up, navigating to his email. He hadn't looked at it in a few days, and he wanted to devote his time to Josie with no distractions. Especially from emails.

He scrolled through his inbox and came across an email that he was sure was spam, but something familiar in the sender's name struck him. "What the?" Marco spat at his computer.

The email was dated from this morning. He opened it, hoping it wasn't some raging virus that would totally fry his computer. In the subject line was the word *Daffodils*.

The body of the email only said the words, "I'm fine."

He was blinking at his computer in shock. The hairs on the back of his neck stood up. He couldn't be seeing this right.

The sender initially looked like gibberish, but the more he stared at it, the more he was able to decipher that it was Lexi's name mixed with her maiden name and the anniversary of their first date. The letters and numbers were all mixed up, but there was enough order for him to put it all together.

"My God, what is wrong with that woman? Why would she even worry about reaching out? Why would she think I would care?" Marco said to himself.

He looked out the window as he heard a car pulling up to the house. He practically ran to the front door to see Josie, thankful that she was safe and he could watch over her.

He opened the front door to greet her and help her with her bag, but instead of Josie, there were two policemen standing on his front doorstep.

Panic rose in his gut. *Oh my God,* he thought. His brain was swimming. The sweat had almost instantly soaked through his shirt. His forehead was wet. He could feel it in his hair.

Calm down, you pansy! He willed himself to follow his own advice. Then Marco remembered that everyone was alive and well. He'd done nothing wrong, and more importantly he didn't really have anything to do with Lexi not being home. This calmed him down enough to wipe off his hand and offer it to the officers. "Hello, officers. How can I help you? Is everything alright?"

The officers glanced at one another. The much taller male officer stood there, looking at his partner to speak.

His partner, a shorter but very solid woman, spoke. "Hello, Mr. Paretti, does your wife happen to be home?"

"Oh, uh, no, she isn't. Is there something I can help you officers with?"

"Do you know where she is?" Marco stared at them, wondering how he was possibly going to answer them. Should he lie to the police? Although he just assumed she was at Anthony's, he didn't really know for sure. If he said he didn't know, it wouldn't be a lie.

"No, I'm not really sure where she is at the moment. Maybe check with her work?" He had no idea why he said that. If they did that, he knew they were going to tell the officers that they hadn't seen her. She was smart enough to tell them she was taking a vacation, but that would lead them right back to his doorstep. He guessed he'd deal with that if it happened.

"OK, we'll do that." The male officer pulled a business card from his back pocket. "Can you have her call me when you see or speak with her?"

"Yes, of course." He thought he should ask why, so they didn't get suspicious. "Can I ask what this is about?"

The female officer piped up to answer. "Yes, we received a complaint about a rental car driving very recklessly, and the rental contract was signed by your wife."

Marco stood there blinking at them.

"From the look on your face, it appears that you have no idea what we are talking about."

Marco softened a little bit, "Uh, no, I'm sorry. I don't."

The officers got in the police car and drove off to look for Lexi.

Marco was thankful that Josie hadn't gotten there yet. He didn't have to explain her presence to the police. He checked his watch and realized that she definitely should have been there by now. *What's taking her so long?*

Chapter 79

Josie was driving to Marco's. She was enjoying the scenery and thinking about the conversation she and Marco had with John. John was really such a nice guy. She was sad that it wasn't going to work out with her and John, but she was finally on the right path with Marco. Even if things didn't work out with her and Marco, at least she would be able to say that they tried.

She smiled. Things were going very well in her life. She spent a lot of time on her work and now it was time to add a relationship to the insanity.

Something was nagging at her about John. Maybe it was something he said, or the way he was acting at her apartment. He seemed perfectly fine, but something was just not right. It could have been the fact that he knew it was over with them, and that's what she noticed. His demeanor was relaxed and confident. It appeared to Josie that he had come to terms with Josie choosing Marco. Josie felt very relieved.

She hadn't heard from Mrs. P in a while, but it was just as well. Now that everything was out of Josie's hands, she didn't want to know what else was happening.

Just as she thought that, her phone rang.

"Hello?"

"Hey, it's me." It was John. Maybe she thought too soon that he was over this.

"I'm sorry to bother you, but I just can't shake a few things. I don't know what it is, but something is just not right with this whole insurance policy thing and Anthony and Mrs. Paretti and her mysterious sister. All of it. There is something else that has been bothering me about Anthony. I'm sure you don't know this, but Anthony mentioned this to Jimmy and me when we went to visit him. He told us that he doesn't go out in public much. Hardly ever, if he can help it. The only thing he does is go for a walk in the park, and usually he's wearing a hat and sunglasses. Why? Why doesn't he go out in public? What is that about?" John sighed. "I know I said I wasn't going to get involved and I was just going to walk away." He stopped and began quickly, trying not to make her think he was talking about them. "Carmine is there, and there is no doubt Lexi is there with him. What's going on, and what does Mrs. P have to do with all of it?"

Josie let out a big sigh. "John, I need to be honest. I was just thinking about you before you called. I was also thinking about Mrs. P. You are one hundred percent right. I think something is off about Anthony and Mrs. P. That must have been what I was feeling."

John laughed. "Isn't there always something off about them? Now that we know they are related, it makes a lot more sense."

Josie laughed. She was sucked into her thoughts of minor shame that she chose that insane family over John, who was quite normal, as far as she knew. The heart wants what the hearts wants. She was rolling with it until disaster struck.

"Josie, are you there?"

"Sorry, John. I'm here. So, what do you want to do about it?"

"Are you still in town?"

"No, I'm almost at Marco's."

"Talk to him and see if he's willing to come back into the city tomorrow. Maybe we should just all go over to Anthony's and see what's happening."

"John, I think that's a little crazy. Don't you think we should just stay out of it?"

"Yes, a very large part of me says run for the hills, don't look back, and let all of them sort it out. But something just keeps drawing me back to it all. None of it makes sense. I obviously don't have all the details and I understand that, but I just can't help but feel like something really awful is going to go down."

"OK, I'll talk to Marco and see what he thinks. I'll get back to you."

She pulled into Marco's driveway just as she was hanging up with John and saw a cop car pulling away from the house.

"Oh, brother. What's happening now?" Josie murmured.

Marco dug his phone out of his pocket to call her and just as he did, she saw her car. He puffed out a giant exhale, realizing that he had been breathing very shallowly since the cops arrived. What a relief. The cops were gone, and Josie was here. Maybe he could get back to some normalcy.

Josie walked up the front steps to Marco, who was still outside from his unexpected visit from the police.

"What's happening?"

"Two cops just came looking for Lexi."

"What? Why?"

"They said someone filed a complaint about a reckless driver."

"That woman is crazy." Josie shook her head.

Marco put his arm out to signal Josie to come in the house with him. He grabbed her bag as they walked inside.

Josie was still processing the conversation she had with John. So now the cops were looking for Lexi. She knew it was important to John to know if something awful might happen, but maybe it wasn't that important to her. She wanted to get over to her parents' house for a quick visit today. This was supposed to be somewhat of a getaway. Compared to this chaos, a crunched deadline for work did not seem so bad.

Chapter 80

Kate was running some errands. Grocery shopping, the pharmacy, and gas. She kept checking her watch to make sure she would get home in time. She didn't want to miss her visitors.

She was beginning to make her way home when she saw that Josie was calling her. She pushed the button on the steering wheel to answer her daughter.

"Hi, honey!"

"Hi, Mom, I'm really sorry for the short notice, but I'm in town. It was sort of an unexpected trip. I was planning on being here for a few days, but I need to go back tomorrow. I was wondering if I could stop by for a little bit, just to visit real quick before I go back?"

Kate paused for much longer than she should have. She wasn't quite panicking, but she got closer and closer to it the more she didn't answer Josie.

"Mom? Are you there?"

She needed to think quick. She wasn't going to give up the chance to hug and squeeze her precious Josie. This was a big day, but she certainly could make time.

"Yes! I'm here. What time were you thinking you wanted to stop by?"

"I was hoping to stop by in a few minutes. It sounds like you are in the car. Will you be back soon?"

Kate rolled the timing around in her head. There would be more than enough time for Josie to come and see them before her visitors arrived.

"That would be fine. Yes, I'm in the car. I was running some errands. I am on my way home now, though, and should be there in a few. Your father is home in case you beat me there. He will be elated to see you," she said. Josie could hear the smile on her mom's face.

"See you soon, Mom."

Kate had a great feeling about today.

Minutes later, she pulled into the driveway and Josie's car was already there. She nearly forgot the groceries, she was so anxious to get in the house.

Joe and Josie were sitting in the living room waiting for her. She beelined for Josie, hugging her. "Hi, honey!"

"Hi, Mom." Josie smiled at the warm hug and was so grateful that her mother and father were still alive and healthy.

Kate sat next to her husband so she could face Josie while they were visiting. She kissed her husband on the cheek to greet him after her short trip of errands. As soon as her lips touched his cheek, she could feel the intensity pouring off him. They made eye contact and she knew immediately that something was wrong.

Her brain drifted to every awful scenario that she could think of. What if the plan had been compromised? What if Antonia and James got cold feet? She almost had to laugh in her head at that one. Those two didn't get cold feet for anything. They made up their minds and didn't look back.

She snapped out of her worried trance and realized that she was just starring at Josie with the smile of an imbecile. She was nodding her head and Josie wasn't even talking.

"You OK, Mom?"

Kate gathered herself from stupidity. “Sure, honey. I thought I forgot something at the grocery store, but I’m pretty sure I got it.”

Joe was able to calm his nerves enough to ask, “What are you doing home, and why do you have to leave so quickly?”

Josie knew one of them was going to ask, and even though she knew, she still wasn’t prepared to answer. She didn’t want to lie, but she felt like that may be her only option at the moment.

“I came home to see Marco, but just as I was arriving, I was called back to the city again.” She really wasn’t lying. She knew her parents would assume it was work-related, but without saying it, she really wasn’t lying to them.

They made some small talk and Josie’s dad asked how the new book was coming along. Josie gave them some details. Even though Joe wasn’t an avid reader, and on the rare occasion that he did read, it was mostly non-fiction, he made a point to read all of her books. How could he not read his daughter’s books?

Josie was beginning to feel on edge. She was slightly bothered by the fact that her nerves were getting the better of her. There was no reason for her to be nervous. Not yet, anyway. She didn’t even know what was going on. Maybe it was her parents acting so odd that made her nervous. Something wasn’t right with them. Maybe they were nervous for the same reason she was. But that couldn’t be. They couldn’t have anything to do with Anthony after all this time. Could they?

She opened her mouth to ask what was going on with them, but against her better judgment she closed it back up and decided to keep her questions to herself. She was not ready to hear what was going on. They would tell her when they were ready.

Josie checked her watch, and maybe for the first time ever, Kate was a little relieved that Josie was leaving.

“Well, I guess I’ll go.”

Josie's mom stood up with her. "Please text us when you get back to the city, so we know you are safe."

"I always do, Mom."

"Your mother is just reminding you, sweetheart," said her dad, giving her a tight hug.

"I know. I love you guys. Text you later."

Josie drove off, waving to her parents who were standing in the front door.

Kate turned to her rattled husband, putting her hand in his to show him she was there for whatever was bothering him. "What on earth happened?"

Chapter 81

Josie drove away from her parents' house, a sickening feeling settling in her gut that they were keeping something from her. She did not want to think the worst, but what if one of them had a terminal illness and they didn't tell her?

She needed to keep it together. She couldn't worry about that now.

On her way back to Marco's she called Mr. P. She needed to know once and for all if it was him who was having her followed or if it was Anthony.

She stabbed at her cracked screen to dial the number. As it was ringing, the urgency to get to Marco and tell him what she spoke to John about was becoming overwhelming.

"Hello, dear, how are you?" Mr. P said.

Josie significantly calmed down at the sound of his reassuring voice. When she was younger, she'd had some fear of this man. She wondered how much of that fear was brought on by Marco and his negative words about his own father.

"Hello. I'm sorry to bother you but I have a quick question for you," said Josie.

"No bother at all. What's up?"

"I noticed a few times walking through the city that I couldn't help but feel as though I was being followed. I had an incident in the park one day when I just happened to run into Anthony. I made eye contact with my stalker and he made a gesture, assuring me that everything would be OK, and Anthony would not be able to hurt me. This pretty much had you or Mrs. P written all over it, but I needed to know for sure, just in case it wasn't you and it was actually Anthony."

"Yes, Josie, it was us. There was no way we were going to let anything happen to you."

"Thank you, Mr. P. I really appreciate it." She could hear him saying something about having dinner when things calmed down, but she was in a hurry to get him off the phone. "Yep, OK, sounds good." She was stabbing at the phone again to disconnect the call.

She was extremely relieved that it was her—maybe soon to be—in-laws who were responsible. Wow, why was she thinking that, at a time like this? She felt herself teetering on the verge of mania. She needed to meditate or something.

Once she got back to Marco's, she would be able to rest shortly, and then they could make their way back to the city. After she told Marco what John called her about.

As she pulled into Marco's driveway again, she was relieved not to see cops, or Lexi, or God knows who else could have popped up.

She went barreling into the house and found Marco sitting at the kitchen table, reading through what looked like work files. He usually worked in his office and not at the kitchen table. She assumed he needed a change of scenery.

"Hey."

"Hey, yourself," Marco blurted, pulling her on his lap.

"I'm getting a little manic. My thoughts seem to be spinning out of control," Josie said.

Marco eyed her curiously. Josie was never the dramatic type. Not like Lexi. He was concerned at her choice of words. "It's OK." He pulled her closer to him, guiding her head on his shoulder. He could feel her heart racing.

"What happened?" Marco asked.

Josie began telling him what happened at her mother and father's house, and how she called his father, and something he said didn't quite sit right with her on top of what her parents had to say. She told him about John and how they spoke, and how she needed to tell Marco what he said.

"Josie, you should calm down. You might be having a panic attack."

Josie looked at him, confused. She realized she was moving from one thing to the next very quickly. She looked into Marco's eyes and took a deep breath.

Marco held her gently, hoping his touch would help calm her down.

Her breathing began to slow. She had stopped talking at this point, and it was easier to gather her thoughts.

"Marco, I think something really awful is going to happen to Anthony."

Marco was sick of hearing about it.

Chapter 82

Joe followed his wife to the kitchen to help her put away the groceries. He wanted to calm down before he spoke to her about his previous state. When they finished, they settled back on the couch in the living room.

"I hated lying to her like that. I don't know if I've ever lied to her," said Kate.

Joe looked at her sideways. "You most certainly have. Not about something this significant, but you have. She'll know all about it very soon, so don't worry about it. Most importantly, she won't be mad at you for it. She will completely understand, and your relationship will carry on as usual with her."

Kate knew her husband was right. It would all be OK once it was over. Everything would go back to normal. Just as she thought that, she noticed that her husband still was rattled. She had pushed that aside while they were waving Josie off and getting the kitchen back to normal, but now, she needed to know.

"What happened? You were so tense when I came home. What's the matter?"

Joe was fidgeting with his fingers in his lap. He tried to hide his concern, but failed miserably. "Well, I received a phone call from Anthony while you were out and about this morning."

She sucked in a deep breath and her body went rigid. Her eyes were darting back and forth trying to process the news. "What on earth are you talking about?" she screeched. "What did he say?" The pitch of her voice cut through his ears like a knife.

"He called to apologize for what he did to us. He said that he wasn't getting any younger and if he dies tomorrow, he wants to make it right with the people that he has hurt the most over the years."

Kate was speechless. She felt like she was going to be sick. She sat there for a few minutes, trying to blink back the tears. Her husband's fingers entwined with hers. As she stressed about this news, it never once came to her mind that they shouldn't see everything through. Her husband didn't falter. This phone call meant nothing to her, despite her emotional reaction. It didn't change anything.

"So, how do you feel about what he said?" she questioned warily.

"As you could tell, I was very rattled at first. I was more rattled at the sound of his putrid voice on the other end of the line." Joe paused while he collected his thoughts. He wanted to make sure his words matched his feelings. "I don't even know if I believe that he is sorry. Also, he can be sorry all he wants, but nothing will get all of our money back. And more important than our money is our family, and all the "I'm sorries" in the world will not change what he did to Josie and what he put her through."

This was music to her ears. It put everything in perspective for her. "I couldn't agree more," she said. "What hurts the most about it is that Josie was too afraid to tell us. I'll never forgive him for that."

They headed to the kitchen to get lunch ready for their guests.

Chapter 83

Marco thought through Josie's comment, wondering what the big deal was; and who cared about Anthony? Wouldn't something happening to him be OK by most people?

"I'm confused. Are we supposed to care? You have such disdain for that man. Why would you care if something awful happens to him?"

She considered his comment and began wondering the same thing. She wasn't really sure why she cared. Wasn't it what she'd always wanted?

Marco watched her quietly while she worked it all out in her head. He did not dare interrupt her thoughts. He wanted her to stay calm.

"I've always wanted him to pay for the things that he did to my family and me, but I don't think I want him to die," Josie finally said.

"Whoa! What are you talking about? What makes you think he's going to die?"

Josie was looking for an answer. "It just seems that way from some things that your mother has said, and I just got off the phone with your dad before I got here and he said they were never going to let anything happen to me."

Marco was confused. They knew his parents were involved after the situation with Lexi, so why was Josie questioning it now? "I don't understand."

"He said it like it was past tense, like I was no longer going to have to worry about Anthony in the future."

"I think maybe you are reading into that a little too much."

"I don't think so. Marco, don't you find it very odd that Anthony hardly ever goes out in public anymore?"

"That's an odd thing to bring up. How would you even know that?"

"John said something to me about it. He told me that Jimmy told him the same thing." Marco felt like she was getting out of control again.

She got up and started pacing. He tried to grab her hand to get her to sit down but, she was not having it.

"John said we should go back to the city," Josie said.

"Why? We just got here."

"I think we should go, and I really think we should go over to Anthony's and see what's going on there."

Marco thought Josie had lost her mind. Why would she even want to go over there? Did she really care that much? She despised Lexi with every fiber of her being. She was always fond of Carmine, but not after what he did with Lexi. She had done everything in her power over the years to have the least amount of contact possible with Anthony.

Marco was beginning to feel like he was trapped. He was beginning to think that Josie was all part of this mess. *No*, he thought. *She couldn't be.*

Marco would entertain, what he hoped, was some form of temporary insanity. He was taking his own car, just in case he needed to get the hell out of there. He was already feeling trapped, even though he was in his own house.

"OK, whatever you want to do, Josie. Let's head back, but let's give ourselves some time to think about what we actually are going to do. If you want John involved, that's OK with me, too."

"I don't need your permission," she hissed. As soon as it rolled off her tongue, she apologized. "Oh, my goodness. I'm so sorry, Marco. I'm clearly getting out of control with this whole thing."

"It's OK, let's just go."

"Now?" Josie asked.

He grabbed his keys and handed Josie her bags, which were still by the front door.

Chapter 84

Antonia was waiting for James. She was letting him drive today. She has been at the wheel the last few times they traveled together, and she knew he wanted to drive. Plus, he just had gotten a new car, and she was itching to check it out.

When he pulled up in front of the house, she felt a flutter in her stomach that she hadn't felt in a long time. She wasn't sure how to feel about it, but she was going to roll with it for now.

They climbed back in the car together after he came to the door to get her. He took in a deep breath. "Are you ready?"

Very confidently, she replied, "Ready as I'll ever be."

They were getting closer to their destination and she was enjoying the new car. James was a safe driver, but took a few chances on this trip to show off what the new car could do. Again, this gave her a flutter of times long ago.

Antonia's cell phone rang. She didn't even want to glance down in her hand to see who it is. She wanted no part in talking with anyone right now. She just wanted to enjoy the moment.

She finally glanced down and saw that it was her sister, Elizabeth. She answered it quickly so it didn't go to voicemail, although for a second, she considered it.

"Hello." Antonia tried to sound calm and emotionally neutral. The slightest thing could set Elizabeth off these days. While Antonia was annoyed at times, she fully understood why her sister was sensitive, but given the new information, that might not even be the real reason. She was hopeful that Elizabeth wasn't really as sick as they thought she was.

James could hear Elizabeth going on and on about who knows what. He made a not-so-very-nice gesture with his finger to his temple, suggesting that she was off her rocker. Antonia gave him a dirty look while shaking her head. He was such an ass sometimes.

Elizabeth was not fond of James at all. James's involvement in tearing her family apart was not something that Elizabeth could ever forgive him for.

James could understand why she was so upset. It was her family. He got it, but Elizabeth knew what kind of man her father was; obviously for her, the family staying together was more important. Even though Anthony was a horrible husband to her mother, Elizabeth still wanted them together. Even though Elizabeth had come to dislike her father very much as she learned more about how horrible he was, she still disliked James. Even though she ended up better off without Anthony in her day-to-day life, she still blamed James. The more he thought about it, maybe she didn't like James because he had been a bad husband to her sister. That had always bothered him.

Antonia hung up with Elizabeth, shaking her head again. "OK, you're upset," said James. "It was rude of me to suggest that she is crazy when she isn't well."

"What are you blabbering about now?" Antonia said, confused.

"I thought you were shaking your head at me for being rude."

"Oh, I was before, but now I'm just baffled by what Elizabeth told me about her wonderful, loving husband."

James's eyebrows shot up. His eyes looked like they were going to bulge out of his head. *What? What on earth is she talking about?* he wondered.

She knew by the look on his face that he was not at all braced for what she was about to tell him. She would have to quickly figure out the best way to break this news to him. The last thing she wanted was for him to go off and try to strangle Carl.

"So, your brother-in-law," she sniggered, "apparently wrote a letter—I know, don't laugh—to Fitz, asking him not to go through with . . ." She stopped then continued, "We already knew this, of course, but she is irate, and all she said was do what you have to do. He put us all through hell, and there is nothing else he can do to hide from all this now."

The shade of crimson that was rising up James's neck was frightening. The last thing Antonia needed was him to have a heart attack. It had been a really long time since she worried about this man. It was scary, at her age, to have this type of anxiety, but at this moment she realized how lonely it had been not having anyone to truly worry about.

Although she had been seeing someone, she never really let herself get too close to him. For so many reasons. All of them led back to her keeping him at a safe distance. He did his thing, and she did her thing. They were separate beings who spent some time together when she felt like it.

"I'm going to kill him!" James shouted into the windshield as they were driving. She laid her hand on his and picked up her phone to call Fitz.

"I will take care of it. I am a bit annoyed that Fitz didn't mention this to me. We are supposed to be in communication on anything that happens before tomorrow afternoon, but I suppose Elizabeth's knowledge of the letter has no bearing on this."

"He did mention it to us," James recalled, "but we never asked what it was about."

"That's right, I'd forgotten. Why would we not have asked about it? Why didn't he tell us that his mother knew?" They started bickering.

The phone began ringing again in her hand and they glanced at each other before looking at the screen. It was Fitz.

Antonia picked up and Fitz barely said hello before he launched into what he had to say. He didn't even give her the chance to say anything. Then he hung up. Antonia hadn't said a word at all.

"What was that about? He didn't even let you say anything."

She sat there, baffled, trying to get her thoughts straight. They were pulling up to their destination and she needed to compartmentalize everything that just happened. *It's all good*, she told herself. *Everything will be fine.* She just needed to gather her thoughts.

"He told me about the letter again and assured me that everything is still on track and not to worry. He said he knew his mother was calling me to let me know, so he wanted to assure me that everything was still set on his end."

James was calm. Almost instantly. He was surprised how, in his old age, he was able to just let things go. Very much unlike his younger days; he was very hotheaded.

Though calm, something kept bugging James. He was not pleased that Antonia told Elizabeth what was going on. He knew she was going to do it, and he'd stayed out of it. It was her business; but in retrospect, he didn't realize that Elizabeth was going to tell Carl. He could see this all going very poorly. As long as Fitz could keep Carl out of it, they should be just fine; but if not, it could be a complete disaster.

Antonia puffed out a sigh. "Let's get in there so we can be one step closer to the end."

Chapter 85

James and Antonia walked in the house, and the ladies hugged and the men shook hands. Kate led them into the dining room so they could sit and have lunch.

James and Antonia shared a quick glance. They were not expecting the spread that the Altieris had out for lunch. They had planned on going in and coming right back out. They now had no choice but to stay and eat. Not that they had much of anything else to do.

James was scanning the room, looking for the briefcase. He spotted it in the corner. He knew they would be leaving with that case today, and he was very happy about that.

His old friends were acting strangely, but he couldn't put his finger on what exactly it was about their behavior that wasn't quite right.

Joe folded his hands and put them on the table and for a minute, James thought it looked like he was going to start a prayer before they ate. It puzzled him; they had never prayed before eating together. What was he doing?

With a big sigh, Joe blurted out, "I'm not going to beat around the bush. I have something to say."

Antonia stiffened. She was positive that they had changed their minds and they were not going to go forward with this. It would be a huge mistake if that was the case. Not to mention that she would look like a fool to Fitz. She had assured him this was a sure thing, and this would be all he needed to take care of Anthony.

Joe continued, saying, "I received a phone call today." He and his wife were nervously looking at one another. It never crossed their minds not to trust their old friends, but Joe was struggling with it now. Everyone seemed to be holding their breath. "Anthony called to apologize for everything that he had done."

James knew that Antonia would speak first, so he stayed calm and kept his mouth shut.

"It doesn't surprise me in the least that he would call you and force out an apology to you. He is vile," Antonia said. She recalled the voicemail that he left her earlier in the day, asking her to call him. He had something *very important* that he wanted to discuss with her. "Are you having second thoughts?"

Joe and Kate said, in unison, "Definitely not." They looked at one another and smiled.

"All the apologies in the world, sincere or not, could not change my mind about this," said Joe.

Antonia, relieved, let out the breath she'd been holding.

Joe stood up and made his way over to the briefcase. He wanted to give it to them before they ate. This way, the small piece of business they had left would done and they could just enjoy one another's company.

He put it on the floor next to James. It was now in his hands, and Joe knew those were the best hands for the information to be in. He had a great feeling about all this, and was finally starting to enjoy the moment. He promised himself that he wouldn't enjoy it until it was over, but the way it had been going so far, he felt that it would be OK to have a pre-event moment of enjoyment.

They laughed together and carried on for a while as they finished eating.

At the end of their meal, they all hugged again, and the men shook hands. On the way out the door, James offhandedly remarked, "We'll have to do this again, when this is all over."

Kate's eyes flew wide open, and she immediately looked to Antonia for her to spill. Antonia rolled her eyes and backhanded James on the arm.

"We'll see about that," Antonia said with a raised eyebrow.

Once the Parettis had left, Kate said, "After all this time, do you think they will get back together?"

"Who knows. It seems to be the cool thing to do these days." Joe looked at Kate with a little worry in his eyes. She knew he was worried about Josie.

Chapter 86

Marco and Josie were back at her apartment, and they were both pacing. Neither one of them could calm down. They were feeding off each other's anxious energy.

"What are you thinking?"

"Marco, this is really eating at me. John should be calling soon, and maybe that will put me at ease, but I just can't help but think something really terrible is going to happen. Maybe it's not Anthony at all, maybe it's Lexi and Carmine. Maybe Anthony is going to hurt them. I know I'm beginning to sound like a broken record," Josie said.

Marco couldn't really care less if Anthony hurt them right now. In the future, it might really bother him if he thought something bad was going to happen, and he just sat back and let it unfold. However, Marco was never good at thinking of the future. He tended to think in the moment.

"I know what you're thinking. You don't care now, but you will if something happens and you don't do anything to stop it," said Josie.

He raised his eyebrows at her. How did she know what he was thinking at any given moment? He tried to take her in his arms, but she resisted. She was too worried right now to snuggle with him.

Marco wanted to say something, but they were interrupted by Josie's phone ringing.

"That must be John."

Marco rolled his eyes. He couldn't help but be puzzled by the fact that Josie and John were so enthralled with this mess. After all, it was Marco's family, not theirs. Not to mention his repulsive wife. Just the thought of that word, *wife*. Ugh. He loathed that woman.

Marco looked at Josie as she checked her phone.

She clicked the button to stop it from ringing. "It's not him. I don't know the number." She put the phone back down.

The last thing Marco wanted to do was go over to Anthony's. Marco was lost in his thoughts, but the alert sound from Josie's voicemail brought him back. He looked at her and saw the panic rising on her face.

"Are you going to listen to that?" he asked.

Josie stood there looking at him, and Marco was getting annoyed. He knew there would be ups and downs in their relationship, but why was she acting so useless? It was out of character for her.

"Josie, this is going to sound insensitive, but what in the hell is wrong with you?"

At that moment, Josie realized she was overreacting. Even though she didn't know what was coming next, she had been attempting to not let on that she knew something was going to go down. She would have been better off just being quiet. Now she would have to gradually pull herself together to show Marco that she wasn't really the crumbling fool she had been appearing to be. Her purposeful actions had backfired.

"You're right. Marco, I need to be honest with you. It's not a huge deal, and I really don't know what's going on, but I spoke with your mother a few days ago and she let on that something was going to happen. I didn't dare ask what, and she didn't offer the information."

Marco wasn't surprised; however, he was annoyed that Josie let this charade continue without telling him. Now that she was calm and collected, he knew she was faking her insanity only moments ago. He was more annoyed now than he was when she was acting.

"So, you're telling me you knew this whole time that something was going to go down and you've been acting like a nutcase just because you didn't want to tell me that my mother shared that information with you?"

When Marco said this to Josie, she realized how crazy she'd been and how upset he was. She was stupid to not share this with him to begin with.

"Yes, I guess that is what I am saying. Your mother scares me sometimes. She told me not to say anything, so I didn't. She would have found out, and then what?"

"She would never hurt you, you know that."

"I know, but I gave her my word I wouldn't, and I guess I was naïve to think that she would have told you herself."

Marco shook his head and thought about what to do next. He was so over this whole thing, and couldn't care less what happened to Anthony, or any of them. This thought was constantly rolling around in his head.

"Alright, so, I'm done with this. I'm tired of talking about it, and more importantly, I'm not going to try to stop whatever it is that you and John think is going to happen to Anthony. I have some work to do. OK if I use your office for a while?"

"Yes, of course. I'll listen to the voicemail and let you know if anything earth-shattering comes out of it."

Marco walked away and Josie picked up her phone. Before she listened to the voicemail, she looked out the window, wondering if she should even bother. Marco was right. They should just walk away and not look back. What did it matter if something happened to him? Did she really care? As she tossed this all around in her head, it occurred to her that it was really Carmine that she was worried about.

Even though he had done really awful things, she recalled all the good times they shared. He never did anything harmful to her. Ever. He was a friend she could always count on for anything she needed. She never called in any favors and rarely needed him, but she knew that if she ever did, he would be there. It had been hard for her to accept that

Carmine did what he did with Lexi. Who does that to their own brother? She was very angry at Carmine for doing such an awful thing. He was not the man she used to know. This was something she had really struggled with. She thought of Carmine's children. *Would they be better off without him?*

She definitely couldn't care less about Lexi, but it was Carmine that she was genuinely concerned for. As her brain continued in overdrive, her phone rang again. It was a private number, though she thought it might be John's office, but she just let it go to voicemail; within seconds, the voicemail tone sounded.

She listened to the other one first, and as soon as the person began speaking, her heart dropped.

Chapter 87

Antonia texted her nephew, Fitz, to let him know they were on their way to his place. With each piece she checked off the list, she felt more relieved. Soon, Anthony would be gone. She recalled the last conversation she had with Anthony in her head.

He had gone on and on about how sorry he was and how horrible it was that he did what he did to her mother. *Blah, blah, blah*, she thought. This was all much bigger than him and what he had done. She no longer thought of him as her father. He was just a man who was now going to be the gateway to something that she had been wanting to accomplish for quite some time.

"What's going on in that head of yours?" James nudged her elbow.

"Oh, you know, this and that." She smiled at him with a raised eyebrow. He knew exactly what she was thinking about, and this invigorated his thoughts towards this whole thing. He'd had his doubts at first, but now he was more assured than ever that they were doing the right thing.

They pulled up to Fitz's place and got out of the car. James grabbed the briefcase, feeling like he was holding the holy grail. He made a joke about it, but Antonia waved him off. She didn't think it was funny; she was too stressed.

They got up to the door and could hear Fitz yelling, but no one yelling back. Very puzzled, Antonia said, "Maybe he's on the phone."

She knocked anyway. She felt bad disturbing him, but she just wanted to drop the briefcase and run. He came to the door in a huff. When he realized it was them, he opened the door wider and waved them in. He puts his hand over the microphone on his cell and said, "It's my father."

James rolled his eyes and Antonia let out a big sigh.

"He doesn't quit, that jackass."

Antonia huffed out a hushed laugh. She knew how much James despised that man.

Fitz was arguing with Carl again. Antonia stuck out her hand with her palm up and waved her fingers, suggesting that Fitz hand her his phone.

He shook his head from side to side, clearly showing his opposition. Antonia cocked her head to one side and raised an eyebrow, still waving her fingers. Fitz turned to James in protest, looking for him to step in, but James only raised his hands and shook his head. He mouthed to Fitz, "No way."

Fitz handed his aunt the phone.

Fitz and James could hear Carl ranting on the other end of the phone.

Antonia calmly said, "Hello, Carl." There was now dead silence on the other end.

"Listen up. You have nothing to do with this, and I will have you know that you are like a hemorrhoid on the ass of society. Please just be quiet. This is happening, whether you like it or not. Whatever involvement you have had with Anthony over the years is your problem. If you are looking to save him, you will have to figure out another way. Interfering with us is not in your best interest right now, or ever, for that matter."

Fitz stood before her with his mouth gaping open. He was completely taken by the way her words flowed effortlessly from her mouth. She didn't skip a beat. It was almost like she had rehearsed it.

It was just a split second, but he noticed a shift in her demeanor. Was it her body language or her facial expression? Something was off. Very slightly, but definitely off. He was trained to detect these exact actions. He noticed that she turned away from them, but she was still on the phone and she was not saying a word.

James did not make a sound, or any sudden moves at all. He also knew something was not right, but not because he was trained; he just knew Antonia too well.

At that moment, Antonia turned back around to face Fitz and James. She raised her hand and clapped her fingers and thumb together, insinuating that Carl was talking and nattering on and on like he was with Fitz. What they didn't know was that he had already hung up, several seconds before.

"I will let everyone know, Carl. Talk to you and Elizabeth in another day or so. Bye, bye."

"What did he say, Auntie?"

"Just that he would leave it alone, and to tell everyone he said hello."

"That was pretty remarkable what you did. I know it's just Carl, my father, whatever you want to call him, but no one seems to be able to shut him up like that."

"I have a gift," she said with a chuckle, tilting her head back for deliberate entertainment.

They all laughed together, and Fitz broke in, "So this is it?" He picked up the briefcase. "Such damning evidence in such a small package."

"Yes, it is. Well, kiddo, we'll see you tomorrow, I suppose?" Antonia was trying to get a gauge on when this was happening without coming right out and asking.

Fitz smiled, "Yep, tomorrow it is." He winked at Antonia, confirming that she went about it the right way.

As the pair drove off, James said, "OK, out with it. What did he say?"

"What do you mean?"

"Really? Are you really going to try to pull that with me? The room seemed to have dropped twenty degrees when you were on the phone with Carl, and it definitely was not because you ripped into him like a dog that just chewed your new Gucci bag."

She smiled at him, recalling the time their very new puppy actually chewed the very new Gucci bag he had bought her for Christmas. They had just started making real money and it was something she had always wanted that he was finally able to get for her. Then the puppy destroyed it, before they even knew what was happening.

"I turned away hoping you wouldn't notice. Do you think Fitz noticed?"

"He is a federal agent, so my guess is he definitely noticed."

"Shit."

"Well, what did he say? I'm not letting you out of this. If we are going to be in this together, then you need to be honest with me."

She knew he was right. They had come so far, and if she lied to him now, he would know it and it would ruin any chance of them getting back together and seeing this thing all the way through.

"It appears as though Elizabeth's disease is getting worse, and Carl can't take care of her himself. He needs to bring in caregivers."

"Oh, OK, well, that's a relief." Antonia looked at him like he was the one who had gone mad.

"No, no, I'm sorry. I mean that's terrible, but from your actions on the phone with Carl, it seemed much worse than that."

Antonia bit her lip. It was much worse than that, but she was stalling. She didn't know why she bothered; she had to tell him, no matter what.

"Well, that's not all." Out of the corner of her eye, she saw him stiffen. "Carl had a caregiver come into the house. He left, but realized that he forgot his wallet, and when he got back to the house, he noticed that the side door to the villa was wide open. He didn't remember leaving it open, so he raced into the house to find the caregiver missing and Elizabeth on the couch, incoherent. There was a glass of water covered in a strange residue on the coffee table . . ." Antonia's voice was shaky.

She trailed off, and James knew she was extremely upset. He let her regain her composure. Antonia was never quite the emotional type.

Finally able to talk, she whispered, "Someone tried to kill my sister."

Not much, if anything, scared James. Nothing really rattled his cage. He'd been through and done so many dreadful things over the years, but to bad people, not that it justified some of the things he'd done, but it was always for the greater good in one way or another. But nothing ever hit this close to home.

He was fully aware that he needed to be calm for Antonia. He needed to nurture her and be there for her. There was no way he could tell her that everything was going to be OK, because at this moment, he knew it was not.

He reached out to touch her hand and she grasped it like it was her last lifeline. "We need to go back to Fitz."

Chapter 88

James pulled up in front of Fitz's home and Antonia was out of the car before he even had it in park.

"Wait, wait, maybe we shouldn't tell him. What if Carl already told him? What if Carl is responsible?" James called after her.

Antonia's head was swimming. "How can you possibly say that?"

"Well, why wouldn't Carl have told him? And if he did, why wouldn't Fitz have told us?"

She stopped. "I hadn't thought of that."

"No, you hadn't, but that's OK. It's too close. We are too close to the awful things that we are capable of causing. We are never on this end of it."

Antonia's cell phone began blasting an awful old-timey ring tone and she jumped back into the car. He held one of her hands while she dug the phone out of her purse with the other. She fumbled with it a few times and finally looked at the screen. She showed it to James. Anthony's name, appearing larger than life, was written across it.

She pushed the green button to answer the phone. "You rotten son of a bitch. What the hell did you do? What were you thinking? How many goons do you still have on your payroll? What kind of sick bastard does that to their own daughter?"

James was staring at her, pleased that she was angry. She was much more aware and on her game when she was angry.

James couldn't hear anything on the other end of the phone. He nodded his head in question at Antonia, and she put Anthony on speaker.

Then, timid and in some odd, old man fashion, Anthony asked, "Dear, what are you talking about? What is the matter? Did something happen to Elizabeth? What's going on?"

"You smug bastard!" she spat at the phone. "Don't you dare tell me that you don't know what I am talking about." There was a knock on the car window and Antonia nearly jumped through the sunroof. Fitz was standing outside of the car, yelling, "Is everything alright?" He didn't realize she was on the phone.

Antonia opened the door so Fitz could see what was happening. James gave her a straight face with a raised eyebrow. She knew there was no way to hide it all from Fitz now.

"Why the hell are you calling me?" she said.

"I called to tell you that I am sorry for everything that I've done in the past. I've been doing some serious soul-searching and I know you won't believe a word I'm saying, and that's OK because I don't expect you to. I'm not getting any younger, though, and I need to make things right with the people who I should have loved enough and held dear to me over the years."

The three of them were baffled. They looked from one to the other in sheer disbelief, waiting for him to burst out laughing and call them poor, disgusting idiots for believing him. But those words never came.

"Are you still there?" Anthony asked.

"Uh, yeah, what? I mean, I don't . . ." She could not find the words to articulate what she was feeling, what she wanted to say to him.

She tried again. "OK, let's back up."

"No, please let me finish. I'll be just a moment and then you can start screaming at me again." Antonia felt a very strange and unwelcome guilt towards him for the way she was yelling at him.

"Have you spoken to your sister lately?" Her blood started to boil. "I called that good for nothing Carl to see if he was with her, and he's not answering. I really want to talk to her. I need to make things right."

Antonia was beyond stunned. She was speechless.

James stepped in. "Anthony, we just spoke with Carl, and it appears that someone tried to poison Elizabeth."

Anthony, very soberly, almost whispered, while Fitz screamed, "WHAT?!" in unison.

Chapter 89

When Josie's heart rate finally slowed down after the voicemail, she began to think she should have the same attitude towards this as Marco did. There was no reason why she should not be moving on with her life. Anthony was taking over again. She swore to herself she would never let this happen.

She went to find Marco to tell him about the voicemail.

"So, that was Anthony who called."

"Wait, what? He called you? What did he say?"

"He said that he wanted me to call him back, but if I didn't, he understood. He was only calling to say he was sorry for everything. Something about him getting old and wanting to make right with the people that he has hurt through the years."

Marco sat back in Josie's desk chair. He ran his hands through his thick black hair. He kept getting sucked back into the drama. He rolled his eyes and puffed out, "Well, are you calling him back?"

It was very obvious to Josie that Marco was still annoyed by it all. "No, I don't think I am. I'm just going to let it go. He said what he needed to say, and assumed that I wasn't going to call him back, so I'm done."

Marco smiled at her and grabbed her hand. He pulled her onto his lap. He looked deep into her eyes and said, "I'm really glad to hear you say that. I want to focus on us. Also, you might tell me to go pound sand, but I noticed you haven't even looked at a computer in days. Shouldn't you be writing?"

Josie was briefly annoyed by his observation, but realized that he was right. She loved being a writer, and all of this had her so frazzled that she hadn't even looked at her latest novel. Her agent called her twice, and Josie never called her back. Even so, something was still nagging at Josie. She knew it was time to just move on and forget about Anthony. When she heard the rest of Anthony's voicemail, her shoulders became much less tense and her mind started to become far clearer. She felt like this was the closure she had been longing for, for quite some time.

"Uh, hello? You still with me?" Marco said.

Josie snapped out of her thoughts and laughed at Marco. "Yes. I have been completely wrapped up in Anthony. Now that I sit down and think about it, this was all just bringing up everything from the past. Nothing going on now really has anything to do with me. His feeble apology doesn't make what he did OK, but at least he's showing some remorse."

"That's the spirit!"

"That's awful. You sound like an old man." Josie laughed. "I think John called. I need to call him back, I guess. See what he wants."

"OK, I'll be right here. I don't have too much work to do, but I would like to get this one project done today."

"I'll be back."

Josie headed back into the kitchen, something still eating at her. She wasn't quite settled. She felt much better when she was talking to Marco, but now that she was in the other room and preparing to call John, she felt anxious again.

She listened to John's voicemail, asking that she call him back as soon as she could.

She texted him first to see if he could talk, and her phone began to ring.

"John." She stabbed at the phone and barked out his name. "What's up? Did you find something?"

"I just got a call from Anthony—"

"Saying that he wanted to apologize for everything he's done because he's getting old and whatever else?" Josie interrupted.

"Yes, I'm guessing you got the same call?"

"I did, but he left it on my voicemail. He said he assumed I wouldn't call him back, so he just said everything he needed to in the message."

There was silence on the other end.

"You there, John?"

"Yes. Is that all he said?"

Josie's stomach turned a little. This couldn't be good. She didn't want to know what that meant.

"Yep, that's all he said. Why? Did he say something else to you?"

John was quiet again, and now Josie's heart rate was back up where it didn't belong.

"After his apology and the awkward pleasantries, he said it was out of his hands now. He paused, said 'I'm afraid it's not over,' and then hung up."

Josie was doing her best not to freak out. Was that a threat? Did it even have anything to do with her?

"What on earth does that mean, John?"

"I don't know, but Jimmy got the same ridiculous voicemail, so he's coming into the city tonight and he and I are going to go over there tomorrow. He needs closure, and he needs to know that his family is safe. Not just Carmine; he thinks this goes way deeper than that."

"I just told Marco that I was done with this whole thing, but maybe I'm not. I want to go with you."

"That's not a good idea, Josie. I don't want you anywhere near that man. Sorry or not, this is obviously not over."

"If I can convince Marco to go with me, then maybe he and I can just stay nearby instead of actually coming up there with you and Jimmy."

This wasn't a question. She wasn't asking John for permission, she was telling him this was what she was going to do. He didn't have a say.

"Convince me of what?" Marco said, startling Josie so badly she jumped.

"Gotta go, John." She hung up and told Marco what she just heard from John about the apparent threat from Anthony.

Marco's shoulders slumped and he sighed.

Chapter 90

Jimmy poured himself a scotch. He had skipped dinner. There was no way he could eat now. After his twilight zone-esque conversation with Anthony, he had called John. Thankfully, John agreed to go over to Anthony's.

He couldn't help replaying the conversation with Anthony in his mind. It was just all so surreal. He was reminiscing about things that Jimmy knew nothing about. Some things he couldn't care less about, but others piqued his interest.

Anthony's life was at the peak of hideousness before Jimmy was even born. He was grateful that he wasn't dragged into that kind of life. Even if his parents were somehow involved, he and his brothers never knew. Never even suspected.

Now he was wondering why his mother had been so standoffish lately. Every time he called her, she was short and tried to hurry him off the phone. He wondered what was happening there. Even more confusing was that she always seemed to be with his father these days. What was that about?

He debated whether or not he should call Carmine and give him a heads-up that he and John were going to Anthony's tomorrow. He didn't want to catch him off guard. Then again, he didn't really trust that Carmine wouldn't tell Anthony.

He swirled the scotch around in his glass, watching it roll around the ice cubes. This used to be a soothing action for him, but it wasn't working like it should. He was on edge. Worried about his family. Worried about what Anthony was still capable of doing to them. It sounded like someone else was running the show, but who? More importantly, why?

He picked up his phone to call Carmine.

Carmine answered, but didn't even say Jimmy's name. He just started talking. Jimmy could barely keep up.

"Carmine, slow down. What are you talking about?"

"Jimmy, look. You're a great little brother and should continue pursuing your dreams. I'm sorry for being such a shit throughout our lives together," Carmine said quickly.

Jimmy thought he'd been drinking; there was something very odd in his voice. Almost sorrowful. Remorseful. *What was up with him and Anthony?* Jimmy thought.

Carmine said goodbye, his tone sounding so final, despite Jimmy saying he'd be over there tomorrow.

Jimmy drained his glass, deciding to end this day and just head to bed.

Chapter 91

Fitz walked into his living room to join James and Antonia. He had just spoken with his brother Joey, who was also in law enforcement. Joey was now following up to see if he could get any information on their mother, Elizabeth. He would also let Joey deal with Carl. Fitz was in no mood for him right now.

"I don't want to be insensitive at all, but I'm guessing this does not affect tomorrow, correct?" Antonia asked.

"No, and if anything, this confirms it's the right thing that we're doing, for sure." Fitz was reeling from the conversation that Antonia had with Carl and now the new information they had from Anthony. He was already stressed about Anthony, and now he had the added stress from his mother on top of it all. She was so far away, and his father was totally useless.

"We still have the matter of the information that John provided about the memory loss medication. Is it possible that this could be the same thing, and it's having this effect on her?" Antonia asked, completely ignorant of medicine.

"Joey is on it. I told him everything. We have to focus on what is going on here, and Joey can take care of what's happening across the ocean."

Antonia looked at James, raising her eyebrows and shrugging her shoulders. James put his hand on hers and said, "Let them figure it out for now. Let's get tomorrow over with."

Chapter 92

Josie rolled over and found Marco's hand to hold as she fully woke up. Her eyelids were heavy, and she desperately wanted to fall back asleep. She stretched and tried to open her eyes but the sunlight coming in through the floor-to-ceiling window was too bright.

She cursed herself for forgetting to close the curtains before they fell asleep. And she couldn't shake the anxiety she felt. She had no idea what was bothering her so much in her sleepy haze.

She could hear Marco breathing heavily, but she wasn't sure if it was sleepy breathing or if it was just waking up breathing. She leaned towards waking up breathing, so she decided to whisper his name.

"Marco? Are you awake?"

He wasn't sure if he wanted to answer her or not. He stayed quiet until she whispered his name again.

"Marco?"

He finally gave into her question and rolled over towards her to confirm that he was awake. "Shh. No, I'm still sleeping." He smiled, eyes still closed. He did not want to be awake.

Josie rolled closer to him, closing her eyes, too. She didn't want to get out of bed. It was warm and cozy, and of course Marco was there. She was very careful with her choice of words. She didn't want to come right out and say, "Hey, let's go over to Anthony's just to make sure he doesn't kill Carmine and Lexi."

"Hey, beautiful, come over here." He moved his arm with a very slight jerk, so her head fell smoothly into his shoulder and rolled onto his chest. He chuckled. "Fits like a glove."

Josie was happy. She couldn't think of anywhere else she would rather be. She glanced at the clock and noticed that it was almost 9 AM. She sat up swiftly. "Holy cow! Did you see the time?"

"Do you have somewhere you need to be?" Marco asked, eyebrow raised.

She bit her lip. She didn't *have* to be anywhere, but she thought she should be. She smiled and crawled back toward Marco. "No, I don't, but I never sleep this late."

"Well then, what are you all aggravated about?"

She calmed down a bit and realized there was no reason at all for her to be riled up. "Nothing, I guess." Just as she was reassuring Marco that nothing was on her mind, her phone vibrated on the nightstand.

She pulled herself away from Marco to see who was texting her. "It's John," she said.

"What could he possibly want now?"

Josie knew exactly what he wanted, but she didn't want to bring it up to Marco. Even though she believed she ended the evening with Marco understanding that it would be a good idea to go over to Anthony's to see what was happening, she wanted to leave it up to him to bring it up this morning.

"Josie, if you want to go to Anthony's today, then I'll go with you. John can come, too," Marco said. He saw her brow furrow and her eyes squint. He'd known her long enough to know that she didn't need permission from anyone to do what she wanted to do. If she was going to do it, she was going to do it, and no one was going to tell her otherwise.

"OK, OK, stop yelling at me," Marco teased.

Josie laughed.

She texted John to find out what would be the best time for them to meet up and head over to Anthony's. They could be ready by 11 AM. Marco just needed to finish up a few things for work and John could meet them at her building.

Marco got up, kissed Josie on the forehead, and headed to the bathroom for a shower.

Josie looked at Marco with obvious stars in her eyes. She thought this mess would have thrown her life off the tracks, but her movie launch was amazing, and she was off to a great start with the second novel, and Marco was back in her life. Even though her life was right where she wanted it to be, the awful feeling she had about Anthony just kept eating at her thoughts. She started chewing at the small piece of skin hanging from her thumb.

Her phone began vibrating again. She was so caught up in her thoughts that it made her jump. She leaned over to grab it off the nightstand and saw that it was from Mrs. P.

Mrs. P: Do not worry about Anthony. Please don't read into his apologies. They are empty and you don't need to worry.

She was annoyed. Mrs. P pretty much confirmed, in her own twisted way, that something serious was going to go down, and Josie knew that it was coming pretty quick.

The second Marco stepped out of the shower, she told him about the text message. "Josie, I doubted your anxiety about this, and I'm sorry." He was being playful so as to not alarm Josie, but she knew exactly what he was doing, and now she knew he was alarmed as well. She knew his mother was telling them to mind their own business and stay out of the family secrets.

Josie sighed. "I'm jumping in the shower, and then we can grab a quick breakfast. Then John will be here and we can head over to Anthony's."

"Yes, ma'am." Marco saluted Josie.

She laughed, then abruptly became very serious. "This is no time for screwing around. We need to put on our game faces."

Chapter 93

Antonia was ready for the day. She had never been more ready for anything in her life. This would close one chapter for sure, but she was fully aware that it could open a whole new book. It seemed to already be starting with Elizabeth.

She spoke with Carl again late last night, and it pretty much confirmed that the medication that Elizabeth was taking was very high dose of anti-depressant. Carl had no idea why, but the doctor said it could definitely be causing her memory issues. Since she was never properly diagnosed with early onset Alzheimer's Disease, the doctor could not say for sure what was happening. They were going to run more tests in the days to come after she had rested and was a little stronger.

However someone, most likely the caregiver that was with her, definitely tried to poison her sister. Antonia believed it was Anthony, although his reaction on the phone when he found out seemed pretty genuine. She was not going to assume until she has more information. She was waiting on that from Fitz.

She heard a car pull up outside. It must be James. She could hear the door open, and James's whistling filled the house. "You ready for this today?"

"Ready as I'm going to be." She turned her head away from him. She didn't want him to see her face. She was not sure if she could hide the expression of slight sadness that she was feeling. There was piece to this puzzle that she hadn't been able to tell him. She knew she should tell him so that he wasn't completely stunned, but James seemed so checked out at this point that he may not even care, in the end. Still, she felt awful for keeping it from him. If they had any chance of having a future together, she should probably tell him.

She turned back to him and saw that he brought bagels for breakfast. She poured him a cup of coffee.

"We have plenty of time to eat and get over there," he reassured her.

"Yes, we do." She sat down with him at the table. She was distant, and she knew he could sense it. She made some small talk to distract him.

"I spoke with Carl last night. Elizabeth is doing fine and she's resting. He still has no idea who could have done this to her."

"You're not surprised, are you? Joey will figure it out and then we will have something else to worry about." He gave her a sideways smile. "You didn't really think this was over, did you?" He put his hand on hers to comfort her as best he could.

"No, I suppose you're right."

They sat in silence while they ate their bagels and drank their coffee. Her mind was reeling. There was so much that she wanted to say to him. So many things that she wanted to share with him, but she didn't want to open up until she knew they were getting back together. She knew they should be talking about that, but she didn't want to discuss it until this was over, and it looked like it might not be over anytime soon. Maybe she could make an exception. Once today was over, maybe they could talk.

"It looks like there is something seriously on your mind. Do you want to talk about it?" James hoped that she would open up. He knew there wasn't much of a chance—that was just how she was—but he still hoped.

"There is actually something that I need to tell you." As soon as the words spilled out of her mouth, she heard the tone for a text message on her phone. It was a message from Fitz. She picked up the phone to show James.

Fitz: Let's do this.

"Sooner than we thought, but we are ready as we'll ever be. Was there something you wanted to talk to me about?" James said.

She briefly considered just blowing it off. He would know soon enough. But she knew for certain that was not the right way to handle it. She needed to face the music. "Oh yes, let's sit down again."

"Should I be worried?"

Awkwardly, she smiled, and he sat down with her.

"OK, let's hear it."

Chapter 94

Josie texted John to see how close he was to her building. She was getting nervous, but she was unsure why.

She was pacing, waiting for a text from John. She was getting impatient.

"Josie, why do you think this is eating at you so badly?"

She was agitated that he was asking. She did, however, understand why. Marco knew how much she despised Anthony, so the pieces were not adding up for how she was feeling. She was acting a little crazy, but it just came down to Carmine.

"I know we've discussed this already, and I was still a little shaky as to what I was thinking. When it comes right down to it, Anthony has hurt my parents, me, John, to an extent, and now Carmine. Not to mention your family. How many more people is he going to hurt?"

"I get what you are saying, but forgive me if my lying, cheating, sad sack of shit for a brother isn't at the forefront of my concern these days."

"I totally understand, Marco. I just . . . Carmine and I were so close. I felt, at one point in time, that he would have done anything for me. He was a true friend. As crazy as that sounds, I really feel that it's true," Josie said.

"I believe that he did what he did with Lexi because he couldn't get you away from me."

"Marco! How can you say that?"

"Because he always had feelings for you, and please don't take this the wrong way, but you were always too buried in your own world to notice."

She wanted to lash out so badly at Marco for suggesting that Carmine had feelings for her, but deep inside, she knew it was true. She valued her and Carmine's relationship so much that she realized that she was just trying to make excuses to avoid dealing with his feelings.

"As much as I want to argue, I know you're right. It just keeps coming back into my head and I can't shake it," she said.

"What can't you shake?"

"That Carmine moved on to Lexi because he couldn't have me."

"Josie, there is no way for me to figure out why Carmine did what he did with Lexi, but I can say that he still made the decision to do what he did. Whatever his motivation, he is the one that betrayed me." Josie buried her face in Marco's chest. It was just all too much to think about.

He pulled her head off his chest to look into her eyes. "I wasn't going to say anything, but I feel like I need to. You're not going to make me go in there, are you?" He smirked to lighten the mood. The last thing he wanted was Josie taking the blame for Carmine's betrayal.

She had not thought past getting to the front of Anthony's building, never mind deciding if she was going to go in there or not. Maybe she would just send John in. If he was willing.

At this moment, she realized how ridiculous she was acting. Again. What was she going to do? Just walk right in there and say, "Hey, leave him alone, you big bully?" She clearly was not thinking any of this through. John had no plan either.

"Well, now that you asked me that, I realized how stupid I really am being. No, I would never expect you to go in there, and honestly, I don't even know if I would go in there. Not by myself, anyway."

She and Marco stared at one another. Neither of them had anything else to say.

She heard the buzz from downstairs that meant John had arrived. She buzzed back, letting him know they would be right down.

Chapter 95

Fitz and his partner reviewed the steps multiple times. They knew what their role was in the process and when each of them needed to step in.

They had both done this sort of thing countless times; it should be like clockwork. They had never had it hit this close to home before. Although Fitz did not grow up with Anthony in his life, Fitz's mother was now involved in this, and she did grow up with him in her life.

There were still so many things to be hashed out and talked about. Maybe this was just the beginning, but Fitz shuddered at the thought of what the future could possibly hold.

He hopped in his car to head over to Anthony's when his brother called him.

"Hey, Joey! What's happening? Do you have more info on Mom?"

The silence on the other end told Fitz that whatever it was, it wasn't good.

"We were able to track down the woman. Dear old Dad identified her as the woman who tried to poison Mom."

"That's great!"

"Well, it would be great if she wasn't swearing that it was Dad who tried to hire her to kill Mom."

Now the silence was on Fitz's end. He had no idea what to say. She had to be lying. His father certainly wasn't his most favorite person on earth, but he loved their mother. Fitz just could not believe that he would do that to her.

"Well, this is obviously not true. I really don't think so, anyway. There is no way of actually knowing the truth at this point, but I just can't bring myself to believe it."

Fitz's head felt like it was going to burst. He was so wrapped up in the events of today that this was the last thing he wanted to deal with. He was so thankful for Joey. For many more reasons than this, but today it was really a blessing to have him in his life and definitely in his corner.

"Listen, I just called to give you the latest update. I know this will fall on deaf ears because you are my brother and we share a brain, but I got this for today. You need to focus on the rest of your day and then we will tackle this. Maybe Anthony will have some information that will be helpful. I'm sure he would never want anything to happen to Mom."

"OK, thanks, bro. I'll call you when this is all over today, and you can give me another update, I hope."

"You got it, bro. Be safe today, please."

"My middle name is Safe."

Joey could hear Fitz smiling on the other end. A big toothy grin. "Yeah." Joey laughed. "That's what I'm afraid of."

"I can't afford to screw this one up. I'll be on my best behavior."

"I never question your ability to do the job. I question that daredevil that sits on your shoulder, urging you to risk everything in the moment," Joey said.

Fitz laughed. "Not this time. There is too much at stake. I will not make a mess out of this one."

Not exactly convinced, Joey said, "Well, call me later, then."

Joey hung up and Fitz was left with his own thoughts. He just needed to shake all that out of his head for now and focus on Anthony.

Fitz pulled up in front of Anthony's building. It was still early enough for the street to be quiet.

His palms were beginning to sweat. He was frustrated by this, as he normally never had an issue with this type of situation. He was usually very calm. As he rolled around the options of why he would be so nervous, the obvious answer was the chance that Anthony could pull something to explode the whole case.

He thought he covered all options of what Anthony was capable of, so now all he could do was hope that his hard work and preparation would pay off. Not every agent had a crazy aunt with inside leads to help him out. He smirked. He knew Antonia wanted this to be over as quickly as he did. Today, anyway.

His partner was close by, and the building was surrounded. There was no way Anthony was getting out before they got to him.

Fitz's partner would deal with Carmine and Lexi. There was not much they could hold them on, but they were going to bring them in for questioning. They didn't suspect that Carmine would incriminate Anthony or give them anything, but it was worth a shot. Fitz had a few things on Carmine, so maybe that would help.

Fitz strolled across the street towards the building, Mr. Altieri's briefcase full of incriminating evidence in hand, when he heard a noise. He stopped when he got to the sidewalk and listened closely. The sound was getting much clearer. It was unmistakable. The sirens were blaring through the city, and most of his worry was shedding away. He was thankful that he wasn't doing this alone.

Chapter 96

Jackie was pacing through the house like a crazy woman. She knew what was happening today. At least, she thought she did. As ruthless as she believed her mother-in-law to be, Mrs. Paretti had at least been keeping her in the loop.

Mrs. P kept insisting that everything would be fine after today, but she didn't explain how, and Jackie couldn't completely understand how that would be possible. She thought the worst might be yet to come.

The kids were in school today, so she had all day to stress and worry.

Her phone was in her pocket and when it rang, she cried, "Oh God!" She pulled the phone out of her pocket and checked to see who was calling before she answered it. Her stomach did a sickening tumble, and she felt like she was going to be throw up. She let it go to voicemail.

Fighting off a panic attack, Jackie practiced her breathing, calming herself down with some techniques she had gotten from her doctor. Her phone rang again, and she answered reluctantly.

"What do you want?" Surprisingly, she was becoming increasing angrier. She realized that she wasn't having a panic attack. It was the adrenaline from her anger. She didn't think she had ever been this angry before.

"I'm sorry, Jackie. I'm truly sorry. I don't expect you to forgive the horrible things I've done to our family, but I need you to know that I know I'm a total ass, and every one of our issues is my fault. I loved you once. I truly did, and I hope you live a wonderful life. You are already a wonderful mother and you deserve to be happy and loved properly." Carmine paused, and Jackie wanted to speak, but couldn't. He started speaking again and she heard his voice catch, "Please tell the kids that their daddy loves them, and try not to tell them how much of a bastard I am." The call ended, and the haunting voice was gone.

Jackie was left trembling, tears streaming down her face. Carmine's voice and apologies were beyond unexpected. She considered calling him back to scream at him and tell him what a horrible father, husband, brother, and son he was. She leaned against the kitchen island and put the phone back in her pocket. She slid down to the floor in a sad heap, put her face in her hands, and sobbed.

Lexi walked through the apartment to find Carmine and saw that he had just been on the phone. He was looking out the windows, his back to her. She walked up behind him and put her arms around him.

By the movement of his ribcage, she could feel his breathing was labored. Almost like he had been crying.

"Hey, what's the matter?"

He didn't answer her. He was repulsed by her touch, but he also did not want her to let go. He needed the comfort.

"You're not getting soft on me, are you?" Lexi said.

"Lexi." He took her hand and guided her to the love seat in the bedroom. "I know we've had this conversation many times, but I don't think you've really heard me at all."

Her brow furrowed. "What are you talking about?"

He was going to have to come right out and say it. He was at a loss as to where to even begin. He figured he would just rip off the metaphorical bandage. "From the way you have been acting, I'm guessing you don't fully understand what is going to happen to us?" He posed it as a question, giving her time to answer.

Lexi pulled away from him.

"What do you mean, Carmine? I gave my whole self to you. I cheated on your brother with you! I was a part, a small part, but a part nonetheless, of pushing your family further apart. I hope you're not saying what I think you're saying."

He knew exactly what was coming over him, but he dared not show Lexi. "Sadly, I'm afraid this is it for us. It's the end of us."

She smacked him across the face. Realizing in that moment that she couldn't leave the apartment, she stormed out of the room.

Carmine was shocked and sad. She never saw it coming.

Chapter 97

Antonia was not able to tell James what was on her mind. Instead, she gave him some bogus information that was insignificant to what they were doing today. He knew she was lying, but he didn't want to press her. He certainly didn't want to fight with her. Definitely not today.

They had made their way over to Anthony's building and were now parked not too far away. They were waiting for everything to unfold. They watched Fitz walk across the street.

They could hear the sound of sirens in the distance. Antonia looked towards Fitz, and she motioned that they were on their way over. Fitz gave her the option of going in or staying outside. He said she could decide whenever she wanted. He gave her the direct contact of his partner, so if or when she decided to go in, she just had to reach out.

James reached across the car to touch her hand. This was always his way of comforting her. This was usually the only type of physical comfort that she would accept. She squeezed his hand back.

As the sirens get closer, James and Antonia could see Fitz's guys moving into the building, dressed completely in black, in full protective gear. "The city cops must be backup, or a diversion," James noticed. "What a commotion for this sad sack of a man."

Antonia laughed at James's nonchalant, sarcastic comment.

Fitz told them specifically where to park so they didn't get caught up in the police barricade or tape. This way, if they wanted to leave and go back, they could. No one knew how long it would take, or what was going to happen.

They were going to stay put for now.

Antonia watched Fitz open the giant, and what seemed to be heavy, front door to Anthony's building. His partner would be entering from an Exit Only door on the other side of the building.

"Listen, I need to tell you something," Antonia said without looking directly at James.

"It's about time. I let it go before because I knew you would circle back to it."

She began speaking very softly. "I'm sorry, can you repeat that?" James couldn't hear what she was telling him. She spoke again, repeating what she said. This time, he heard what she said, loud and clear. Words could not express his anger.

Chapter 98

Carmine was prepared for a reaction, this reaction, so he let her go cool down and blow off some steam. He busied himself with a few more things that he needed to take care of before he went out to find Lexi.

He fired off a few emails and sent a few text messages. He sent one to his mother, which was the hardest to write, and he sent another one to his father. It was short and sweet, but apologetic.

There was a small kitchenette in his bedroom, which Anthony put in when Carmine ended up at his place. It was more of a mini wet bar, but Carmine used it as a multipurpose area. He reached into the cabinet and grabbed two tumblers and filled them with ice. Then he poured two shots of a very expensive bourbon for himself and two shots of Crown Royal Peach for Lexi.

He pulled a tissue out of his pocket with two pills. He took a deep breath and exhaled. He knew how badly this really sucked, but he also knew this was something that needed to be done.

He crushed both pills and dropped equal parts into each glass. He stirred them both, then headed out to find Lexi.

She was sitting with Anthony in the living room, still in tears.

Carmine walked up to her, both eyes slightly welling with tears, and handed her a glass. "Come on," he said. "Let's talk. I'm willing to talk for as long as you want, about everything."

There was a knock at the door as Carmine and Lexi walked back to their room. Anthony stood up to get it.

They got to their room, and Carmine closed the bedroom door, leaving them isolated from whatever might be happening in the living room.

Lexi was still crying, "Just give me a minute to calm down, if I even can."

He tapped the lip of her glass. "This will help." She smiled at him, oddly calm.

He did not drink out of his glass until she did.

She could smell the peach in the glass, anticipating the warmth that would flow through her body once she took a sip.

"I don't want to do this," she whispered, and for a moment, Carmine thought she finally understood how it would end.

"It will all be OK. I promise." This time, Carmine didn't urge her to take a sip. He wanted her to do it on her own.

They sat in silence again for a minute or two. "I think I am calm enough to talk now," Lexi said, and took a gulp of her drink, almost half of what was in her glass. Carmine tried not to look surprised. He was expecting her to take only a sip. Now it would be faster than he thought, but that was probably for the best.

"Carmine, I deeply care for you. I know how horrible of a person I can be at times, and how selfish I can be, but I believe I truly love you. I know my selfishness is what got us in this mess to begin with, and there is a part of me that is sorry for that, but the selfish part of me believes that we belong together."

Carmine swallowed hard but didn't say anything. She eyed him cautiously. He could feel the inside of his stomach clench as he fought a dramatic sob.

At his silence, she drained her glass, and Carmine quickly took a giant gulp of his as well.

"Carmine, I thought you would say something. I'm not asching fro uu ta prfsss . . ." Her words were slurring now, and he downed the rest of his drink. Carmine picked her up in his arms and placed her on the bed with him. He looked right into her eyes. "Lexi, I love you with all my heart. You are the only woman I have ever truly loved."

He could tell by her eyes and her contorted mouth that she had realized what was happening and he said, "I'll see you soon, my love."

Chapter 99

The team was armed and ready in the stairwell, not far from Anthony's door. They were directly connected to Fitz and his partner via radio. They would enter with force as soon as they had word to do so from either one.

Fitz assumed when Anthony realized it was him at the door, they would have to force their way in. He knocked and could hear someone walking. There was a brief hesitation on the other side of the door, and Fitz put his hand on his radio. Fitz hoped his bureau windbreaker would be enough to hide the Kevlar vest he wore, just in case Anthony decided to make this harder than it needed to be and fire a weapon. Fitz was ready for whatever might come next.

Only a few seconds later, the door swung open and Anthony stood in the doorway.

Anthony firmly brought his hands together in a giant clap. He was smiling from ear to ear, like a sweet grandpa being visited by his grandchildren.

Fitz was very taken aback by this. Whatever he was expecting, it wasn't this. He wasn't going to let his guard down, though.

"Son, come in, come in." Anthony closed the door behind Fitz, too quick for him. Anthony gave Fitz a one-armed hug and, feeling the vest underneath his jacket, quickly pulled away from him. With genuine concern, Anthony said, "What is this? What's going on?"

Fitz was beyond flabbergasted at Anthony's actions. "I'm not sure why you thought I would be visiting you for fun. Did you think this was a reconciliation visit? Especially after I think you tried to poison my mother. Your own daughter, for God's sake!"

Anthony was quiet. He searched for clarity. Searched for the right words to say. *Why is Fitz really here? It can't be because of Elizabeth. Not with a bulletproof vest on, anyway.*

"What are you doing here?"

"Let's sit down somewhere. I have some things to show you." Fitz motioned at the table for Anthony to sit down.

Anthony quickly reviewed his escape plan, just in case. If things went downhill, Anthony had a secret exit in the apartment that he could sneak out of. Fitz had anticipated that this might be the case, and he made sure the apartment was surrounded. No way in and no way out.

Anthony led Fitz to the dining area so they could sit at the table. Fitz flung the briefcase on the table. "I'm sure you don't know what's in this. I don't want to hear a word out of your mouth, unless of course it will get you in even more trouble. Then, I'm all for it."

Anthony was quiet. He'd been involved in enough bad things for as long as he could remember that he knew not to say a word that would incriminate him.

Fitz opened the briefcase to uncover several old mini cassette tapes, bank statements, and a handwritten journal. The journal documented each time Anthony forced Joe to give him money, as well as dollar amounts that Anthony forced him to launder. Joe had all the proof that Fitz needed.

"I don't need to explain what you are looking at here. You are going away for a very long time. There are sixteen briefcases filled with just as much incriminating evidence as this one, from multiple stores you pulled this crap with, right around the same time."

"Why now? Why now is this all coming about? This was years ago," Anthony said.

"Let's just say that no one knows why people choose to do the things that they do. And if I find out you had anything to do with my mother's poisoning, you will regret every misstep through your career in organized crime."

"The situation with your mother is complicated, as I stated to you and your aunt on the phone. It's complicated, but I didn't try to kill her. I was confused as to why that's what you all kept going on about. What happened?"

Fitz's stomach clenched. "What are you talking about?"

"Most situations like those our family creates are bigger than what they seem on the surface."

Fitz shuddered. They were nothing alike.

"I'm nothing like you, old man, so don't say 'Our family,' as if I'm just like the rest of you. Neither is Joey, so don't rope us into this."

Anthony shrugged.

Fitz was thrown slightly off his game, but regrouped quickly as he pulled out his cuffs and read Anthony his rights.

Anthony was ridiculously cooperative. Fitz was pleased, but wary all the same. Fitz sent his partner a message—"Come in, but no need to break down the door."

Once his partner was in the apartment, Fitz asked Anthony, "Where are Carmine and Lexi?"

"Back in his room, I assume. They haven't left the apartment since they arrived."

Fitz and his partner glanced at one another.

Anthony was cuffed at the kitchen table, so Fitz and his partner left him and hurried down to Carmine's room.

Fitz knocked. "Carmine, open up!" Nothing. Fitz put his ear up to the door to see if he could hear anything, but again, nothing.

Fitz wound up to kick the door and he heard Anthony yell, "What's going on back there?" He wanted to tell the old man to zip it, but he wound back up and kicked the door down. As he and his partner entered the room, they saw Carmine and Lexi lying on the bed, motionless.

"Carmine?" Fitz said, looking around the room. He saw the glasses, and his hand moved to his mouth. He knew instantly what they'd done.

Fitz rushed over to them. He put his fingers to Carmine's neck to feel for a pulse. He looked at his partner and shook his head. He moved onto Lexi for the same thing and shook his head again. "Call downstairs, hurry."

Chapter 100

Josie and Marco met John downstairs.

"Jimmy was coming, but decided against it at the last minute. Something about not wanting to deal with the chaos," John said

Marco shook his head, but held back his comment.

"Are we taking a cab over there, or do you want to walk?" asked Josie.

"It's probably better if we walk. It will give us some time to figure things out," John suggested.

Against Marco's better judgment, he said, "Why did Jimmy really decide not to come?"

"He said this was all started to consume his every thought, and he wanted to try to move on. He thought we were crazy for doing this and there was nothing else he had to say to Carmine."

"I don't blame him." Marco slowly moved his gaze towards Josie.

John and Marco spent the next fifteen minutes teasing Josie for dragging them into a nightmare, as it surely would be one.

"Very funny!" Josie teased back.

"Let's be honest here, Josie, this was not a good idea after all," mused John. They were all trying to keep the moment relaxed.

"This was practically your idea, John. Do not blame me for being on board."

While John and Josie were picking on one another, Marco looked up ahead and saw enough cop cars and ambulance lights to practically light up the whole city.

"What the . . ." Marco put his arms in front of Josie and John to stop them from walking. They both finally looked up to see the chaos.

"Oh my God!" yelled Josie. "What is happening?"

"See, I told you something was going on," said John, laughing. Josie and Marco rolled their eyes at him.

"Whatever is happening, it looks like we are right on time," blurted out Marco.

"Or maybe we are too late," Josie whispered.

They slowly made their way closer, shocked at what they saw.

They were about a block away when they ran into Mr. and Mrs. P.

"Mom? Dad? What are you guys doing here?" Marco looked from his mother to his father. Mrs. P looked flustered, but still in control, while Mr. P looked completely bewildered. Marco was worried. He had never seen his dad like this.

The group walked closer to Anthony's building together. Josie put her hand to her mouth as two bodies were rolled out of the building, covered in sheets. She reached for Marco, who was right behind her. "Marco!" He put his arm around her and laid a hand on John's shoulder. Marco was hoping that John didn't try to go running in there. He thought he had more restraint than that.

Marco was looking around slowly, as if time had stopped. He knew full well who was under those sheets. He knew the reality of it all would not sink in until the shock wore off. He searched for his parents; they weren't far behind. His father's distance from his mother told him that his father knew his mother was responsible for this. He needed to let them sort that out. He needed to be right here for Josie, and reluctantly, John.

Josie turned around and buried her face into Marco's shoulder. She was not crying, but she didn't want to watch any longer.

They remained standing there, and only a few moments later, Anthony was walked out in handcuffs.

John and Marco glanced at each other. "He didn't kill them?" John fired his question to Marco. It was rhetorical, of course, but by the look on Marco's face, he knew they were both thinking the same thing.

"No, I highly doubt it. Although we don't have any reason to think he didn't, or that he did," Marco said

Antonia was watching intently as the bodies were brought to the ambulances. She could see Carmine's hand hanging out over the gurney. She watched. She kept watching. She was waiting patiently for something.

She grabbed James's arm and bobbed her head over to the ambulance. "Just watch," she said. They watched together. He was angry at her still, but he followed her lead. Finally, they saw what they were looking for: Carmine's hand slowly slipping back up underneath the sheet.

Epilogue

Antonia knocked on the front door of a very beautiful home in the suburbs. James was with her. Antonia glanced around the neighborhood and saw a very out-of-place, bright-looking house. She rolled her eyes in distaste.

A very attractive brunette opened the door. "Can I help you?"

"You must be Angie! Hi, I'm, well, everyone calls me Mrs. P, but you can call me Antonia." She paused while Angie cocked her head; her eyes went wide with wonder. "I'm Elizabeth's sister."

Angie shuddered at Elizabeth's name. Fear spread through her whole body.

A man appeared behind Angie, as if for protection. Antonia eyed him up and raised an eyebrow.

Angie was dumbfounded. "I don't know where she is, so I can't help you." Angie began to close the door, but James slipped his foot into the door jam.

"I don't want to burden you with all the details, but Elizabeth was poisoned," Antonia said.

Angie couldn't help herself. "Oh my God, is she OK?" She didn't know why that slipped out of her mouth with such force. A minute ago, all she wanted was for this woman to leave her alone, and now she was sympathizing with her. "Who would do such an awful thing, and to an already sick woman?"

Antonia was filled with delight to see this fire and conviction in Angie. Maybe she could use her as an ally in the future. She raised an eyebrow at Angie. "Thank you for the concern," she said. "However, Elizabeth does not have early onset Alzheimer's."

"What?" Angie deadpanned.

"It turns out that our loving father was somehow giving her medication that was causing her to lose her short-term memory. When my sister saw a doctor, he told her she had Alzheimer's, but there were never any proper brain scans done, or anything official, and she just went with the diagnosis. She never got a second opinion. Until the poisoning, that is."

"But your father . . . I mean, what?"

"He's been here in the states, but Elizabeth never put two and two together until she was looking through her medication and found a bottle of pills that our father sent her. She must have mentioned, in one of the few conversations that they had, that she was struggling with pain in her shoulder from a car accident that she had been in years ago. He said he would send her something natural for the pain. I don't have the slightest idea why she trusted him, but she had been taking it and that's how she figured out where the memory loss was coming from. He kept sending a new bottle each month, and she kept talking it. Obviously, it was not for her shoulder." Antonia felt close to Angie in this moment. She hardly ever shared anything, and here she was dumping out a piece of her life to this stranger.

"Well, that's something, isn't it?" Angie was at a loss. She was getting deeper and deeper into this the longer Antonia was there, and she wanted nothing to do with it. "So, why are you here again?"

Antonia glanced at the strikingly handsome man standing behind Angie and sort of stumbled over her next words. "I know I've already overstayed my welcome,"—they still stood on the front porch—"but Carl, my sister's husband, said he had some business to tend to with a man named Jeff." Antonia rushed through Jeff's name, as it was obvious that if he lived there once, he didn't now.

Angie softened only slightly. "You mean my ex-husband?" The two women shared an awkward laugh, and Angie rolled her eyes.

James briefly thought Angie was referring to Carl, but then realized she was talking about Jeff.

"Did Jeff ever say anything that might indicate where Carl might be?" Antonia asked.

"Last we heard, they went back to Italy to live in Elizabeth's home over there so he could take care of her." Angie really didn't want to get involved, but she feared she was already roped into it. "Why? Are they in some kind of danger?"

"Our father has been arrested and is facing numerous charges for extortion, and, well, faking his own death."

Angie stood there, blinking at Antonia. "Faking his own death? Your father is alive? Oh yeah, you just said that about him sending those pills to Elizabeth." She felt the need to inquire deeper. It seemed like everyone was putting on a show. She was stewing over the fact that her ex-husband, Jeff, had subjected her to the nonsense that was this family. Now here, on her doorstep, was another layer of the family who had tracked her down, believing that she was privy to the whereabouts of the rest of the nutcases in this family. As angry as she was, she felt a strange and welcome connection to these lunatics.

Rolling her eyes, she said, "Well that's all I know, so if you will excuse me, I need to rest. I just had major surgery and I'm still recovering. Please leave me out of any of this going forward. I never had communication with Elizabeth. Ever." Angie turned around to find Derrick's open arms ready to help her back to the couch so she could rest.

"Thank you for the help. We're sorry to have bothered you. Oh, one more thing. Fitz says hello. He and his wife are expecting."

Angie's heart leapt for them. She was thrilled, but she wasn't going to show her enthusiasm. "Oh, that's nice. Tell him I said congrats."

Angie closed the door and Derrick took her in his arms. She looked up at him and said, "Something tells me this visit is just the beginning of a twisted and very surreal saga." Derrick held her tighter.

Angie shivered slightly in Derrick's arms. Anthony had visited her in the hospital the morning he was arrested, but she was not about to share that information with Antonia. That would be her little secret . . . for now, anyway.

About the Author

Jolynn Angelini is the author of the fast-paced thriller, The Protectors. Next up in the exciting series is Family Secrets, which continues the thrill ride and can be read as a stand-alone novel. Jolynn holds a bachelor of science degree and a master of education degree. Jolynn lives with her husband and daughter in Pennsylvania.